BEAVERIN(

GREAT N

David Yeandle was born in 1955 in Cambridge, where he was educated at the Perse School and Jesus College. He graduated with a BA in Modern and Medieval languages in 1977 and received his PhD in 1982. He is Emeritus Professor of German at King's College, University of London, where he taught for over thirty years, specializing in historical linguistics and medieval literature. Since taking early retirement in 2010, he has taught part-time at Cambridge University. He has published widely on German language and literature and latterly also on Anglican Church history. He lives with his wife in an East-Anglian village. They have one son.

DAVID YEANDLE

GREAT MINDS

A TALE OF ACADEMIC INTRIGUE

BEAVERING BOOKS

BEAVERING BOOKS

Set in Garamond 11

ISBN 979-8-4726-1825-0

For Peter H., with thanks

'Great minds seldom think alike.'

Morris Henry Hobbs

‘

1. RESTRUCTURING

Sunday, 14 September

'Why do campus novels always start with the beginning of a new academic year?' Professor Peter Lampton mused as he busied himself with preparations for the impending meeting of the 'RRE'. A campus novel, he thought, belonged to the essentials of any academic journey, and the Research Restructuring Exercise offered scope for quite a few of these journeys. This latest exercise had been introduced by the Government, following the previous 'highly successful' Research Excellence Exercise and Research Assessment Framework. It promised to do little for the participants' mainly sedentary lifestyles and possibly even less for their mental well-being.

Peter, the Head of the Department of Other Languages at the University of London Bridge, was delighted to have been appointed to an RRE subpanel, but the pride that he felt at this honour was kept well hidden from family and colleagues alike. Peter's twenty-five-year commitment to 'other languages' had obviously been recognized at last in his appointment to Subpanel Z, the enigmatically named 'Other Languages and Problem Areas' of the main panel Literature, Languages and Linguistics, which was already being nicknamed LiLaLi or LaLiLa, which Peter took as a sign of disrespect for his subject at large and wondered whether such a panel, with its connotations, might run the risk of seeming faintly absurd, so peripheral to

1

everyday life as to be no longer worthy of funding. This was a danger that the panel members must fight with all means possible. His thoughts turned, however, to his own title and the subpanel's role. He remembered that at Cambridge, where he had been a student, there was a Department of Other Languages, and this distinguished association served to confirm in his mind the importance, prestige—and dare he say Her Majesty's Government's devotion to 'impactfulness'?—of the work that he had been entrusted to perform. And so, he went about the house, looking for things to put into his suitcase, ready to travel the 300 miles north to Scotland, where the first really significant Subpanel Z meeting had been arranged.

Maybe his own comparative study of glottal stops in politicians' English, a follow-on from his thesis, would benefit from the restructuring exercise. He had found it difficult enough to find a publisher who was even remotely interested in the pages of his carefully conducted research on this topic, despite the painstaking transcriptions and the exhaustive analysis. Now, however, he hoped that the magnum opus that was nearing completion would be the crowning glory of his career, designed, as it was, to show that the use of the glottal stop was on the increase amongst the younger, ambitious politicians, who showed their solidarity with the electorate by adopting the speech habits of the man in the street.

Dr James Lubbins had been a late addition to the subpanel. He had been recommended by the chair of the LiLaLi main panel as one skilled in the medieval dialects of Upper Bavaria. Lubbins and Lampton shared things in common besides the initial letter of their surnames. They were both graduates of Cambridge, but whereas Lampton coveted a post at the prestigious ancient university, Lubbins had been fortunate enough to secure one there at a time when departmental politics played a major role. When had it not? Peter wondered. Not just in universities, but almost universally, preference and prejudice had always held sway. Lubbins had been appointed as the inferior candidate to exclude a very well-qualified applicant, whom the Head of Department wished to eliminate at all costs, anxious as he was that this candidate should not outshine him with his progressive views and forward-looking research. A Yorkshireman through and through, Lubbins did not even pay lip service to the niceties of academic convention. He spoke his mind, and anyone who disagreed with him could sod off. He was almost universally admired by his students and almost universally avoided by his colleagues. If Lampton was a refined, shy, unassuming academic, whose goal in life had always been to secure a job at the prestigious university and then settle down to a gentrified existence of scholarship, mixed with agreeable socializing, Lubbins was a strident professional northerner, who spoke with a pronounced north-country accent and eschewed the customs of social intercourse within the university. His form of eccentricity ran contrary to the norms of the august seat of learning. He dressed like a city gent, although his pinstriped suit was probably from Burtons rather than Savile Row; hence he stood out among the tweed jackets and sloppy dress of most Cambridge dons. He deliberately did not conform, to the point of being bloody-minded, especially in meetings and on exam boards. But in one respect, Lubbins was a leader amongst men, and that was in the pursuit of the opposite sex. He fancied himself as a lady's man, though he was seldom fancied by ladies. He usually set his sights on younger colleagues and willing undergraduettes.

Jim brought with him the same approach to the RRE. It was a chore for him that had to be endured. It might yet lead to a senior lectureship or—who knows?—to a more prestigious post at another institution. The couple of published articles, culled from his thesis, were hardly likely to lead to promotion on their own, but together with the experience of the RRE, they might give him a chance.

Peter and Jim had both booked tickets, as it happened, on the same train, the 10:18 from Peterborough, via Edinburgh, to Glasgow, and thence connecting on to Ayr, arriving with any luck sometime after 5 p.m., allowing for disruptions and engineering works.

Neither was aware that the other was travelling on that train. Peter went to the rear of the platform, awaiting the arrival of the first-class carriages, a privilege that was accorded the academic travellers and one that Peter never normally allowed himself. Jim waited further along the platform for the second-class carriages. He disapproved on principle of first-class travel, though he was not averse to charging the rate for first on expenses and then travelling second. When the train pulled into the station, Peter cast an eye up the platform and espied a familiar figure. He hastily turned to look towards the approaching train and boarded it without looking round. He found a single seat and set out his laptop, his novel, and other essentials on the small table in front of him, hoping that no-one would fill the seat opposite.

Jim got into the second-class compartment and looked round for suitable females with whom he might strike up a conversation. There were two twenty-somethings who looked like students, probably foreign, on a tour of the country, to judge by their backpacks. Jim went and sat next to these.

The train pulled out of the station, and Peter looked out of the window at the passing buildings, thinking himself safe from disturbance until the first stop at York. A voice roused him from his reverie, 'Excuse me, is this seat free?' He looked up to see an attractive middle-aged woman with a suitcase, standing beside the seat opposite him.

'Yes, of course,' he said with a polite smile, mindful of his manners. He pulled his laptop nearer to him.

'Oh, please don't worry,' the woman said. 'I don't need much of the table, just room for a coffee.'

'Thanks,' Peter said. 'I'll fetch a couple from the buffet car when you're ready. Let me know, won't you?'

The woman gave him a friendly smile and a chuckle.

'I should introduce myself,' she said. 'My name's Vicky.'

'Peter, Peter Lampton,' Peter said and proffered an embarrassed hand, raising himself slightly from his seat.

Jim meanwhile was unfolding his copy of the *Sunday Mirror*; he looked over the top of it and smiled suggestively at the two girls.

'Are you going far?' he asked. 'Let me guess,' he said with a twinkle in his eye. 'You're going all the way.'

'No,' one of them said, embarrassed. 'We get off at York.'

'Ah, grand,' Jim said, 'God's own county. That's where I'm from—Harrogate, the posh part,' he said, making sure to pronounce the 'haitch' with extra aspiration. 'What brings you to these parts?'

'We are doing our Rail Rover, seeing Britain in a week,' the blonde said with a hint of a foreign accent.

'Kommt ihr aus Deutschland?' Jim asked.

'Excuse me,' the brunette said. 'We are from Sweden.'

'Oh, well, yeah,' Jim said, wishing he knew the language better. 'Ha en bra resa,' he said, dredging up a phrase that he had learned as a student backpacker and smirking at the Swedish word for 'good'. 'Send me a postcard. Look me up if you visit Cambridge. I'm the only Lubbins in the phone book.'

The girls smiled at his feeble chat-up attempt. *No need to try harder*, Jim thought. *Now, if they were in one of my supervisions …* and his thoughts drifted off into the realms of fantasy.

Peter, in the meantime, had opened up his laptop and was perusing documents for the first round of RRE meetings. He began to read through the list of attendees for the first scheduled meeting at 10:00 on Monday morning. He knew all of the colleagues on the Other Languages subpanel, of course, but one name stood out as unknown to him—*Victoria Atherton*. The unknown lady was due to give an introductory lecture on the principles of Research Restructuring. Her affiliation was given as RARE (Eastern Region). Peter later learned that this stood for 'Rational Restructuring'. He had never heard of such a concept in industry before, not being the least interested in anything so mundane or practical, but he supposed that the civil servants in Whitehall had thought up the ruse of applying industrial restructuring to the ivory towers of academe, whose inhabitants, though a necessary part of any civilized nation, were perceived as bumptious and in need of taking down a peg or two. After all, the Whitehall mandarins themselves had been restructured. Peter was now no longer sure which Government Department was responsible for universities. When he was a research student, he received a grant from the DES, but the Department of Education and Science had since been re-named. He thought that it might now be the Department for Education, but where had the science gone, and what was the difference in the prepositions? Was that just a rebranding or did it imply something more sinister? he wondered. Something more akin to *re*-education? Wasn't that what they did in China and such ideologically motivated countries? It couldn't happen in Britain, though, could it? Peter had been suspicious of governments ever since Mrs Thatcher and her ideologues had nearly killed off his entire academic career. He had just slipped into post before the onslaught against universities came in the Eighties. He feared he, as the last one in, would be the first one out, but he had been lucky and gradually made his way through the hoops that the new, ideologically motivated Tory government had set up. His work had scored well in the earlier assessments, one of his articles even achieving a top mark, but he was afraid that the glottal stops of politicians might be seen as just a bit too rarefied, too lacking in practical application, with little potential for financial exploitation. Would he be restructured?

Jim was oblivious to the concept in either a university or industry. It is true that his first job had been in commerce. After leaving Cambridge, he had joined a firm of City stockbrokers, with the intention of achieving a six-figure salary, a brick phone, and a Lamborghini, but his achievements did not match his expectations. He proudly displayed his bulky phone, especially in female company. This was the only visible achievement of his financial career. Sadly for him, a ride in his battered old Triumph Stag did not have the same allure for the opposite sex as a Lambo or a Porsche. He seemed thwarted as a professional northerner in his attempts to equal the successes of the Essex men with their slick manner and their lazy Estuary English. His *oops* and *owts* and his mashing the tea sat uncomfortably beside the *yahs* and *nahs* of the Hooray Henrys and the Essex boys with their Champagne cocktails and fast cars. But it was here that he acquired his penchant for pin-striped suits. As he was travelling on a Sunday, however, he had not shaved and was dressed in an ill-fitting blue pullover, brown trousers, and black shoes, with scant regard to elegance or pulling power.

Peter occupied himself with the documents on his laptop. Although it was a Sunday, he felt it his duty to look like a serious business traveller, for which reason he had worn a suit and tie for the journey. His suits were off the peg but bought from John Lewis. His shirts and ties from Tie Rack were well co-ordinated. Hence, he looked like the serious *homme d'affaires* that he was trying to emulate, even if his character was ill suited to this role.

At 11:00, he looked at his watch and then over to Vicky.

'Time for a coffee?' he said with a smile.

'I think I could manage one,' his new-found, smart travelling companion said.

'How do you take it?' Peter asked.

'Just a dash of milk, no sugar,' Vicky replied.

'Two great minds think alike,' Peter said with a smile that might suggest an attempt at flirtation. He wasn't sure himself. He set off along the train towards the buffet car. 'Back in a tick,' he ventured. 'Don't go away.'

Vicky smiled politely, accepting his awkward chat-up for what it most likely was—nothing more than an embarrassed response to the situation he was in, a way of making the journey more pleasurable, with no further implications. And yet, Peter meant to impress her. A piece of cake might do the trick, he thought, definitely some shortbread, perhaps a Danish pastry. He bought a selection of all that was on offer—two of each—and returned to his seat with the coffees in each hand and the food in a paper bag with carrying handles, which he managed with his right hand.

'I hope everything is to your satisfaction,' he said with a hint of irony. 'There are some biscuits and other things in the bag. Do help yourself … Oh, sorry!' he said. 'Where are my manners?' He reached inside the bag and spread out the food on the table. 'Not much of a selection, I'm afraid. The Danishes look quite nice, though.' Calling the pastries Danishes was a concession to being with it, almost trendy, Peter thought. He objected to the term, partly as a linguist and partly because he generally eschewed Americanisms. Danishes were in the same category as pastrami on rye or bagels for him—something smart New Yorkers ate rather than modest academics from second-rate British universities.

'You're so kind,' Vicky said and reached for her elegant handbag. 'How much do I owe you?'

'£6.99,' Peter chuckled.

Vicky opened her handbag and began searching for money.

'That was a joke, of course,' Peter said. 'I would never accept money from a young lady.'

'You flatter me,' Vicky said. 'But thanks very much. Lunch is on me, then.'

'Thank you,' Peter said, 'but I couldn't possibly accept.'

'Well, then, I insist on paying for this,' Vicky said.

Peter held out his hand to restrain hers. Their eyes met, and they smiled.

'We don't want a scene like Mrs Doyle and Mrs Dineen,' Peter said.

'No, we don't. Are you a fan of *Father Ted*, too?' Vicky asked.

'Yes. It's one of my favourites. I can watch it over and over again,' Peter said. 'Brilliant casting.'

'And so true to life,' Vicky commented.

'Yes, I expect so, but I've never been to Craggy Island, not even to rural Ireland, and I'm not a Catholic, so I'm not the best judge,' Peter said.

'Ah, well,' Vicky said. 'I'm one up there.'

Peter was intrigued. He wanted to know more, but he didn't want to appear nosey.

The train stopped in York at 11:34. The two Swedish girls got up.

'Don't forget to look me up when you get to Cambridge,' Jim said, handing them a handwritten note with his phone number. 'I'll give you a guided tour. You could stay with me. I've got tons of space.'

'Hej då,' the girls said.

'Yeah,' Jim said with a grin. 'I'll remember that.'

Another group of passengers boarded the train. Jim looked up for suitable company. He was disappointed when a married couple came and sat opposite him, so he opened his paper again and studied the football results. At 11:40, he got up and went to the buffet car with the intention of getting a coffee to go with the sandwiches that he had brought from home. There was a lone woman, still wearing a scarf and coat, waiting in a queue to be served. Jim assumed she had got on at York.

'Hullo,' Jim said. 'Are you all on your own?'

'Excuse me,' the woman said, pretending not to have heard.

'Isn't that a Girton scarf you're wearing?' he asked. 'Jim Lubbins, Department of Other Languages, Cambridge University. What did you read?'

The woman, who looked about 25, realized that not to answer would appear very rude, said, 'Classics' and gave a forced smile.

'Gallia divisa est in partes tres,' Jim said. 'See, I'm not just a pretty face.'

'No,' the woman said curtly. 'I'm just getting some things for lunch before it gets too crowded.'

'I've got some nice bacon butties further down the train. Come and join me. Let me buy you a coffee,' Jim said. 'Two coffees, please,' he called out to the steward.

Jim paid and picked up the coffees. 'You bring the milk and sugar,' he said and set off in the direction of his seat.

The young Girtonian had no option but to follow if she wanted her coffee. She decided to spare Jim a couple of minutes in return for his generosity. He seemed genuine enough, and anyway, what harm could possibly come to her on a train full of people?

'What's a Girton lass doing so far from home?' he asked. 'What's your name by the way? Mine's Jim, but I've told you that already.'

'Isabelle,' the refined young lady replied. 'I'm on my way up north. I've just finished my PhD and have got a new job as a secretary. It's only temporary. I'm really hoping to get an academic post.'

'Well, I just might be able to help you there,' Jim said. 'I have many contacts in Cambridge. Employment for young ladies is a speciality of mine.'

Isabelle looked worried.

'Do you have any research students?' she asked.

'Well, no, not at the moment,' Jim replied.

'Have you got jobs for all your students, then?' Isabelle asked.

'It's early days still,' Jim replied unhelpfully.

'How many have you had?'

'I've lost count,' Jim said with a smirk.

'You must be a very popular supervisor,' Isabelle continued.

'You're right there,' Jim boasted. 'The young ladies are always knocking at my door.'

'Don't you have any male students?' Isabelle asked tauntingly.

'One or two,' Jim said.

They finished their coffees and bacon butties.

'Well, thanks ever so much,' Isabelle said. I must be getting back to my seat. I've left my bag there. Maybe see you in Cambridge one day.'

'Yeah, hope so,' Jim said. 'Lubbins, Other Languages—don't forget.'

'Thanks, I'll remember that,' Isabelle said and determined to forget it, but then she thought maybe it might come in handy one day. She was keen to advance in academia.

Peter began to become more adventurous with his conversation. His curiosity about Vicky was getting the better of him. What had she meant by that reference to *Father Ted*? Had she visited the place where it was filmed? Or did she mean she was a Catholic or Irish? Perhaps all three? He wanted to find out more about her generally. Why was she travelling alone, smartly dressed on a Sunday? *Start simply*, he thought to himself.

'How are the Danishes?' he asked, then thought that was never going to get him anywhere. 'I always think those from Ole & Steen take some beating. I pick one up whenever I'm near the Haymarket. Do you know the shop?'

'No, I can't say I do,' Vicky said. 'I don't often go to London, and if I do, it's to the City. My absolute favourites are the Chelsea buns from Fitzbillies. I'm based in Cambridge, you see.'

'Hah!' Peter chuckled, 'I know them well. I was a student in Cambridge. We sometimes had them as a treat on a winter afternoon for tea. I was at Caius—only a short walk along King's Parade.'

'Yes,' Vicky said. 'I was at Newnham—further to go, but I'd pick some up when I went into town for my Management Studies lectures in Mill Lane.'

'Wow!' Peter said. 'It's a small world. My lectures were out at Sidgwick—just over the road from Newnham. I wonder if we ever met.'

'I went up in 86,' Vicky said. 'How about you?'

11

'Oh, me, I'm afraid I was there much earlier. Class of 77, as they say. I hope you don't mind Americanisms.'

'No, not at all,' Vicky said. 'They crop up in my work all the time.'

Peter hoped that she might divulge more, but she took another bite of her Danish pastry.

'Mm, not bad,' she said, 'for a train buffet.'

'Not up to Fitzbillies' standard, of course, but any port in a storm, I suppose,' Peter said.

'Yes,' Vicky agreed. 'Tell me more about yourself. You're a businessman, I suppose.'

This was Peter's chance.

'Oh, no, but I'm on business. That's why I'm dressed like this. I'm on my way to an academic meeting,' Peter said.

'Similar to me,' Vicky said. 'But you must tell me more about yourself.'

'Not much to tell, really,' Peter said. 'I'm rather in the doldrums, stuck in a boring academic job with no hope of any excitement. University of London Bridge, Professor of Phonetics and Linguistics.'

'What's your specialism?' Vicky asked.

'Glottal stops,' Peter said with furrowed brow. 'I don't know how I got into them, but I'm stuck with them now.'

Vicky made a glottal gulp, then chuckled. She realized that one of the items on her personal agenda was a research project on glottal stops, ripe for restructuring. *Say no more*, she thought. *He mustn't know.*

'Sounds very academic,' she said.

'Yes, that's the problem,' Peter said. 'English is peppered with them nowadays. Quite appalling! The politicians are adopting the speech habits of the common man to sound more trendy and relevant, but no-one's interested in the academic study of the glottal stop.'

'Oh, I don't know,' Vicky said. 'I am.'

'Well, we seem to have more than fine pastry in common,' Peter said.

'Yes, that's nice,' Vicky agreed.

'I didn't like to ask, but since I've told you what I do, maybe you'll tell me about yourself.'

'I work for a company called RARE—Rational Restructuring. We're based in the Cambridge Science Park,' Vicky said.

Peter had a sinking feeling. Had he made the connection correctly? *Which was more important, his research or a flirtation?* he wondered. *Keep schtum for the time being,* he thought.

'Sounds fascinating,' Peter said as if through gritted teeth.

'Not at all,' Vicky said. 'It's a dog-eat-dog world in industry. Restructuring can be very harsh,' she said, as if to prepare him for something that might come in the future.

Peter thought it was time to change the conversation.

'Have you been to Craggy Island?' he asked.

'Good gracious, no!' Vicky said. 'You know it's not a real island, surely.'

Peter didn't know but didn't want to admit it.

'Yes, of course,' he said. 'But the parochial house must exist.'

'Yes, somewhere in County Clare,' Vicky said. 'My husband's family was from there. I've never been there myself, though.'

Peter looked disappointed.

'Excuse me,' Vicky said, 'but I need to brush up on some reading for my meeting.'

'No problem,' Peter said. 'I think I'll read my book.'

He picked up *Changing Places Again* and began reading.

'Very funny,' Vicky said. 'I can't get enough of his books.'

'Yes,' Peter agreed, 'quite the best campus novelist. That's another thing we share in common.'

Jim picked up his newspaper again. He looked at his watch. Four more hours to go before Glasgow—*Bloody 'ell!* he thought. He filled out the quick crossword with his fountain pen and put the newspaper down again. He looked out of the window and began to doze off. When he awoke, the train was waiting in Newcastle. The couple opposite had gone. No-one

13

had come in their place. Jim felt disappointed. He would have to do some work.

He got out an envelope marked RRE—Confidential and opened it. *Bloody 'ell!* he thought again when he saw the small print of the two hundred pages of papers to be discussed from 11:00 to 1:00 on Monday. *Bloody 'ell! We'll be ready for lunch and a pint after that lot!* he sighed to himself. He looked at the agenda and read the accompanying letter: 'Please ensure you have read all the papers for Monday's meeting. In particular, be prepared to speak to the individually assigned paragraphs.' The words were underlined to indicate their importance. The list contained synopses, penned by the authors, of all the books and articles to be assessed for potential restructuring. Those deemed in need of restructuring would be read in full—in theory at any rate—by one or two of the great minds on the subpanel, who would then make recommendations, which had, of course, to be approved by the full subpanel. Jim had not paid attention to any of the detail before. He thought he could charm his way through any meeting, using techniques he had learned in his former job in the City. He liked to think he could similarly charm any female who crossed his path. Thinking on your feet he called it. Yes, thinking on your feet in your black shoes and non-matching red socks. He supposed he would wear his pinstripes on Monday. That should impress the rest of them. 'Bloody 'ell!' he said out loud when he read the allocations:

Other Languages
Lubbins (dialectology): Submissions 1–25, pp. 1–20
Lampton (phonetics): Submissions 25–50, pp. 21–41

He stopped reading the rest as soon as he read the word literature, which was assigned to many of the names. Other languages had to deal with language *and* literature. Dr Lubbins and Professor Lampton were the odd ones out—the pure linguists, who had to cope with all the languages that no-one else could manage but who were spared the literature. That was a word that, when Jim heard it, caused him to recoil. *Literature's for wimps* was his verdict. *Hard facts* (with a *haitch*) *are what I deal in* was his motto. He was oblivious to the fact that most of his colleagues laughed at him. He looked hastily through his assignment. One in particular caught his eye: *Glottal Stops in Twentieth-Century English Political Discourse: A Phonetic Perspective* (book, 350 pp. + transcriptions, P. Lampton). *Bloody 'ell!* Jim thought. *That's going to be tricky.*

After an hour, Peter put down his novel and returned to his laptop. He pushed it further towards the middle of the table. Vicky smiled.

'I hope I'm not getting too close,' he said.

'No, of course not,' Vicky said. 'Be my guest.'

Peter felt excited. He had already read all the papers in preparation for Monday's meeting, of course. But having seen Jim further along the platform in Peterborough, he thought he ought to look over his allocated submissions. *Oh dear!* he thought when he read '"Undes ars in tine naso": Insults and Injuries in Old Bavarian Dialects' (article, 16 pp., J. Lubbins). *That might prove embarrassing. Typical Lubbins. He always has to be different.* Not being a medieval scholar, Peter didn't know what the quotation meant. *Something to do with art? Was it a strange form of medieval Latin?* he wondered. *Whence comes art?* was the best he could do. He would have to look it up. He typed the words into his laptop. The first translation that he found was 'le cul d'un chien dans ton nez'. Supposedly, that was something the French said to each other. He hadn't come across it before; he doubted whether many had. *Typical Lubbins!* he thought. It caused him to do a minor glottal gulp.

Vicky looked up.

'Are you reading something exciting?' she asked.

'I'm afraid it's confidential,' Peter said. 'Business, you know.'

'Oh, I'm sorry, I don't mean to pry,' Vicky said. 'International man of mystery!'

'Hardly,' Peter said, 'but I have to preserve my colleagues' confidentiality … Do you know French?'

'I did it for A Level and have always been interested,' Vicky said.

'How are you on idioms?' Peter asked.

'Not bad,' Vicky replied. 'I did a bit of waitressing one summer. You meet all sorts on the job,' she said with a knowing smile.

'It's just, I've never come across this one before. I know what it means, but I can't believe people really say it.'

'Go on, tell me,' Vicky said.

'Promise you won't be shocked,' Peter said.

'Yes, promise.'

'Le cul d'un chien dans ton nez! Would you believe it?'

'I'd believe anything of the French,' Vicky said.

'But "a dog's arse in your nose?",' Peter said disapprovingly, 'Apparently, it's medieval in origin.'

'No, I never came across that one,' Vicky chuckled.

'Just as well, I think,' Peter said. 'I may have to explain it in a meeting tomorrow.'

Vicky smiled.

'You seem like a broadminded sort of chap,' she said.

'There are limits,' Peter said and looked back at his computer. Vicky read her novel.

The train pulled into Glasgow Central. 'All change please' came over the Tannoy.

'Is this where we part?' Peter asked. 'I must say, chatting to you has made the journey pass quickly and very agreeably,' he said. 'Maybe we'll be able to meet up again one day in different circumstances.'

'Yes, that would be nice,' Vicky said. 'Maybe in London for one of those Danishes.'

'Or a Chelsea bun,' Peter said. He scribbled his mobile number on the back of his university business card and gave it to her.

16

'It's been lovely meeting you,' he said. 'Please look me up sometime.'

'Yes,' Vicky said enigmatically and walked over to Costa.

Jim put the envelope into his coat pocket and hurried to platform 13, having looked up the number in advance at home. He looked at the various locomotives in the station and noted down a few numbers. He would look them up in Ian Allan, as he still called his guide to rolling stock, when he got into the train.

Peter looked at the departure board for connections to Ayr. He discovered that the 17:30 train would leave from platform 13. *Not a bad omen, I hope*, he chuckled to himself. While he was standing in his reverie looking for the platform, he noticed out of the corner of his eye a young man of disreputable appearance, clad in a grey hoodie, with the hood up, his eyes looking down, leave a group of similarly dressed youths. He was now making a beeline towards him. Peter turned abruptly, and the man diverted away from him in a curve and back to the group of youths. *A narrow escape*, he thought. He had never encountered a pickpocket before. He kept his belongings close to him and proceeded, unsettled, to the platform. *Bad things come in threes*, he thought to himself. He would be more circumspect from now on.

When he arrived at the platform, he walked along the ScotRail train, looking in the windows. 'Damn! Lubbins again,' he muttered as he passed the third carriage and quickly looked ahead. *That was number two, I hope*, he thought, as he got into the fourth carriage.

Vicky spent fifteen minutes over her coffee, popped into WH Smith's to buy *Homes and Gardens*, and made her way to the departure board. *Blast!* she thought, *just missed it*, as she saw the 17:30 pull out of the station. The next train was at 18:00. She walked to platform 13 and sat down on a bench.

Peter found a seat away from most of the people, whom he judged to be disreputable, since most were clothed like the would-be pickpocket in Glasgow. He passed the hour-long train journey reading his novel and occasionally looking out of the window.

Jim surveyed the Scottish travellers—a different type from what he was used to, he thought. *Where are all the pretty young lasses?* He could see only sullen-looking mothers with babies and children, all dressed in cheap, unattractive clothing and mostly without a man. *No point in looking out for talent*, he thought. He'd better look at his papers again, on which he had made a few notes. He reached for the envelope. 'Bloody 'ell!' he said loudly enough for the mothers to look round at him, 'The bugger's gone.' Although not a man to be concerned about minor details like this—there was nothing of intrinsic value in the envelope in any case, but he was worried that the contents might fall into the wrong hands. The notes he had made could be incriminating. He remembered having labelled Peter Lampton's work a load of crap, doubly underlined. There were similar disparaging remarks about many of the other works on which he had to comment. More problematic still was that he would have to remember now his reactions to the submissions that he'd made on the previous train journey. He wasn't prepared to read through all the paragraphs again. *Bloody 'ell!*

The train arrived in Ayr at 18:20. Peter and Jim both got out and headed towards the taxi rank. Peter wondered if he could avoid sharing a taxi with Jim. There was no point sharing, since he could claim the price on expenses anyway. When he got there, there were no taxis waiting. He would have to stand and wait. A few minutes later, he felt a tap on the shoulder.

'Ey up!' Jim said. 'Fancy seeing you here. You'll be wanting to share a taxi, I expect.'

Peter looked disconcerted but agreed that he would share a taxi with Jim.

'I thought I might see you,' Jim said. 'I've been reading about your work—I've got to speak to it tomorrow.'

'Yes,' Peter replied, 'I've been doing the same with yours.'

Both men looked at each other to try to detect a hint as to how their own work had fared, but each remained inscrutable.

'Fascinating topic,' Peter said.

'A much-neglected subject,' Jim said.

After a few minutes waiting for a taxi, Peter spied a notice: *For taxis please use phone inside the ticket office.*

'I'll do it,' Jim said.

He walked away and came back in a couple of minutes.

'Coming in five minutes,' he said.

'Well done,' Peter said. 'We want the Argyle Hotel.'

'Hoo can I help you gents?' the driver asked.

'We want the Hargyle Hotel,' Jim said distinctly.

'That's the Argyle,' Peter confirmed.

'Aye, very posh,' the driver said. 'Are you gents here on business?'

'No,' Jim said simultaneously with Peter's 'Yes'.

'We're here for a conference and perhaps a round of golf at Troon,' Peter said.

'Yeah,' Jim said. 'I play crazy golf. He's just crazy.'

Peter looked unamused. The driver chuckled.

They arrived at the hotel and checked in at reception.

'Dinner's from 7:30 to 9:00,' the receptionist said. 'Your group's in the Silver Dining Room.'

Peter and Jim went up to their rooms, which were at opposite ends of the corridor on the first floor.

'See you later,' Jim said.

'Perhaps,' Peter replied unenthusiastically.

Peter had a shower and changed into more casual attire for dinner. A beige golfing pullover seemed appropriate. Jim changed his pullover for a green one. Neither felt it necessary to shave. Peter still looked cleanshaven from the morning, Jim had grown a fair bit of stubble. Jim felt it wasn't necessary to shower. Not only literature, but also showering, was for wimps. He was an alpha male, he reminded himself; showering kills the pheromones, ergo only shower occasionally and not when you want to pull.

Peter came out of his room at 7:25, just as Dr Beatrice Frensham, known to her friends as Beebee, was coming up the stairs.

'Hi!' Beebee said. 'I'd hoped I'd see you.'

They exchanged a modest kiss in the French style on both cheeks.

'We're next to each other,' Beebee said.

'Great,' Peter said.

'I hope you'll be quiet,' Beebee said with a glint in her eye. 'I don't want keeping awake.'

'I'm hardly likely to make a noise all on my own,' Peter said suggestively. 'Shall we go down to dinner together?'

'I've got to get myself ready,' Beebee said. 'Come in for a moment.'

They went into her room, and Peter sat on a chair beside the writing desk.

'I must change out of these clothes and do my hair,' Beebee said.

'Fine by me,' Peter said.

Beebee went into the bathroom and emerged wearing an elegant top with buttons down the back. The top two were still undone. 'I need someone to do up my top buttons. Any volunteers?' she said.

Peter looked worried. *What did she want? Was she coming on to him?*

'I'll look the other way, then,' he said.

Beebee chuckled as Peter did up the remaining two buttons. He felt embarrassed as he took the opportunity to look more closely at the job in hand and to ensure that the clothing did not become entangled with Beebee's gold chain around her neck. He tried to avert his eyes from anything below the neck. Beebee thanked him and put on a smart blue jacket, and they went downstairs together.

The panel of restructurers was gradually filling up two tables. At the head of the first, sat Niamh O'Loughlin, the chairperson, with Ólaf Ólafsson, a gentle, unassuming man, who

20

was in charge of Nordic languages, on her right. Derek Brown, a man of many talents but few graces, was on her left. They had already fetched their food from the buffet. Bottles of red and white wine were placed strategically along the table.

Peter was horrified when he saw Brown. He had encountered him as a supervisor when he was an undergraduate and had got on well with him at first; indeed, he liked him and admired him then, but Brown had shown his difficult side as Peter progressed in his career and became successful, so that the initial felicitous relationship had turned sour, culminating in a dispute over Brown's failure to acknowledge Peter's work in a footnote. He hoped Beebee would choose to sit next to him on their return from the buffet. He could then get to know Ólafsson better, who appeared to him from the preliminary meetings to be perfectly affable.

Beebee and Peter fetched their food. Peter waited with a gentlemanly smile for Beebee to choose her place. She sat next to Ólafsson. Peter had no choice than to sit next to Brown. At Cambridge, he had had to suffer the quaint, old-world practice of being called by his surname only, something that had all but died out in universities well before he was an undergraduate. By that time, its use appeared as rude and unfriendly, especially when combined with the nonreciprocal form of address that Brown still expected of him. No, Peter would not indulge him; Brown would not be addressed by name, Peter had resolved.

'Hello, Lampton,' Brown said grudgingly in greeting.

'Hello,' Peter said, adding 'arsehole' inaudibly and smiling disdainfully at him. 'I didn't expect to see you here.'

'No,' Brown said. 'It was a last-minute decision. Lubbins got me involved. He wasn't up to Romance.'

'No, I suppose not,' Peter said. 'Do you know Dr Frensham?'

'I haven't had the pleasure,' Brown said superciliously.

Beebee shook hands across the table.

'What is your specialism?' Brown asked.

'A bit of everything,' Beebee said, 'with a sprinkling of Scandinavian.'

'Beebee reads six languages,' Peter said. Brown smiled disdainfully at her paucity of expertise and helped himself to more wine.

'May I offer you a glass, Dr Frensham?' he said.

'Yes, please … Do call me Beebee; everyone does.'

Brown smiled.

The company was in full flow; the noise levels were rising. At just before 8:00, Jim walked in together with a young lady. They had evidently struck up a friendship. He sat down next to Beebee, while the young lady sat next to Peter.

'This is Isabelle,' Jim said, as he filled her and his glasses. 'We met on the train, would you believe? She's our secretary for the meeting.'

Peter introduced himself, proffering a hand and raising himself slightly.

'I don't think we've met,' he said. 'Peter Lampton.'

'Ah, yes,' Isabelle said. 'I've read a lot about you.'

Peter did not know whether to be alarmed or not. His research was not of such calibre or centrality as to have made it stand out, he supposed. He feared the worst.

'Only good, I hope,' he said optimistically.

Isabelle smiled and nodded very slightly. Peter was even more worried.

'Would anyone like more wine?' Brown asked in an effort to appear more friendly than his reputation warranted. 'It's not very good, I'm afraid.'

Jim held out his glass, which was already half-empty.

Gradually, the other members of the subpanel came in. Raúl Feliciano, a youthful researcher seconded from Spanish for his competency in Galician and other Romance dialects, came and sat next to Isabelle. A couple of minutes later, in walked Pilib Ó Súilleabháin, whose specialism wasn't clear to Peter. Jim should get on well with him, he thought with gleeful irony. The second table next began to fill up. Yoshanna

Greenfield, an expert in Yiddish, Ralf Whitby, an expert on the European courtly romance, Kurt Grabowski, some kind of political expert from Berlin, whom Peter found most trying, took their seats one by one.

Shortly before 9:00, Niamh rose and gave a welcome speech, reminding colleagues to get a good night's sleep before tomorrow's business. 'You'll need to have your wits about you for a talk that may well shock you all. It will certainly give your ideas a jolt. I don't think our speaker has arrived yet,' she said. Just as she was about to sit down, in walked Victoria Atherton.

'I'm so sorry I'm late,' Vicky said. 'I missed the train, and the next one broke down. I hope that's not a bad omen.'

A warm glow came over Peter. His suspicions were confirmed. Victoria Atherton and Vicky on the train were one and the same person. He went over to her and shook her hand with delight.

'Well, fancy that. Why didn't you tell me you were coming here?'

'Why didn't *you* tell *me*?'

'I was scared of you, I think. I didn't want to make a wrong impression,' Peter said. 'Come and sit down. I'll fetch you some food. Let me introduce some of the others.'

Beebee looked on, intrigued. *Did Peter have designs on her?* she wondered. As they approached the first table, Brown made his apologies, got up, and left. Peter now had access to both desirable women.

Gradually, the company dwindled. Some of the men went off to the bar, while stragglers remained at both tables and moved closer together.

'I'm very tired,' Beebee said at just before 11:00. 'It's been such a long day. Would you excuse me.'

Peter and Vicky were left alone in the dining room. At 11:30, Vicky began to make a move.

'Aren't you tired?' she said. 'We ought to be getting back. Loads of restructuring to be done tomorrow. How about a quick nightcap in my room? The minibar's well stocked, and it's all on expenses.'

Peter perked up. They went back up to the first floor and towards Vicky's room. They met Jim and Isabelle in the corridor, as Jim let Isabelle into his room.

'I hope you're keeping the pheromones going,' Jim whispered to Peter with a smirk, as he disappeared into his room. Peter hoped Vicky hadn't heard.

Peter slept unsoundly. He often did in a strange bed. He lay awake at 3:00 a.m., turning over the events of the previous day in his mind. The three choices that presented themselves to him were perplexing. He had long fancied Beebee, ever since that first Subpanel Z meeting in London when she had turned up in tight-fitting brown leather trousers and revealing white blouse. Her untypical attire for an academic meeting had put him in the mood for excitement. He had hoped for a chance to meet up in more relaxed circumstances. Then he had met Vicky, and she had shown interest. She was sophisticated but level-headed. He fancied Beebee had led a wild youth. He knew she was divorced. Had she had enough of men, or was she on the lookout for a new steady partner? That was more likely, he thought. She had left and gone to bed, whereas Vicky had taken him up to her room, and they had enjoyed mirthful, flirtatious conversation. But she wore a wedding ring, so did he. It was 60-40 for Beebee for sexiness and only 40-60 for his being in with a chance. With Vicky, the odds were reversed, he surmised. Which should he pursue if any? *Damn!* he thought when he remembered he hadn't phoned his wife to tell her he'd arrived safely. *Damn!* He'd do it after breakfast. That was his third choice, the one he knew he ought to make. Chastity and obedience, faithfulness to Becky. What a dilemma! He needed to count sheep or better still he would count backwards from 100, 99 … 29, 28, 27—he fell asleep.

Monday, 15 September

Peter's phone woke him at 7:30. He had another shower and chose suitable attire for breakfast. He intended to change for the meeting. At 8:30, he emerged from his room, tired and slightly disoriented. The whole situation seemed to him surreal. Not only had he, a much-neglected academic from London Bridge, been elevated to what must, he thought, be the most important subpanel for language and literature, but he had attracted the attentions of two desirable females. Things could only get better. As he passed Beebee's room on his left, he smiled. *Yes, maybe*, he thought to himself. Next, he passed Vicky's. *A distinct possibility* was the thought that was reinforcing itself in his mind. *Damned restructuring!* That thought brought him back down to earth. He went down to the Silver Dining Room, where the breakfast buffet was laid out. *Damn!* he thought, as he saw Brown, sitting alone at the second table, waiting for someone to join him. The first table had already been nearly fully populated with people he could take or leave. Under the circumstances, he had little choice of where to sit, but could he take another dose of Brown's superciliousness? No, he would delay at the buffet, pondering the offerings, waiting for the conveyor toaster and possibly order a herbal tea—though he preferred normal coffee—in the hope that someone else would sit at Brown's table first. Two minutes of pondering brought no change. Peter left his plate, half filled, at one end of the table, looked at his watch and feigned sudden surprise, necessitating his leaving the room, with eyebrows raised and an expression of realization for anyone to see who was watching him. He glanced back at Brown, who still showed no interest and had not acknowledged his presence. *Damn the man!* He would almost have foregone the honour of subpanel membership, had he known in advance that his nemesis would be there. Outside in the corridor, he bumped into Beebee. Her expression was one of slightly puzzled annoyance. There was no friendly kiss in greeting. *Damn!* Peter thought again.

'Everything all right?' Peter asked cheerfully as an ice-breaker.

'No,' Beebee replied. I was kept awake until 12:30 by the noise from the next room—loud laughter and banging. Goodness knows what they were up to in there.'

'Oh, that's so annoying,' Peter said sheepishly. 'I expect it won't happen again.'

There was no banging! he thought to himself. *Would that there had been …*

'A word of warning,' Peter said. 'Brown's in there alone at a table. I can't stomach him on my own. If you sit with him, I'll come and join you. I need to make a phone call first,' he added, thinking that, if he phoned Becky now, that would get it over with and allow Beebee to engage in conversation with Brown.

Beebee smiled and entered the dining room. Peter followed five minutes later. He went back to the buffet and finished filling his plate. Beebee fetched herself a yoghurt and a croissant. Peter felt embarrassed at having chosen a full Scottish, including haggis. He held it away from her and waited for Beebee to sit opposite Brown. He could then sit beside her.

'Good morning, Dr Frensham,' Brown said courteously but unfeelingly.

'Beebee, please,' Beebee insisted.

'Beebee, then,' Brown said more cheerfully. 'Good morning, Lampton,' he said with a less friendly tone.

Peter attempted to make his grimace into something resembling a smile and said 'Good morning' back, without addressing him, of course.

'Did you sleep well, Derek?' Beebee asked.

'Yes, like a top,' Brown said.

'Ah,' Peter said. 'An interesting etymology! Something to do with a mouse in Italian if I remember rightly.'

'Oh, that old chestnut!' Brown said. 'I'd have expected better of you, Lampton.'

Peter glared at him and stopped speaking. There was an awkward silence.

'Would you mind passing the butter, Lampton,' Brown said. Peter complied with a forced smile.

'Have you read all your submissions, Derek?' Beebee asked.

'Yes, of course,' Brown replied. 'Not just the synopses like most of you. I've read the full submissions that are ripe for restructuring, too—that's most of them.'

Peter thought he wished he had to restructure Brown—not just his research but his whole personality, but he wasn't on his list. He would check later and nobble the person responsible, he thought with glee. Brown finished his toast and marmalade and left the table after politely taking his leave.

'Damn that man!' Peter said to Beebee. 'Such a stuck-up prick!'

'Oh, I don't know,' Beebee said. 'I think he's rather charming.'

Peter thought it politic not to comment further.

Vicky came in and walked to the buffet.

'Excuse me if I go and talk to Vicky for a moment,' Peter said. 'Don't go away. I'll be back.'

Peter exchanged a few words with Vicky, which evidently amused her. They both returned to the table, Peter carrying Vicky's breakfast for her. He put it down in the free place opposite him.

Beebee smiled and exchanged a few pleasantries with her.

'Are you all prepared for the big lecture?' she asked.

'Of course,' Vicky said. 'I'm always prepared. Aren't you?'

What a daft conversation! Peter thought. Was he prepared though? For all eventualities? Probably not.

More colleagues entered the room, eyed carefully by Peter, who was dreading having to converse with some of them, should they sit next to him. Kurt Grabowski, who was up there in the ranks of those to whom Peter really didn't wish to speak, came and sat beside him. Peter introduced Vicky and Beebee politely. Grabowski explained how he had been involved in a similar exercise in Berlin and how much he was looking forward to the process.

Jim came in with Isabelle. He was wearing his blue jumper again and still hadn't shaved. *Typical Lubbins!* Peter thought. *But had he scored?* He told many a tall tale about his 'conquests'. How many of them were true, if any, though?

After getting their breakfast, Jim and Isabelle came over to the table and sat down, Jim beside Vicky, Isabelle beside Jim. Jim looked over to Peter, winked, and mouthed 'pheromones' with a smirk.

'Do you know where we can get papers from?' he said to Grabowski. 'Do they sell the *Daily Mirror* north of the border even?' Grabowski looked at him disdainfully. 'I think you can buy the *Scotsman* at Reception,' he said.

'That's no good,' Jim retorted with a grin. 'I'm a Yorkshireman.' *Stuck-up prick!* Jim thought to himself as he tucked into his black pudding.

'Done any good restructuring lately, Kurt?' he asked facetiously.

'Yes,' Grabowski replied. 'Actually, there's a very interesting correlation between age and restructuring required,' he said and continued to explain without Jim listening.

'Oh, yeah,' Jim said and turned to Isabelle.

'You'll have your work cut out, writing it all down when this load of windbags gets going,' Jim said.

'I can always check the facts with you later,' Isabelle said with a grin and nudged him.

Gradually, the restructurers left the dining room and returned to their rooms. Peter changed into a jacket without a tie. That asserted his gravitas, he thought, without the need for the formality of his grey suit.

Jim went back to his room and shaved. He got dressed in his blue pinstripe suit and wore a polyester tie, which, only in his estimation, matched.

The colleagues reassembled in the Conference Room where Niamh introduced Vicky's speech.

'Ladies and Gentlemen, Esteemed Colleagues,' she began. 'You probably think that the concept of restructuring is totally alien to academia. So did I when I was first approached to address the RRE, but experience with some of the other subpanels has led to me observing the benefits being acknowledged by their members.'

Jim stifled a yawn. Peter skimmed through the list of attendees that each of them had in front of them. He was amused at some of the designations on the closely printed sheet:

Z – Other Languages
Chair
Professor Niamh O'LOUGHLIN (University of Bristol, All Other Languages and Literature)
Members
Professor Derek BROWN (University of Oxford – Romance and Germanic Languages and Literature, Others)
Dr Raúl FELICIANO (University of Newcastle – Iberian languages and Literature, Others)
Dr Beatrice FRENSHAM (University of Essex – Germanic, Romance, and Scandinavian Languages and Literature, Others)
Professor Kurt GRABOWSKI (Universität Berlin – Politics, Languages, Others)
Professor Yoshanna GREENFIELD (University of Manchester – Yiddish, Romany Languages and Literature, and Others)
Professor Peter LAMPTON (University of London Bridge – Phonetics and Linguistics, Others)
Dr James LUBBINS (University of Cambridge – Dialectology and Dialects, all Others)
Professor Pilib Ó SÚILLEABHÁIN (University of Ulster – Language, Politics and Religion, Others)
Professor Ólaf ÓLAFSON (University of London – Scandinavian and Others)
Professor Ralf WHITBY (University of London – Courtly Romance (except Romance), and other Others)

Consultant
Ms Victoria ATHERTON (Industrial Restructuring)
Secretariat
Dr Isabelle CHESHAM (Subpanel Secretary)

'Why would a university restructure?' Vicky asked. 'More importantly, what are the benefits of restructuring research?'

'None,' Jim whispered to his neighbour and received a glare from Vicky. She turned to her PowerPoint presentation and began to go through a list of bullet points:

- Viability
- Effectivity
- Turnaround
- Stakeholders
- Streamlining
- Non-performing
- Downscaling
- Profitability
- Disinvestment

Peter looked on aghast. Was the sophisticated, attractive woman, whom he had only recently got to know, a hard-nosed businesswoman with no empathy for the likes of him? His thoughts drifted off to a linguistic analysis of business speak while the words drifted over him. He wasn't interested in *what* she was saying but *how* she was saying it. There was the nub. He began to count the times she said *paradigm, streamlining, outreach, best practice, touch base*. He wanted to reach out to her, to touch her base even, to shift her paradigm and streamline her. She was welcome to run things up his flagpole. He could leverage her assets and empower his own.

On a more academic level, he disapproved of her American pronunciation of *leverage*. Why had British speakers adopted it? It was almost as bad as *pry-vacy*. Pri-vacy! he would shout at his students if they mispronounced it. And woe betide anyone who used a misplaced glottal stop. He drew their attention to those dreadful adverts from the Eighties, in which it was proclaimed 'Milk has gotta lotta bottle.' It was the pronunciation of *bottle* that really got him going. But, of course, the adverts were unknown to his students, who weren't even born then, so he had to do a feeble imitation of it or sometimes play them a clip from YouTube, which he incorporated into his Power-Point presentations, being quite tech-savvy, despite his linguistic conservatism.

'And that, Ladies and Gentlemen, concludes my assessment. Thank you for listening. Go forth and restructure!' Vicky said.

Peter was jolted out of his reverie by the applause, in which he hastily joined, smiling at Vicky. In the coffee break, he congratulated her on her lecture and told her how it had given him new ideas for his own research.

'You won't mind so much if your magnum opus on the glottal stops is restructured, then,' she said with a chuckle.

Peter made a gulping sound with his glottis, thereby trying to put a brave face on it. *Lubbins wouldn't dare, would he? Sixteen pages of medieval vulgarity against 750 pages of close phonetic research. You just couldn't compare the two*, he thought.

After the coffee break, the restructurers sat round the table once more and prepared themselves for the nitty gritty as Peter called it, or in the words of Jim, they got down to brass tacks— to rhyme (after a fashion) with hard facts, his *raison d'existence*.

Niamh introduced the discussion with an air of relief that they had eventually arrived at discussing some examples of restructuring after so many preliminary meetings on the theory and dry runs.

'I think the best way to proceed,' she said, 'is if we each speak to one of the synopses on our list that you have deemed in need of restructuring, keeping the author anonymous, and then discuss it *in pleno foro*.'

31

Jim raised his eyes to heaven at the pretentious use of Latin. Peter stared at the table in front of him. Brown fixed his eyes on Niamh.

'In the afternoon,' she continued, 'we'll begin with the submissions for each institution. This will, of course, mean discussing our own contributions, and I'll naturally ask you to each step out of the room for your own institution. But for now, we'll take turns in no particular order, starting with Derek. I know I'm safe with him, as he's always prepared. The last speaker chooses the next, so the rest of you will have to be alert! You can each choose a submission at random. Ten minutes maximum for each.'

Bloody 'ell, Jim thought. *I'll be lucky if I can keep going for one.*

'Over to you, Derek,' Niamh said.

Brown rose to his feet and got out his neat pile of hand-written notes.

'I propose to take one of the most salient works in need of restructuring from one of our best-known universities. I make no apologies.'

Brown proceeded to expatiate for exactly ten minutes on the demerits of the work, in particular mentioning its lack of structure and order and concluding that anyone who had authored such a piece of research ought to be asking themself whether they—he used the plural pronouns advisedly for anonymity, despite his distaste for them—are suited to the academic profession.

Peter looked concerned and mouthed 'arsehole' but was relieved that he wasn't in the same discipline. Jim grinned. He thought he was all right for the same reason.

'Whose turn now, Derek?' Niamh said.

'I think Whitby,' he said with ill-concealed schadenfreude.

Ralf smiled.

'Thank you, Derek, for your confidence,' he said and thought, *touché.* 'I'll try to keep this succinct.'

After ten minutes, people began to look at their watches with a frown.

'Just a couple more minutes,' Ralf said. 'It'll be worth it in the end.'

After five minutes, Niamh cut him short, firmly but politely.

'Sorry, Ralf, but we need to keep to schedule, so a final sentence, please.'

Five sentences later, Ralf concluded, 'So, on the one hand, it's fine as it is, on the other, it needs to be restructured.'

Colleagues either shook their heads or looked heavenwards; some muttered. Jim whispered something in Isabelle's ear—she laughed embarrassedly.

Gradually, they went round the table. Isabelle made pages of notes. Jim, who was sitting next to her, nudged her from time to time and pointed to something she had written with a smirk.

At the end of the session, Niamh summed up.

'I forgot to mention at the beginning,' she said, 'with regard to this afternoon's session, since we don't have two of all subject specialists, Derek has offered to take on any submissions that require a second opinion, especially any problem cases.'

Everyone looked concerned. Jim thought that that needed preventing, but how?

'This afternoon,' she said, 'when we're discussing each other's work, I expect you to be scrupulously honest. Even though you won't be in the room for your own, word has a habit of getting back, and don't forget, Derek is the final arbiter. Have a good lunch!'

At the coffee urn, after lunch, Jim had a word with Peter, with Isabelle in attendance.

'Keep this under your hats,' he said, 'but we don't want Brown buggering up our chances. We need to dish the dirt on him, and I know there are a few skeletons in his cupboard.'

'I'm not sure that's ethical,' Peter said, 'though I have one or two things in mind myself.'

'You'll help, won't you, love?' he said.

'What are you offering?' Isabelle asked suggestively.

'You want a good job, don't you?' Jim said.

Isabelle chuckled.

'I'll expect an IOU,' she said, 'signed and sealed.'

'You'll give me a good hearing, won't you?' Peter said.

'Of course, lad,' Jim answered. 'What do you think of my paper on the dog's arse?' he asked. 'Good, isn't it?'

'First-rate,' Peter said. 'Couldn't possibly be improved. What about my book? Two volumes, eh!'

'I thought it was a load of crap,' Jim said, 'but I'll give it top marks. You'd better write me a quick paragraph for this afternoon.'

'I'll write it during the presentations, seeing we're not on until later, and then send it to Isabelle. She can slip it to you under the table,' Peter said.

'We're being like naughty schoolchildren,' Isabelle said. 'I don't want putting into detention!'

'I'll see you're all right,' Jim said, 'but you'll owe me.'

Peter looked embarrassed.

'We need to pool our information on Brown,' he said. 'Let's all meet in a corner of the bar after dinner.'

The three conspirators looked pleased with themselves.

'Not a word to anyone,' Jim said.

'Not a word,' they agreed.

The afternoon session began with a brief introduction by Niamh.

'Welcome back, colleagues. I hope you all had a good lunch.'

Brown smiled inwardly and thought of the half-bottle of wine he had consumed. Jim patted his belly and breathed stale beer in Isabelle's direction, suppressing a burp. Peter looked across at Beebee, who was making eyes at him discreetly. Vicky opened up her laptop for the session.

'Well, if you're all sitting comfortably, let's kick off! Over to you, Derek,' Niamh said.

Peter winced at her use of kicking off. *For heaven's sake, this isn't a damn football match*, he almost said out loud.

'It looks like you're speaking to Ralf's submission now.' Peter winced again. *AS IF!* he shouted silently at her. 'Sorry, Ralf,' she said with a chuckle, 'this looks like victimization, but I can assure you it's pure chance. Just the order on our list. Scrupulous fairness will be observed, so would you step outside, please.'

Brown gave his own résumé of Ralf's work, an essay on the theme of order and disorder in the courtly romance, which differed substantially from his own synopsis. 'In conclusion,' he said, 'the title of the work is symptomatic of the author's approach. The essay shows little in the way of originality, significance, or rigour. If this were an undergraduate essay, I might just give it a II.2. If it can be improved at all, it needs substantial restructuring, better still the author should start again from scratch in an orderly manner.'

'Thank you, Derek, for that frank assessment,' Niamh said. 'You've certainly kept to the guidelines. What grade would you award, then?'

'C,' Brown said.

Jim looked over at Peter and mouthed, 'Bloody 'ell!' Each gave a knowing frown to the other. A lip reader would have been able to make out 'arsehole' by looking at Peter's lips, but there were no lip readers present, even though many had the same thought and fears for their own work.

Ralf was called back into the room. His expectant smiles were met with glum expressions round the table. He scrutinized Brown's expression but got no hint of how he had fared.

They continued through the list. During the next presentation by Raúl Feliciano, who examined the work of Yoshanna Greenfield, Peter wrote assiduously, looking up from time to time at Raúl, to suggest that he making notes on what he was saying. Just as Raúl was summing up on Yoshanna's book on Yiddish academic humour, giving it an overall A- and noting its strong originality, significance, and rigour, Peter folded his sheet and wrote Isabelle's name on the front. He passed it discreetly further.

Yoshanna was called back in, looking glum, but met with a sea of beaming faces. Ralf took note and determined to find out how he had fared and, if possible, to improve his rating. He would ask Peter later discreetly.

'We've reached Beebee now,' Niamh said. 'Ólaf, it's your turn to step out of the room,' she added with a smile.

Beebee smiled at the assembled company and dug out her notes. Peter's eyes fixed on Beebee. *60–40*, he thought and sailed away in his mind to distant times. A Viking longship had rowed in the early morning mist up the mouth of the Thames as far as where the ULB would be situated in 900 years' time. It was now returning to Sweden, laden with plunder and blonde maidens, one of whom bore a certain resemblance to his colleague. Erik Erikson, the captain, who looked not dissimilar to him, would later take his trophies home and enjoy … He was awakened from his reverie by Beebee's summing up. 'A modicum of restructuring required, I think,' Beebee said, 'but overall a good A-'

Ólaf returned. He was unconcerned with his ratings. Why would anyone give him less than he deserved, anyway?

'Lampton comes before Lubbins,' Niamh said. 'Out of the room, Jim, and over to you, Peter.'

Jim cast a knowing glance at Peter and closed the door behind him.

'I should just point out that, although Jim and I are both linguists, our fields are very different; however, I'll do my best to be scrupulously fair. He read out the title of Jim's essay. Brown looked thunderous at his mispronunciation. He clearly didn't have a clue, he concluded from this one faux pas. He would need to intervene. Peter waxed lyrical about the exceptional originality of Jim's paper, the astonishing rigour, and the international significance of his research.

'No restructuring required,' he concluded. 'A clear A for all three.'

Jim was called back in. He had been trying to memorize the contents of what Peter had written, while he had been out of the room.

'The next on the list is Lubbins,' Niamh said. 'Lampton and Lubbins—it would make a good double act,' she said. Peter looked sheepish and smiled at Jim as they exchanged places.

'Well,' Jim said. 'Some people might think this is a load of crap, but it will be referred to for a hundred years to come, long after Tony Blair is just a dim memory. And why is that? I'll tell you. Hard facts. That's what it is, hard facts. None of your intellectual pap. He gets down to brass tacks. Not bad for a namby-pamby southerner, but we can't hold that against him. A- for originality, A for significance, A for rigour—no restructuring required.'

Brown looked apoplectic. There was no way he was going to let them get away with this stitch-up, he thought.

Peter came back into the room to a discreet wink from Jim. Isabelle whispered in Jim's ear. Beebee gave Peter a broad smile. Peter felt elated. Niamh looked perplexed.

Pilib spoke next about Kurt's work.

Over dinner, many enquiring looks and glances were exchanged and not a few knowing ones. The seating arrangements had changed, despite a habit on these occasions to keep to an established pattern. Niamh considered it her duty to move position and talk to others. She located herself at the head of the second table. Brown stuck to his original position. Peter ended up sitting at the second table next to Beebee and opposite Vicky. Jim and Isabelle found a place at the other end of the first table, as far away from Brown as possible. Ólaf, who was something of an outsider, ended up sitting at the head of the table next to Brown, opposite whom sat Yoshanna, and next to him Grabowski.

'Bloody 'ell!' Jim whispered to Isabelle, 'That's going to be a laugh a minute at t'other end of t'table.' Isabelle chuckled and smiled at Ralf, who came and joined them.

'I got the impression that Derek may have been less than fulsome about my work,' Ralf said.

'Couldn't possibly comment,' Jim said with a smirk. 'You and he go back a long way, don't you?' he said. 'You must have a lot of stories you could share about him. Some embarrassing, eh?'

Ralf began to relate discreetly, weighing up the situation in his inimitable manner, but disclosing only hints about what he knew. Isabelle looked at her watch.

'More wine, Ralf?' she asked, in an attempt to curtail Ralf's enthusiasm.

'Where can we find you tonight after dinner if we need you?' Jim asked.

'I'll be in my room,' Ralf said, 'preparing for tomorrow's session. I need to write my assessments for the departmental session.'

Bloody 'ell! Jim thought. *Waste of time!* He'd bluff his way through his.

After dinner, Peter, Jim, and Isabelle reconvened in a corner of the bar. Grabowski came over, evidently wanting to join them.

'Sorry, mate, linguists' conflab. We're talking shop and don't want to bore you,' Jim said.

'I'm sure it would not bore me,' Grabowski said, 'but I can take a hint. Tschüss!'

'Yeah,' Jim said, adding under his breath, 'bugger off!'

Peter went up to the bar and fetched drinks for the three of them—a pint for Jim, a Cabernet Sauvignon for Isabelle, and a Talisker single malt for himself.

After they had said 'cheers,' the three of them drew their heads closer together.

'I'm not a vindictive person,' Peter said, 'but Brown shouldn't be allowed to get away with this. We can't let him ride roughshod over us all.'

'So what's your big plan?' Jim asked.

'Well, when I was a research student,' Peter continued, 'I let him read an essay of mine on the glottalization of sonorants in thirteenth-century Romance and Germanic. I had it accepted by the *Zeitschrift für vergleichende Phonologie*, but their lead time was two years at the time, and before mine was out, Brown's "seminal article" on thirteenth-century phonology had appeared in the *Handbook of Comparative Phonology* that he was co-editing. He had lifted great chunks of mine, so I had to withdraw mine from the *ZvP*. When I challenged him, he claimed he had come up with the same conclusions independently and denied all knowledge of having seen my article. He threatened me with oblique references to my chances in the job market. What could I do if I wanted a job? When I got one, with his help, there was no point anymore in complaining. The matter was forgotten about, and I was one article down on my CV.'

'Yeah, but how can we make the dirt stick now?' Jim asked.

'I've still got the letter of acceptance and the dated, edited essay from the ZvP,' Peter explained.

'Hard facts!' Jim chuckled.

'Hard luck, Brown,' Peter said.

'Yeah!' Jim said.

'How do I come into it?' Isabelle asked.

'You send out the papers, don't you?' Jim said. 'You can always slip in an extra official-looking paper into his envelope. He won't know where it comes from, but it will get him worried.'

'A genial plan!' Peter said and smiled with delight.

'Actually, I've got another bit of dirt to dish,' Peter said. 'You know he never works in a library—he always takes books home. I just happened to discover one on his shelves one day stamped *Université de Lausanne*. I'd asked him if he had a copy that I might borrow. He said no, he'd used it in London years ago. Funny how he kept on quoting it in his research, I thought. Of course, I never let on, but now's the time, I think.'

'What was the book?' Jim asked.

'*Comparative Phonology of Sonorants*,' Peter said.

'I think I know where I can lay my hands on a copy if we ever need one,' Jim said, 'but maybe we could remind him in some other way. I'll give it some thought. Isabelle will help, I'm sure.'

'I wonder what Ralf meant, when he was rabbiting on about Derek's amorous exploits,' Isabelle said. 'I can't really imagine him as a lover.'

'Yeah, well!' Jim said. 'You might say the same about me, but I've already proved you wrong, haven't I?'

'Wishful thinking,' Isabelle said.

Peter looked embarrassed.

'Well,' Jim said, 'I'm going to pay Ralf a visit later. Something about Niamh Ralf was hinting at.'

'What a pair!' Peter said.

'A pair of what?' Jim asked.

Tuesday, 16 September

The following morning, the conspirators reconvened over breakfast.

'How did you get on with Ralf last night?' Peter asked.

'Well,' Jim said, 'it was a long time ago after a college feast. Brown had invited Niamh as his academic guest to the feast at Needham, and they both had a lot to drink. Niamh was staying in college overnight. Apparently, the bedder discovered signs of amorous activity the following morning and told all and sundry. It got back to Brown's wife and caused a rift. Only a few people remember now. Ralf's one of them.'

The restructurers reconvened for the morning session. Niamh recapitulated the events of the previous day and asked for any questions or comments. Brown rose to his feet.

'I think you'll find, Niamh, that we need to reflect carefully on some of the submissions yesterday. I can think of two in particular that need to be revisited. I don't wish to mention them by name now, but I was concerned that not everyone kept to the guidelines.'

'Thank you, Derek,' Niamh said. 'We can have a word later and revisit the matter if necessary.'

Brown sat down, looking smug. Jim winked at Peter and nudged Isabelle. Ralf smiled. The others looked perplexed.

'Well, today we're going to have a preliminary look at results per institution in our UOA,' Niamh said.

Jim put his hand up.

'Yes, Jim?' Niamh said.

'We're not all mind-readers,' he said. 'What the bloody 'ell's a UOA?'

Smirks went round the table at his ignorance about one of the most fundamental aspects of the exercise.

'It's on the list of abbreviations, Jim,' Niamh said. 'Hasn't Isabelle given you one?'

'Not one of those,' Jim said with a grin.

'It's a Unit of Assessment,' Isabelle said. 'Here, have one of these,' she said, as she handed him the list.

'Yeah, I've got one of those,' Jim said. 'We're Other Languages, right? Well, why didn't you say that?'

Niamh looked perplexed.

'I think, Niamh,' Brown said, 'that if we are repeatedly delayed by these kinds of queries, we shall be here until the cows come home.'

'How now, Brown cow?' Jim said at half volume.

Colleagues tried to suppress giggles. Brown looked furious.

'May I request that all colleagues are acquainted fully with abbreviations and all papers well in advance.'

Peter winced. *BE acquainted*, he screamed silently.

'Excellent request,' Jim said. 'May I in turn request that we aren't held up by smart-arse requests from know-it-alls.'

BE NOT, no NOT BE—Oh damn! Why am I such a pedant? Peter asked himself in torment.

'You'll live to regret that,' Brown muttered.

'Well, we've got that little matter out of the way,' Niamh said. 'I'm sure we shall all manage to preserve a sense of humour, even if things do sometimes get trying. Vicky is going to start the ball rolling.'

'Damn football metaphors,' Peter whispered to Beebee.

'Croquet actually, Lampton,' Brown said sotto voce.

'Over to you, Vicky,' Niamh said.

'Thank you, Niamh,' Vicky said. 'I hope you can all see the screen,' she continued. 'First of all, have a look at this spreadsheet for all 33 departments in the UOA. I've ranked them in order of numbers of submissions, then by numbers of potential restructuring required, and finally by geographical location. The next slide shows my typical paradigm, taking into account the viability of restructuring the resources available. Here we're going to have to think outside the box,' she said. Peter winced and wondered what box of delights Vicky might have in store.

'Blue sky thinking is the order of the day,' Vicky said. 'We all need to become change agents. Pivot your ideas. Give the task 110%.'

'Bloody 'ell,' Jim spluttered, 'translation please.'

'Don't worry, I'll keep you all in the loop,' she said with a grin. 'I'll make sure we're all singing from the same hymnsheet.'

It dawned upon people that Vicky was being deliberately provocative. Peter began to chuckle.

'We shall need to have a thought shower,' Vicky continued, tongue in cheek. Peter was beside himself, not because Vicky had used these terms, since he realized she was teasing them, but because the English language had sunk to such depths. *Was that the bottom line?* he asked himself with revulsion.

'I blame the glottal stop,' he whispered to Beebee. She patted him on the knee. He raised his eyebrows and smiled knowingly.

'We could touch base offline sometime,' Beebee said.

'Take it to the next level even,' Peter joked.

Brown glared at them.

When Vicky had finished, Brown got up and said, 'This is the most preposterous waste of time that I've ever experienced. Thank heaven my university doesn't teach anything as vulgar as business studies.'

'I hate to disabuse you, Derek, but I have an MBA from the Saïd Business School,' Grabowski said.

'An ex-stockbroker, me,' Jim said. 'Business and pleasure always mix in my book.'

Peter winced.

'I think that's the signal for coffee,' Niamh said, exasperated by the way the session had developed.

'Bloody 'ell,' Jim said to Peter, 'what a lot of fannying around.'

'Did you hear what Brown said?' Peter asked.

'Yeah, well,' Jim said. 'He may change his tune when he hears what we're planning. Isabelle's going to type something up tonight, aren't you, love?'

Isabelle smiled.

After coffee, the restructurers would be asked to comment on the extent of restructuring that was feasible in a number of pre-selected departments.

Niamh explained the criteria with an example.

'I'm going to take the University of the Roundabouts as a paradigm,' she said.

Peter looked heavenward. *Not you, too!* he thought.

'Derek has kindly worked out the grades for the institution in conjunction with me. The University has submitted four FTEs in our UOA.'

Jim looked heavenward and whispered in Isabelle's ear. She pointed to the list of abbreviations. 'Gobbledegook,' Jim whispered again. Isabelle looked embarrassed.

'Sadly, there were no submissions awarded an A overall,' Niamh continued, '10% awarded a B, 60% awarded a C, and 15% each for D and E. I'll now ask Vicky to speak to these results.'

'Let me begin by saying that for a new university that has little history of teaching Other Languages,' Vicky said, 'this is a creditable performance. The institution showed no submissions of world-class significance in need of no restructuring, a handful of submissions of international significance in need of only some restructuring, a substantial proportion of submissions of national significance in need of more serious restructuring, a significant proportion of submissions of sub-national importance in need of significant restructuring, and a substantial proportion of submissions needing comprehensive restructuring. As regards rigour, there was a substantial proportion of those submissions of international significance in need of only some restructuring that showed a significant amount of rigour. The submissions of national significance in need of more serious restructuring showed a slight amount of rigour in a significant proportion of the submissions, while the submissions of sub-national importance in need of significant restructuring showed an insignificant amount of rigour in a significant proportion of the submissions, and the submissions needing comprehensive restructuring, showed a significant lack of rigour in all the submissions.'

'Bloody 'ell!' Jim exclaimed.

'Coming now to originality,' Vicky said, 'the institution showed no submissions of world-class originality in need of no restructuring, hardly any submissions of international originality in need of only some restructuring, a substantial proportion of submissions of national originality in need of more significant restructuring, a significant …'

The restructurers began to giggle until most were convulsed in fits of laughter. Brown sat stony-faced. Niamh looked embarrassed. Vicky smiled and attempted to continue, but it was useless.

'Ten minutes' comfort break,' Niamh said. 'I hope colleagues will have composed themselves by then.'

She went over to Derek and appeared to agree something with him. After the short pause, Niamh made an announcement.

'Derek and I have decided that a fixed seating arrangement would be preferable and suit our discussions better. I'm going to ask you to move according to the following plan. Going round the room, starting on my right, Derek, next to him Jim, then Kurt, then Beebee, then Ralf, then Ólaf, then Peter. On my left, Isabelle, then Vicky, then Pilib, and finally, Raúl.'

'And what, may I ask, is the purpose of this change?' Jim asked.

'You'll have to ask Derek,' Niamh said. 'It was his idea.'

'Yeah, well, I for one am not prepared to be treated like a schoolboy.'

Niamh sensed a rebellion and thought it politic not to pursue the idea further.

'We'll review the matter over lunch and make any necessary changes this afternoon,' she said.

Lunch saw groupings of restructurers into distinct camps. Peter, despite his earlier attempt to avoid Jim on the journey, had now established a firm bond with him and Isabelle for the purposes of the manoeuvrings in opposition to the machinations of Brown, who was in a minority of one, but still exerted a hold over Niamh, going back to the episode after the feast in the late Sixties. Both Brown and Niamh had since divorced and remarried. He reminded her that her new husband would probably not approve of the liaison, which he was currently doing his best to revivify. Under the circumstances, she was a pliant chair. Of course, Brown thought the episode was forgotten about by all but a handful of older colleagues, amongst whom Whitby could be named. But Whitby daren't say anything, dare he? He, too, had his skeletons in the cupboard. He knew Brown could give tit for tat—a technique that he had frequently used in his ambitious rise to prominence in academia.

Peter observed how Brown and Niamh were in deep, animated conversation over lunch and that both seemed in unusually high spirits, caused not just by Brown's enjoyment of three quarters of a bottle of house red. They had clearly organized something to their advantage.

To Peter's conspiratorial group could be counted Beebee and possibly Vicky, both of whom joined him, Jim, and Isabelle for lunch. He observed how Kurt and Raúl, as younger colleagues, had formed a duo, to which Ólaf and Pilib, who were loners, had attached themselves and thus formed a clique. Ralf wasn't sure where he fitted in—he tried to get on with anyone and everyone, except perhaps Derek, who grudgingly granted him the use of his first name—and ended up sitting next to Yoshanna. Peter had labelled these the misfits, Jim the ragbag or, with little justification, the hoity-toity crowd.

Peter needed to test Vicky's allegiance. He could count on Beebee, whom he had known for a long time and with whom he had long hoped to be more intimately acquainted, but Vicky? She definitely seemed interested on the train. They were contemplating a meeting in Cambridge or London even after their first meeting. But Peter didn't know what drove her, nor had he experienced her in 'business mode' with her thought showers and thinking outside the box. How much of this did she believe? Was it just for effect? On balance, he would rather touch base with Beebee; Vicky could always be held in reserve for a future meeting. *Damn!* he thought, as he remembered Becky and the kids. *Damn!* He'd better phone tonight. Still, he needed to find where Vicky's loyalties lay. He would pursue this later.

After lunch, the restructurers reconvened. The new seating plan was implemented only insofar as Isabelle was persuaded to sit on Niamh's left. Jim went and sat next to her, but the proximity to Niamh and Brown on her right, hampered their clandestine communications during the meeting.

The purpose of the afternoon's meeting was to recapitulate the work done on the synopses and finalize that as far as possible, excepting any problem cases, which would be dealt with later. The next day, they would each be required to speak to institutions allotted to them after the model of the University of the Roundabouts. This would require some individual preparation, for which reason, the afternoon's session would end at 4:00 p.m.

Before they began with the afternoon's agenda, Niamh announced a change in the proceedings.

'Seeing we still have much business to conduct, tomorrow,' she said, 'I propose that we start at 9:00 instead of the usual 10:00 and that I hand the chair over to Derek, who will speak to the problem cases that he has identified so far. I will resume with the main business at 10:00.'

Jim put up his hand.

'I hope you don't mind if we bring our bacon butties into the meeting in that case,' he said.

'If you must, Jim,' Niamh replied.

Brown looked furious.

After the meeting, Isabelle was asked by Niamh to prepare a list of problem cases that had been identified by Brown for the extra session next morning. Amongst those listed were two marked with an asterisk, denoting a substantial disagreement between the original assessors and himself:

Glottal Stops in Twentieth-Century English Political Discourse: A Phonetic Perspective (book, 350 pp. + transcriptions, P. Lampton)
First assessor: Originality A-, Significance A, Rigour A
Second assessor: Originality B, Significance C, Rigour B-

*'Undes ars in tine naso': Insults and Injuries in Old Bavarian Dialects (article, 16 pp., J. Lubbins)
First assessor: Originality A, Significance A, Rigour A
Second assessor: Originality B-, Significance B-, Rigour C

*Substantial disagreement

Isabelle put the papers into the envelopes after photocopying them and alerted Jim to the developments. He gave her a handwritten sheet for her to type up and put only in his, Peter's, and

Brown's envelope, ensuring that it was uppermost in his pile of papers. It read:

Please add the following essay to your list of submissions, which is in preparation for submission to the *Zeitschrift für vergleichende Phonologie*, 'The Glottalization of Sonorants in Thirteenth-century Romance and Germanic', (revised edition of the original, unpublished article, 1978, 33 pp., P. Lampton). A synopsis and comparison with the entry on thirteenth-century phonology in the *Handbook of Comparative Phonology*, ed. D. Brown (1979), will be tabled for discussion. At Professor Brown's request, please prepare yourselves thoroughly by reading the above.

Isabelle next had the task of taking the envelopes round to each of the colleagues' rooms.

'Be sure to give Del Boy his envelope half an hour before all the rest,' Jim said disrespectfully. 'He always reads papers straightaway, and he'll get a shock when he reads this. I wonder what he'll do next.'

He gave Isabelle a kiss and a squeeze.

'I'll make it up to you tonight,' he said.

'You'll be lucky,' Isabelle retorted.

Jim apprised Peter of the plan.

Ten minutes later, Brown was to be seen knocking at people's doors, asking them to return the envelopes, owing to an omission.

Most colleagues explained that they hadn't yet received theirs. He next rushed to Isabelle and demanded she give him all the envelopes. She asked him why he needed them.

'I'm afraid there has been an omission in the papers for the 9:00 meeting,' he said.

'If you let me have the additional material, I'll put it in for you,' Isabelle said with a grin.

'No, I don't want to put you to any trouble after you should have knocked off for the evening,' Brown said.

'It's really no trouble,' Isabelle said.

Brown seized hold of the envelopes and took them away. He was perplexed when he discovered that the extra sheet was not in the recovered envelopes. He would need to take action in the meeting itself.

At dinner, colleagues regrouped in the seating arrangement they had occupied at lunch.

'So far, so good,' Jim said with a big smirk to their group. Vicky looked perplexed.

'Care to cut me in on this?' she said.

'We can't tell you now,' Peter said. 'Come to my room at 9:00, and I'll fill you in on the details.'

'OK,' Vicky said. 'I can't wait.'

Peter wondered if his chance had arrived. It was Beebee he wanted really, but Vicky was fun, too. At least they could have a flirtatious evening together.

Jim went over to Brown and enquired whether he had sorted out the problem with the envelopes.

'Yes, I think you'll find that the problem is now solved,' Brown said.

'Oh, I discovered another envelope after you'd gone,' Jim said. 'Isabelle had forgotten to put the extra sheet in mine. She gave it to me later. I don't suppose it's important, is it?' he said tauntingly. 'But I suppose, in view of what you said about being well prepared, I'd better read it first.'

'No, I would advise against that,' Brown said.

'You've changed your tune, then, have you?' Jim said with a poker face.

'Have you opened it yet?' Brown asked.

'No, it's on the desk,' Jim said.

Brown hoped that, if Jim's was the last incriminating sheet in circulation, to remove it and substitute duplicate papers for the 10:00 meeting would solve the problem. But how to gain entry to Jim's room? He knew Jim would be in the bar after dinner.

The conspirators and Vicky met in the bar again. Brown popped in briefly to ascertain whether Jim was there.

'Come and join us, Derek,' Jim said. 'I'll buy you a drink. I was a bit rude to you earlier. No hard feelings, eh? What's your poison?'

'No hard feelings,' Brown said grudgingly, 'but I need to get back to my room and prepare for tomorrow.'

'Yeah,' Jim said. 'we should be here all evening.'

Brown hastened back to Jim's room and opened the door with a technique he had learned in the military. He closed the door behind him and swapped the envelopes.

Jim went back to his room and opened the door as noisily as possible. Brown had to secrete himself under the bed, again using a technique he had learned in the military. Jim was relishing the intrigue. After an hour, he went out of the room and back down to Peter, Vicky, and Isabelle. Peter and Vicky went back upstairs just in time to see Brown exiting Jim's room. They smiled at him but said nothing. He muttered something in embarrassment.

'The plan's working,' Peter said to Vicky. 'Come in, and I'll tell you all about it.'

Peter opened the minibar and poured out two gin and tonics. He next began to initiate her into the intrigue. Vicky was enthralled, and the two of them enjoyed each other's company with considerable mirth. Would Vicky seduce him? Peter wondered. He was ripe for seduction, but Vicky was expecting a move on his part, and Peter's mildly suggestive comments without actions were insufficient to initiate anything. At 10:00, his phone went. *Damn!* he thought, as he recognized his wife calling. *Damn!* After the brief conversation with Becky, his conscience was pricking him. All amorous intentions had evaporated. He made his excuses—he needed to get an early night—and Vicky departed, disappointed.

Damn!

Jim and Isabelle left the bar and went up to Isabelle's room.

'I told you I'd make it up to you,' Jim said. 'But I need you to do me another small favour first.'

Isabelle looked worried.

'I'll keep you company for a quick drink from the minibar,' she said, 'but I need an early night. I'll have a quick G&T.'

'Yeah,' Jim said. 'I'll mix you one.'

He poured out Isabelle's drink and opened a can of beer for himself. He went up to Isabelle from behind and reached over her shoulder while handing her the drink.

'I hope the gin doesn't kill off the pheromones,' he said. 'Do they turn you on?'

'Honestly, no,' Isabelle said. 'I prefer a good Cologne, but even Old Spice would do the trick for me—you know the slogan, *Smell Like a Man, Man.*'

'Yeah, well,' Jim said. 'I smell like a *real* man.'

'What was that little favour you required?' Isabelle asked.

'I want you to get out your laptop and go online,' Jim said.

'There must be a catch somewhere,' Isabelle said.

'No, just sit at the desk and search for *Comparative Phonology of Sonorants* in the publisher's catalogue. Right, copy that and write "Reprint of the Lausanne 1958 edition" on it. I need a printout then.'

Isabelle used her computing skills to mock up a convincing-looking flyer.

'Well done, lass,' Jim said. 'I want to press your *print* button,' he said suggestively and reached over Isabelle's shoulder to send the document to the hotel's printer.

'Ah, pheromones!' he said hopefully as he repositioned himself for a more amorous embrace. Isabelle looked concerned.

'Come on, you know you want to,' he said, as he tried to persuade her to follow him to the bed. There was a knock at the door.

'Bloody 'ell,' Jim said.

Isabelle went to the door.

'A printout for room 137,' the hotel employee said. Isabelle took the sheet of paper and put it carefully away in her briefcase.

'Let's have it, then,' Jim said.

'You'll have to behave yourself if you want it,' Isabelle said. 'I'll bring it along to your room later.'

She gave him a brief kiss and said, 'Goodnight, see you later.'

Jim returned to his room and waited expectantly. At midnight, he went to bed, unfulfilled.

Wednesday, 17 September

In the morning, Jim went down to breakfast and discovered Isabelle sitting at a table with Vicky.

'I was waiting for that printout last night,' he said.

'Yes, sorry, I fell asleep,' Isabelle said. 'Anyway, here it is.'

'Yeah, thanks a lot,' Jim said sullenly.

Peter came and joined them.

'Look, here's the plan,' Jim said. 'Vicky, we want you to take this and hand it to Derek just before the meeting, while we watch his reaction. Tell him you think it might be of interest.'

Niamh introduced the meeting and handed over to Derek, who proceeded to run through the list of synopses for restructuring.

Jim put up his hand.

'I don't seem to have page 1,' he said. 'Nothing on linguistics, then?' he asked.

'No,' Brown replied sullenly.

'So you approved of our ratings, then,' Jim said tauntingly.

'Yes,' Brown said through gritted teeth.

'Well, that's a relief,' Jim said.

At the coffee break, Jim and Peter reflected on the progress.

'That's an A for stratagem,' Peter said, 'to add to our As for originality, significance, and rigour.'

'Yeah, we outwitted him,' Jim said. 'But he'll be plotting his revenge. We may yet need to focus his attention on one night in Cambridge in 1968.'

'Shades of Mrs Biggs,' Peter quipped.

'A very sharp observation,' Jim rejoined.

'I wonder if my old landlady's still around,' Peter said. 'She was old enough to be my mum, but she fancied us undergraduates—called us "my boys". She used a special posh voice to speak to us and then reverted to her common accent when talking to her family. Maybe that's what got me interested in glottal stops. She would know the bedder from Needham if they're both still alive.'

'Yeah,' Jim said, 'that might come in handy.'

The restructurers held a final morning session to wrap up the business of the three days, finishing with lunch. In the afternoon, Peter, Jim, Vicky, Beebee, and Isabelle went for a walk along the beach towards Troon.

'Let's just pop into the clubhouse and ask how much a round of "goff" is,' Jim said. 'Very hoity-toity here, y'know. You'd better ask, Peter. We can get a pint anyway.'

Peter went and asked. He came back ashen-faced.

'200 bloody quid,' Peter stammered.

'That's fifty quid each,' Jim said.

'No, 200 quid each,' Peter said.

'Bloody 'ell,' Jim said. 'I'll ask them if they do special rates for distinguished academic visitors from England.'

'Sir's joking with me,' the assistant said. 'You might wish to try Darley municipal course down the road. Their green fees are a tenth of ours. I'm told it's quite good as municipal courses go.'

'Stuck-up Scottish prick!' Jim muttered as they walked away towards the bar.

'Excuse me, sir, but I'm afraid you need to wear a tie in here,' the barman said.

'A dog's arse in your nose!' Jim said in a German accent. 'Old Bavarian, you know!'

53

Peter hurriedly ushered him out of the bar before there was any response. The three ladies looked embarrassed. They would not be returning under any circumstances.

On the walk back to the hotel, Jim put his arm round Isabelle, who hadn't the heart to reject him. Peter walked between Vicky and Beebee. Which should he choose? *Let them decide!* he thought. He walked back alone.

A couple of the restructurers had already departed for home, leaving the remaining ones feeling demob happy. Now was the time for unrestrained liaisons on their final night in the hotel. Now was also the time for Brown to gather intelligence on more than an academic plane.

The seating arrangements at dinner changed, too, as did the voluntarily adopted dress code for many. For the first time, Brown was to be seen sporting an open-neck shirt and pullover rather than the ill-fitting 1960s-style jacket and skinny tie that he habitually wore. His style was not consciously retro—his wardrobe had scarcely changed in forty years. It apparently did not bother him that his jackets could not be done up, let alone meet in anything like the middle. To his students, he was a curiosity, a product of a bygone age. Even if his dress was once fashionable for the likes of the Beatles, his attitudes went back to the forties. Neither had changed. Students were puzzled, however, that the legs of his skinny trousers, which were understandably bulging below the overtightened waistband, were now two inches above his shoes and the sleeves of his jackets seemed either to have got shorter or else his arms had got longer, possibly in tandem with the expansion of his cranial anatomy, which, with the acquisition of ever-greater knowledge and intelligence, had begun to show an excrescence on the right-hand side. His espionage techniques, learned in the military, could now be put to good use on the final evening in plotting his revenge. He had realized not only that he had been rumbled by Jim and Peter but that they had deliberately gone to pains to humiliate him in the pursuit of their aims. Revenge would be sweet, he thought, but he needed to put his victims off their guard, and that had already started with the change of attire to a postmillennial pullover. Normally the first one to arrive for dinner, he had deliberately come exactly ten minutes later than the official start time, which today was 7 p.m. Thus, he was the third person to be seated at the second of the two tables, which had that evening begun to be occupied first. Changing places, he thought, was not only a passable novel but a good ploy that evening. Niamh entered the room and went to sit next to him. Brown hastily whispered something in her ear, and she moved opposite him, next to Raúl, who sat opposite Grabowski. Niamh engaged in conversation with Raúl, leaving Brown to converse in very formal tones with Grabowski, something that afforded neither of them much pleasure but which fitted Brown's plans admirably, certainly far better than his unchanged trousers, the circumference of which would be further challenged by his intention to consume an entire bottle of house red and indulge himself with three courses that evening.

Jim and Isabelle looked cautiously round the door into the dining room. There was no lingering at the buffet that evening, since dinner was served *à la carte*, which meant choosing a seat immediately on entry. Hence, Jim and Isabelle exited the room and waited ten minutes in the bar over a pre-prandial drink. In the meantime, Yoshanna had gone and sat opposite Brown, and Ralf had grudgingly found a place beside his old adversary. The conversational dynamics were awkward. Ralf's good manners precluded him from interrupting the conversation opposite him, in which Yoshanna had also become involved, but did not extend to engaging Brown even in a perfunctory conversation; hence he sat alone, not speaking until he was able to converse with Yoshanna in a lull in her conversation. Ralf was used to such awkwardness from the time when he was a research fellow in Cambridge, where the configuration of High Table was dependent on seniority, the number of guests present, and deliberate attempts at avoidance, which did not always work, so ten minutes without an interlocutor was no hardship for him.

Meanwhile, Jim and Isabelle had been joined in the bar by Peter, Vicky, and Beebee, after Peter had cautiously ascertained the lie of the land in the dining room. The five of them were then able to seat themselves at the second table and converse relatively unhampered, save that an eye had to be kept on Brown, who was, however, not well placed for espionage.

The mood of the conspirators—for that was now the accepted name they had given themselves—was especially jovial. Jim regaled the company with tales of his amorous exploits, conveniently omitting to mention the unsuccessful conclusion of most but rather hinting that he had scored. Peter found this amusing, since he knew better the true history of this would-be Casanova of the linguistic world; he was able to laugh along at the exploits, in the knowledge that Jim was making a rather absurd and sorry spectacle of himself. Jim was blissfully unaware that he was being laughed at rather than that he was amusing the company by his wit. Isabelle, who was apprehensive about Jim's amorous intentions, began to fear more, unsure whether the succession of tales about Jim's young ladies indicated merely a sexual, rather than a more emotional, interest. Peter steered the conversation away from its focus on Jim by asking Beebee about her academic plans. She was one of three panel members who did not bear the title of professor. Peter wanted to know both about this aspect and, more importantly, about her love life. He knew she was divorced, but he couldn't come straight out with it and ask whether she currently had a partner. *Stratagem, Peter!* he thought to himself.

'You must be really well placed to observe the speech habits of estuary English, Beebee,' Peter said. 'Is glottalization something that interests you, too?'

Beebee looked surprised. She knew Peter had more than a scholarly interest in her, and she also found him quite attractive, but she knew he was married. She wanted to find out how happily. To do that, she would need to show interest.

56

Vicky looked bored and slightly disturbed at Peter's greater interest in Beebee than in her. She hadn't indicated to Peter that she was divorced from her husband and potentially on the lookout for some extramarital action.

At the other table, Brown had become involved in a scholarly conversation with Ralf and was in the process of superciliously putting him down by comparing Ralf's modest article on the courtly romance with his substantial book that subsumed the topic of Ralf's work.

'You're lucky restructuring wasn't advised, Whitby,' he said, ostensibly forgetting that they were on first-name terms. 'I expect you'll have a job placing that article.'

'Actually, no,' Ralf said. 'It's already been accepted for the *International Journal of Arthurian Studies*. I only submitted it to the RRE to show willing and to test the system.'

Brown looked on disdainfully and was about to speak again when he felt a foot brushing against his leg. The source of the stimulation was indicated by a slight smile from Niamh. Jim, who had become bored by Peter's interest in Beebee, had been looking over at the next-door table and had detected an overture to 'amorous activity', as he was wont to call his attempts to bed young ladies. He smirked and nudged Isabelle, nodding discreetly in the direction of the activity.

Beebee agreed that her situation in the University of Essex was indeed the perfect place for the kind of study Peter was interested in. Indeed, she had been reading an article on the subject in the university magazine on the train.

'It's in my room,' she said. 'You can come and fetch it after dinner if you like.'

Peter was surprised that his maladroit opening gambit had actually achieved the more important of his two goals—a private encounter with Beebee. He didn't want to appear too eager, so he said he would come along after coffee if the offer still stood.

'Of course,' Beebee said. 'We can go up together.'

Jim smiled knowingly at Isabelle.

'We'll be wanting to go back to mine this evening, too,' he said. 'Get the old laptop out again and go through those papers like last night,' he said to intimate that amorous activity had taken place.

Vicky looked left out.

'You can come, too, love,' he said, thinking that a three-some might not be out of the question.

'That's very kind,' Vicky said. 'But I have some economies of scale to work through for another subpanel.'

'Oh, yeah!' Jim said with a wink, but secretly thinking amorous activity *à deux* would be much easier to achieve. 'If you change your mind and feel like joining us, you can make your economies of scale with us. Three's better than two.'

Vicky looked faintly disgusted but smiled politely and kept her mouth shut.

'Well, it's been a lovely few days,' Peter said. 'Who'd have thought that an RRE meeting could be such fun? I'm dreading going back to London Bridge and all the dreary admin—exam boards, boards of studies, departmental meetings, introductory meetings for students, enrolment for courses …'

He stopped with no real conclusion, the list of tedious activities having dried up.

'You forgot the most important bit,' Jim said. 'Teaching the lasses.'

'That's a bit sexist, isn't it?' Isabelle said.

'*I'm* a bit sexist,' Jim retorted. 'The lasses know where they're placed with me.'

'And where's that?' Vicky asked.

'If they stay on the right side of me, they know they stand a good chance of a First. A bit like the RRE, eh, Peter? You scratch my back, I'll scratch yours. Only with the young ladies it's somewhere else.'

Vicky gave Jim a strong stare.

'Only joking,' Jim said. 'Subtle's my middle name, phero-mones my secret weapon.'

It was now Isabelle's turn to look disapproving at the thought of the pheromones, which she had experienced at close range.

'I'll buy you a bottle of Eau Sauvage, Jim,' she said. 'You might stand a chance with the young ladies if you splashed it on all over. Remember Henry Cooper.'

Peter looked perplexed.

'I don't get it,' he said. 'That was Brut. Actually, it quite turns Becky on.'

Nothing much else does, he thought.

'Pheromones would do the trick better,' Jim said.

'Well, you're not trying it with Becky,' Peter said.

'Nor me,' Isabelle quipped, half in jest.

'Is this what you call an academic conversation?' Vicky asked. 'We may be a bit more practically oriented in business, but we keep to our own kind.'

'Yeah, well,' Jim said. 'I'm always kind. I'm going to get you a job, aren't I, Isabelle?'

'We'll see,' Isabelle said.

'By their fruits shall ye know them,' Peter said.

Jim wanted to make a joke about fruity young maidens, but propriety got the better of him.

'We'll go online tonight and look for academic jobs. All you need is a good reference from J. Lubbins, eh, Isabelle?'

Isabelle smiled an uncertain smile.

'What about the research?' Vicky asked. 'You won't just go away and forget about those articles you're writing and how they might be in danger of restructuring.'

'No chance of that,' Peter said. 'We've beaten Brown at his own game.'

'I wouldn't be too sure,' Vicky said. 'I've heard it said that he never accepts defeat.'

'Oh, yeah? Who told you that?' Jim said.

'His wife, actually. I met her at a May Week party once, soon after he'd got remarried. He was in full flow, quaffing champagne and stuffing himself with strawberries and cream, while she stood beside him, looking out of place. For want of anything better to do, she had had a few glasses herself, and evidently that loosened her tongue. Would you believe it? She took me to one side and told me about Brown's wooing technique and how she wished she had resisted his "charms". Something along the lines of "I think you'll find that marrying me would be to your advantage, Marion." He wouldn't take no for an answer. Apparently, her main function, apart from keeping house for him, is to type up his work and put the books away after he's used them.'

'Yeah, well,' Jim said, 'he seemed to be cosying up to Niamh this evening.'

'I think it was the other way round,' Isabelle said. 'Goodness knows why.'

'Might be worth keeping an eye on that,' Jim said.

'Sorry, but if we're going to fetch that article, we need to go up now, otherwise I'm going to fall asleep at the table,' Beebee said.

'Excuse us,' Peter said.

Jim gave him a wink. Peter returned the gesture with a frown, but was that just a ploy? He opened the door for Beebee and accompanied her in gentlemanly fashion to her room.

'Do come in,' Beebee said. 'Sit down while I make myself more comfortable. These shoes are killing me.'

She kicked off her shoes and loosened her top two buttons, revealing some cleavage. Peter looked embarrassed, thinking back to the first evening when she had asked him to do up her buttons.

'Should I look the other way?' he said.

'No, of course not,' she said. 'You're not embarrassed, are you?'

'Well, just a little,' Peter said. 'I've always been a rather shy person, you must understand.'

'I was, too, once, but I've grown out of that now,' Beebee said.

He'd always imagined she had been a bit of a goer in her youth. Maybe she was now. Was she telling the truth? He supposed so. Peter had an endearing trait of always trusting people, but it had got him into trouble. In his naivety, he thought that people always tell the truth, as he—mostly—did. He never lied outright, even if he occasionally cunningly and subtly moulded his utterances to suit his intended veracity. Was Beebee coming on to him now? If he seemed overkeen, that might put paid to the whole enterprise. He lacked finesse in wooing females. That was not to say that he blundered his way in, all guns firing. No, that might be Jim's technique, but Jim shrugged off rejection, even if he might once have been hurt by it. Now, after fifty or more—he had no idea how many it was in reality—he must be so used to it that it was water off a duck's back. Peter envied him for it. He, on the other hand, shyly stood aside and bided his time, which usually never came. He could look longingly at a woman but never act upon it. How did it ever come about that he ended up sleeping with Becky in those halcyon days? he wondered. He supposed it was because they were both up for it and all that was needed was a flint to spark the fire and ignite their passion. They both smoked in those days, so a cigarette lighter sufficed. Now, however, if it wasn't his innate shyness, then it was his conscience pricking him. He tried to duck out of the way of conscience's darts, but they always found him and hit him, usually in his most vulnerable spot—Becky was such a good wife to him. He felt guilty for taking her too much for granted. Steady and loyal and faithful—at least he supposed so, and there was no evidence to the contrary. Like him, steady and boring in bed. The glottal stop of lovemaking. Beebee, on the other hand, was wild, brimming with gay abandon. He loved that term and insisted on still using it despite the inevitable smirks with which it was met. Abandon or abandon? Yes, should he abandon any hopes of an illicit liaison? He was very poor at reading the signals from a woman, but they were so damned contradictory, and semiotics was not a branch of linguistics that he had warmed to. Gay or gay? Definitely not gay. Straight or straight? Definitely never straightforward. Nothing ever was with women. *Abandon hope, all ye who enter here* or, as he preferred it in the original, *Lasciate ogne speranza, voi ch'intrate.* He had already entered her room. But should he seek the entrance to her inner sanctum or run for the exit?

Beebee sat down on the bed nearest the pillow and beckoned to Peter to come and sit beside her.

'Are you as shagged as I am?' she asked.

What the hell does she mean? he thought. She reached over and took out the *Essex Uni Magazine* from the bedside table, opened it and moved closer to Peter. Beebee turned to the start of the article. It was entitled 'Estuary English—Campus Lingua Franca?'

'Fascinating,' Peter said as Beebee passed it over and onto his lap. She reached across him and turned the page, smiling up at him as she did so.

'Look, here's a bit that even mentions your glottal stops. "Lampton's long-awaited work on politicians' English promises to finally settle the dispute as to the status of glottalization in a historical context."'

Peter winced.

'Glottal stop or no, he has no business splitting his infinitive,' he said.

'You're splitting hairs, Peter,' Beebee said. 'Can't you see? You're famous. It's certainly something when you get written about by a student journalist in the *Uni Mag.*'

'You flatter me,' Peter said. 'I'd assumed you weren't interested.'

'Who couldn't be interested when a handsome man like you throws himself into such a fascinating study with such far-reaching implications?' Beebee said.

'You may be taking the micky,' Peter said, 'but it'll become a standard work of reference. Remember what Jim said. People will refer to it in 100 years' time.'

Beebee laughed.

'Where exactly is your glottis?' Beebee asked.

'You're having me on,' Peter said.

'No, of course not,' Beebee said with a grin. 'Point it out to me.'

Peter tilted his head back and stroked his Adam's apple with two fingers.

'Let me feel,' Beebee said.

Peter smiled in embarrassment.

'Open wide,' she said. 'I want to see from inside.'

Peter opened his mouth cautiously while Beebee positioned herself nearer to him.

'Now shut your eyes,' she said. 'I don't want to poke anything.'

'I think I can just see,' Beebee said. 'I wonder how far back I can see. I need a closer look.'

Peter felt a sensation. A tongue had penetrated his oral cavity and was well past his alveolar ridge, he thought.

'Have I reached it yet? Shall I stop?' Beebee asked.

'No, of course not,' Peter said.

Which question was he answering?

'Is that as far as it goes, then?' Beebee said.

Peter looked apprehensive. Was she really coming on to him or just teasing him?

Beebee continued her exploration of Peter's mouth. She looked up and smiled at Peter, who by now had nearly lost his inhibitions. They kissed passionately.

Damn!—Becky!—I'm sorry! There was a knock at the door. Peter was relieved. He'd overcome temptation. Or had he?

'Don't you think you'd better answer it?' he said.

'No, you're more important,' Beebee said.

Outside, Jim could be heard talking to Isabelle.

'D'you think they've got down to business yet?' Jim asked. 'Randy bastard!' was just audible from inside.

Peter felt insulted. He wasn't a randy bastard. That might be an appropriate designation for Jim, but he was a shy, sensitive, honourable man. He had seldom scored, even less frequently set out with the intention of scoring. His honour was impugned. He must defend himself. He opened the door.

'Ey up,' Jim said. 'Fancy finding you here. Read any good articles lately?'

'Yes,' Peter said. 'We're in the process of that and currently discussing glottalization.'

'Oh, aye?' Jim said. 'The happlication of the glottal stop in poncy stuck-up hacademics.'

'Well, at least I'm not a randy bastard,' Peter said.

'Nor am I, am I, Isabelle?' Jim said.

Isabelle smiled.

'Did you two want something?' Beebee asked.

'Yeah,' Jim said. 'Derek's in with Niamh. He was on the prowl earlier, listening in at all the doors. He stopped a long time outside this one. He seemed to be using one of those handheld Dictaphone machines. Only it looked rather old-fashioned, like something Q would have given to James Bond.'

Peter frowned.

'He didn't get any "intelligence" out of us, though, did he love?' Jim said to Isabelle.

'He's just kidding,' Isabelle said. 'Wishful thinking again.'

'Anyway,' Jim said. 'The night is young for amorous activity. We've hatched a plan, and we thought you two would like to be involved.'

'We were rather busy,' Beebee said.

'What's the plan?' Peter asked.

'It'll cost you a couple of quid,' Jim said, 'but it'll be worth it.'

'Don't keep us in suspense,' Beebee said.

'Aren't you going to invite us in, then?' Jim asked.

Beebee grudgingly complied. Peter looked annoyed.

'Tell them the plan, Isabelle,' Jim said.

'You tell them; it's your idea,' she said.

'Well, we worked out that it's 40 years since that feast in Cambridge. That's your ruby wedding anniversary, right?'

'I don't know,' Peter said. 'We haven't got to that yet. Our next one's pearl if we make it that far.'

'Well, that doesn't matter.'

'Jim thought we should club together for a bottle of champagne and have it taken up by room service with a note saying, "Congratulations on your 40th Anniversary from all at Needham College",' Isabelle said.

'Isn't that a bit childish?' Beebee said.

'Isn't it a bit expensive?' Peter added.

'Thirty quid each and ten for the ladies,' Jim said. 'I can't wait to see his face in the morning. And here's the best bit, Isabelle's got this pen drive that's also a voice recorder. If we tip the waiter twenty quid, he'll secrete it somewhere on the trolley, and we can listen to their reaction later plus any other activity.'

'Steady on, that's a hundred quid all told,' Peter said. 'I'm not sure I want to waste my money on a silly prank, even if it would be fun.'

'It might be your glottal stops at stake yet,' Jim said. 'He hasn't finished with us yet. Weight of evidence, you see—hard facts. A nicked library book and a borrowed research idea against sounds of amorous activity from you two. Which would win in your opinion?'

'OK, here's forty quid. I can't expect Beebee to pay,' Peter said.

Jim picked up the phone and rang room service.

'I want a bottle of champagne for room 106,' he said. 'And bring one of those cards saying, "Congratulations on your 40th Anniversary from all at Needham" ... Yeah, Lubbins,' he said, 'put it on my tab.'

Ten minutes later, the waiter arrived.

'It's not for us,' Jim said. 'It's a surprise for two love birds. They're celebrating their ruby anniversary. Put this under the ice bucket, where they won't find it, and bring it back to us when you clear up.'

'I'm not sure I should, sir,' the waiter said.

'Would twenty quid help?' Jim said. 'It's all a surprise anyway. Room 121, right?'

'Yes, sir.'

Thursday 18 September

In the morning, Peter went down early to breakfast. The staff were still setting out the buffet. At exactly 8:00 a.m., as was his wont, Brown entered. He went and sat at his normal place. Peter fetched his breakfast and went and sat next to Brown.

'Good morning, Derek,' he said cheerfully.

'Good morning, Lampton,' Brown replied.

So far, one – nil to him, he thought. He had made Brown feel awkward by his change of address and by obliging him still to use his surname.

'Isn't it time you and I were on first-name terms?' he said. 'Everyone else on the panel is. I'm Peter.'

He held his hand out for Brown to shake it. Brown grudgingly complied.

'Derek,' he said.

Two – nil.

'Did you have a good night, Derek?'

'Yes, thank you, Lampt … Peter.'

Three – nil.

'I think there were a few celebrations yesterday evening,' Peter said. 'A few of us were celebrating a successful conclusion to the three days. Did you manage to celebrate, Derek?'

Four – nil.

Brown began to look uneasy. Was he going to admit to anything, or would he tell a barefaced lie?

'No, I had a quiet evening, reading,' he said.

Five – nil.

Peter was satisfied that he had made Brown squirm enough.

'I'm going to fetch another coffee. May I get you one, too?' he said.

'That would be very kind,' Brown said grudgingly.

Six – nil? At this rate, Team Peter was in line for promotion to a higher league. Jim and Isabelle came in and joined Peter at the coffee urn.

'I had a good shower this morning after last night's activity,' Jim said with a wink. 'Washed the pheromones away, eh, Isabelle?'

'Yes, Jim,' she said.

Peter assumed he had scored, but he didn't care.

'Go and ask Derek how he got on yesterday, Isabelle,' Peter said. 'No, wait. Not yet. He might be suspicious.'

Peter returned to his place, followed by Jim and Isabelle.

'Ey up, Derek,' Jim said. 'Mind if we join you? Or would you prefer we keep a place free for Niamh? You probably have important business to conclude before we all go home.'

Seven – nil, Peter thought. *This is getting embarrassing.*

'Go ahead,' Brown said. 'I shan't be waiting around.'

Niamh came in and sat at the other table. Brown cast a glance in her direction, which was met with a discreet smile. Beebee came down and joined Niamh. Peter cast a glance in her direction, which was met with a broad smile. Peter felt embarrassed and chuffed at the same time. His inhibitions were fast melting away, but opportunity was now spent. Vicky came and joined Peter's table.

'Are we all going to go back on the same train?' she asked.

Brown got up and excused himself.

'Have a good journey home, Derek,' Peter said.

'Yes, see you next time in Berlin,' Isabelle said.

'Or maybe before,' Jim said. 'I'm externalling in Oxford, as you probably know.'

'Yes, I had heard,' Brown said. 'I was on sabbatical when you were appointed.'

'You got a pleasant surprise, then,' Jim said tauntingly.'

Brown smiled.

'Goodbye all,' he said and walked over to Niamh.

'Good morning, ladies,' he said. 'I'll see you later,' he said to Niamh. 'Goodbye, Dr Frensham—Beebee, I mean.'

'Goodbye, Derek,' Beebee said. 'Until Berlin.'

'Until Berlin,' Brown said and departed.

'Are you externalling anywhere this year?' Niamh asked Beebee.

'Peter asked me to look after phonetics at London Bridge. It's a bit of a tall order in view of the RRE, but I'll fit it in somehow,' Beebee said. 'How about you?'

'No, only a DPhil for Derek in Oxford,' Niamh said.

'Oh, how interesting,' Beebee said. 'What's it on?'

'Sonorants in Germanic,' Niamh said.

'Isn't that Peter's field?' Beebee asked.

'Yes, but he had his reasons for asking me.'

Beebee smiled and didn't enquire further. She could think of at least two.

The waiter from yesterday's room service came in and went up to Jim.

'I have something for you, sir,' he said and handed him the pen drive discreetly.

'Ta very much,' Jim said. The waiter smiled.

'It might be worth another tenner, what's on there, sir,' the waiter said.

'I'll let you know once I've listened,' Jim said. He slipped him a fiver. *Maybe next time*, he thought.

'We'll pop up to your room with this after breakfast,' he said to Isabelle.

Vicky joined Niamh and Beebee.

'Does anyone want to share a taxi to the station?' Beebee asked.

'I need to check with Peter first,' Vicky said. 'I expect we'll all be catching the same train back.'

Beebee wondered whether there was a particular attraction to the sharing proposal. She supposed she might catch the same train down south, even though she had flown on the way north. She popped over to the other table to enquire, then returned to Vicky and Niamh.

'It looks as though we can all catch the same train,' she said. 'Peter's decided the 10:07 from Ayr is best, getting to London at 16:36. You'll only be with us as far as Glasgow, I suppose, Niamh. You go via Preston, don't you?'

'No, I think I'll take the Euston train and keep Derek company. We've agreed to leave later,' Niamh said.

'I hope you have a great journey, Beebee said. 'I'd better get back and pack.'

'Yes, so had I,' Vicky said.

They said their goodbyes and went over to the other table.

'It looks like we need two taxis,' Vicky said.

Peter winced. If one of his students had used *like* as a conjunction in an essay, it would have been circled round in red. But since he had a soft spot for Vicky, she was spared this indignity in its verbal form. The scarcely perceptible wince amounted only to a few dots under the word, such as he might use to indicate displeasure in a research student's work.

The conspirators agreed that they would order two taxis and set off together for the 10:07. They all went up to their respective rooms to pack.

Peter got into a taxi with Beebee and Vicky; Jim shared one with Isabelle.

'You never told me where you live,' Jim said.

'You never asked me,' Isabelle replied.

'Are you getting off at York, then?' Jim asked.

'No, I'm going through to Peterborough.'

'Where do you live, then?'

'Cambridge—in Rustat Road.'

'But you got on at York.'

'Yeah, I was visiting a good friend.'

'Oh, yeah, was she at Cambridge, too?'

'He was at Jesus.'

Jim didn't know whether to be thrilled that Isabelle lived in the same city or worried that she had a good friend of the male sex. Pheromones will overcome any hurdle, he thought.

'Put this somewhere safe,' Jim said, as he handed the pen drive to Isabelle. She unzipped her laptop bag and put it into a pocket inside, zipping it up for extra safety.

'I'll have a brief listen on the train with my earphones,' Isabelle said.

'Yeah, well, perhaps you'll let me have a listen, too,' Jim said. 'Can't we share them? You know, one in each ear.'

'No, that's gross,' Isabelle said. 'Full of bacteria.'

'Not with Jim Lubbins,' Jim said. 'You'll have got a few of mine already anyway,' he said with a smirk.

'Sorry, Jim, you'll have to wait.'

The two taxis arrived at Ayr station. Jim bought the *Scottish Daily Mirror* and Peter the *Scotsman* from the kiosk. Vicky bought the *Scottish Woman* and *Business Women Scotland*.

'A right poncy lot you are,' Jim said. 'Isabelle can share my *Daily Mirror* with me if she gets bored.'

'Thanks, Jim,' she said. 'I shan't get bored, and anyway, I've got all my notes to go through from three days of meetings.'

The hour-long journey to Glasgow was uneventful, spent reading newspapers and idly chatting. Isabelle waited until they were in the intercity train before getting out her laptop. She read through some of her handwritten notes. Jim amused himself making frivolous suggestions about how she should write up aspects of the three days' proceedings.

'Put "Prof. Brown expressed great satisfaction with the results of the linguistics members of the Subpanel and noted that no restructuring was required."'

'I don't think Niamh will approve that,' Isabelle said.

'I think she will if she knows what's best for her,' Jim retorted.

'I'll try to remember when I get the laptop out,' Isabelle said.

'Yeah, which of those jobs are you going to apply for?' Jim asked her.

'I haven't decided yet,' she said, 'but I know your reference will make a big difference.'

'Accuracy, efficiency, and attention to detail are the hall-marks of Dr Chesham's work,' Jim said. 'Is that what you want me to write?'

Isabelle smiled.

'No restructuring required,' she said.

Peter and Vicky grabbed a quick coffee at Glasgow Central while Beebee purchased a ticket and Jim arranged an upgrade to First class for himself and Isabelle. They boarded the train for Euston. Jim and Isabelle sat opposite each other while Peter sat in a group of four seats with Beebee and Vicky. When the train got underway, Isabelle opened her laptop and started working.

'Aren't you going to listen to what's on that recording, then?' Jim said.

'I'm in no hurry,' Isabelle replied. 'Why are you so keen?'

'I'm not,' Jim said, 'but it's boring just sitting here. Go on, let me listen.'

'Sorry, pheromones or no, I'm not having any of your bacteria in my ears,' Isabelle said.

'Yeah, well, play it on the loudspeaker then on low volume.'

Isabelle looked round the carriage to see if they could be overheard. The noise of the train would seem to preclude that, she thought. She looked over to the other three colleagues.

'All all right with you?' she asked.

'We're fine, thanks,' Vicky answered.

Isabelle went ahead and connected the pen drive to the laptop. She clicked play. There was a lot of indistinct clatter as the trolley with the champagne was wheeled along the corridor. A few minutes in, the conversation started, preceded by a knock at the door.

'Room service, sir,' the waiter said.

'I think you'll find we haven't ordered anything,' Brown said.

'No, sir, but this is for you, it's a surprise from your friends on your anniversary.'

'Niamh, do you know anything about this?' Brown asked.

'No, not a thing,' came the reply.

'I'll just leave it with you, sir, then,' the waiter said. 'It's all paid for. Just leave it in a corner of the room, and it'll be collected in the morning.'

'Damn it, man, we didn't order it,' Brown said. 'Put it there, anyway.'

'Thank you, sir,' the waiter said and paused in the expectation of a tip, but none was forthcoming.

The recorded conversation continued of Niamh and Derek's puzzlement at the unexpected events.

'I smell a rat,' Brown said. 'Lubbins or Lampton or Whitby is behind this,' he said angrily.

'What does the note say?' Niamh asked.

'"Congratulations on your 40th Anniversary from all at Needham",' Derek read.

'Curiouser and curiouser,' Niamh said.

'They'll not get away with this,' Derek said.

'Who knows about our fling in Needham anyway?' Niamh asked.

'It was the talk of the staff, I'm told,' Derek said. 'But it's long since forgotten now, unless Whitby …'

'Oh, forget about it,' Niamh said. 'Here's to us. We've got something to celebrate, after all.'

A cork popping was audible, followed by the sound of two glasses of champagne being poured out.

'All right, Niamh. I think you'll find that we could take up where we left off,' Derek said.

'Yes,' she said. 'Do you want to be my little chocolate Brownie again?' she said with a giggle.

'I'm not one for levity,' Derek said, 'but I'll make an exception in your case.'

Jim and Isabelle listened, intrigued. The conversation faded away to be replaced by sounds of amorous activity.

'I think we do it better,' Jim whispered to Isabelle.

'You wish,' she said. 'Have you heard enough yet?' Isabelle asked.

'Yeah, well, enough of the banging,' Jim said. 'See if you can find any more conversation.'

Isabelle fast forwarded the recording an hour and found more talking.

'All right, Niamh,' Derek said. 'I think you'll find it's time for you to go back to your room. Thank you for a pleasant evening.'

'Good night, Choccie,' she said with a giggle and shut the door after her. The recording captured only sounds of Derek's movements and occasional muttered words: *Good God! … All right, Marion … Lubbins … Whitby … Lampton … Restructure the lot of them …* Minutes later, the room went quiet and sounds of gentle snoring began.

'Make me a copy of that, lass,' Jim said.

'D'you think it'll give you ideas? Hone your lovemaking skills?' Isabelle asked.

'Sod off!' Jim said.

'Pheromones to you!' Isabelle said and mouthed him a kiss.

'Did that make you feel horny?' Jim said.

'No. I found it faintly disgusting,' Isabelle said.

'Have you heard of the mile-a-minute club?' Jim asked.

'No,' Isabelle said. 'I want to get on with my work.'

She looked over at Peter's group. They had shown no interest in them, so she supposed no-one else in the train had heard anything. She continued to work on her laptop, typing up her notes.

'It's like the mile-high club,' Jim said, 'only on a train. How about a quickie later?'

'You wish,' Isabelle said. 'Randy bastard.'

'Make sure you get your references right,' Jim said.

'Maybe later,' Isabelle said, thinking, *Maybe not today … Oh no!*

The five colleagues continued the journey uneventfully through to Peterborough, where four of them said goodbye to Beebee, who continued on to Euston.

'Looking forward to seeing you soon in London Bridge,' Peter said, as he made his farewells to Beebee. 'You'll be scrutinizing the papers soon and may be called upon to do a few orals.'

Beebee chuckled. The four remaining restructurers got out at Peterborough and walked to the car park.

'You're a lucky lass,' Jim said to Isabelle. 'You can have a lift to Cambridge in my Passion Wagon.'

Isabelle wasn't sure what to expect but decided to wait and see.

'Thanks, Jim, I could've got a taxi, but I expect I'm in for the ride of my life,' she said.

They went to their respective cars.

'It's been great meeting you,' Peter said to Vicky. 'We really must share a Danish together soon.'

'Or a Chelsea bun,' Vicky chuckled.

'Keep up the streamlining!' Peter said. 'I hope we'll get to know each other better soon. There's too much going on at one of these RRE meetings to chat with people properly. Oh, well! Back to the wife and kids now,' he said with a sigh.

'I wish I could say the same,' Vicky said.

'You mean you have a wife?' Peter asked perplexed.

'I'll explain when I see you,' Vicky replied.

They embraced briefly and said goodbye.

Peter got into his VW Passat and Vicky her BMW coupé. *Crikey!* Peter thought when he read the amount to pay. He was glad that his local station charged half the amount at Peterborough, whereby he saved himself a great deal of money on his usual commute. He pressed the button for a receipt and stowed it carefully in his wallet.

Vicky sped away while Peter adjusted the seat and made a slower exit. On the drive back home, Peter was melancholy. The three days in Ayr had been such a change, such a relief from home life with dependable Becky and the kids. He'd had an adventure. The five of them had made a great team. They called themselves the conspirators, but maybe the Famous

Five was almost appropriate. *Five on Kirrin Island?* he chuckled. He'd read it when he was about eight and had loved the sense of adventure and excitement that Enid Blyton's simple, but so alluring, stories conjured up in his childish imagination when life and society were so much simpler.

It came as a shock to him when, at prep school, the works of his favourite author were disparaged by the teachers and the boys discouraged from reading them. Was that not a form of restructuring? he thought. What right did the teachers have to restructure their pupils' thinking? It was fine to introduce them to higher literature and greater aspirations but wicked to stifle their youthful passions and pleasures. The same applied to the RRE.

He tried assigning the five colleagues to the characters in the book. He supposed he was Julian and Jim was Dick, but got stuck when it came to the females and wasn't sure where the dog fitted in. Nevertheless, they had had their adventure. They had thwarted their villain.

Peter was a simple soul at heart. He liked things to be straightforward and above board, to know right and wrong, but he was never strict in dividing sheep from goats. People weren't either black or white. He liked the good person who had his or her flaws, just as he did, just as Jim did. The five conspirators, it seemed to him, each had a warm heart, each wanted to see right prevail. He supposed they were the sheep of the subpanel, even if they might have ugly painted markings and less than pristine hind quarters. That's how sheep are, Peter thought. But he also had a soft spot for goats. They were a part of his vacation experience in Fuerteventura, where he and his family had once rescued a young kid that was lost among the sparse vegetation. He stopped. He was taking the analogy too far. Derek, as he now called him, was quite patently a goat—not to say the alpha male of the herd—but there was good in him, too, Peter supposed, and if in saving their own work from his restructuring zeal, they were in danger of over-maligning Derek, that offended against his sense of fair play.

But where to find that spark of good in him, and how to let it develop into a beacon of hope for research in other languages? Was such a thing even possible? Peter swerved to avoid a piece of debris on the road. He came back to his senses—the RRE was just a dream, wasn't it?

When he got back home to Bluntingham, the village where he lived in modest tranquillity, a respected if not notable, member of the local community, he turned into the drive and parked his car. He supposed Becky would be eagerly awaiting his return, but her car wasn't there, and he found the house locked. She might have told him, he thought, but then, he had been dilatory in phoning her. Only twice briefly in three days, and he hadn't actually told her the time he was coming home. Ben and Richard, their two sons, were out at school or doing some after-school activity, he supposed. He felt guilty on that score, too. When they were young, he had devoted a lot of time to his kids and had even forced himself to kick a ball around with them. He had occasionally indulged their passion for football by taking them to see their favourite team play, but with increasing years, the glottal stops had taken over, his career had become dominant, and his interaction with his kids—oh, how he hated that word, but its ubiquitousness had led even him to use it sparingly—had almost ceased. It was not so much different with Becky. But where was she now? He unlocked the house and took his suitcase into the bedroom. He unpacked the clothes and left them lying on the marital bed. That would annoy Becky, but she committed worse domestic transgressions. She left the kitchen in a tip and only put her shoes away when people were coming. He went to his study and put the papers from the RRE on his desk, together with his rather cumbersome laptop, which contained the fruits of ten years' research on the glottal stop. Of course, he had made the odd backup, but these were haphazard and disorderly. He never knew where the latest one was, and so, if his laptop were to be lost or stolen, anything from a week to a month's worth of glottalization might be lost, to say nothing of his admin and exam papers, depending on which backup he could find. Peter was organized in his disorder, though. He usually knew where to look for something, even if he could not always find it.

At 7:10, Peter heard the sound of Becky's car on the gravel. He went to greet her.

'You're very late back, aren't you?' he said.

'What kind of a welcome is that?' Becky retorted, annoyed.

'Sorry,' Peter said. 'It's been a hectic few days. I'm just unwinding. Where are the kids?'

'At school, at a rehearsal,' Becky said. 'They want picking up at 7:30.'

'Where have you been?' Peter asked. 'I was expecting to find you at home.'

'I was in town, shopping.'

'What did you buy?'

'Oh, this and that. Food mostly.'

'Let me help you carry it in.'

'No need, I've already put it away in the kitchen.'

Peter discontinued the conversation. He hadn't seen a bag or heard any sounds of groceries being packed away, nor had Becky been long in the kitchen on her return. What was she hiding? She was normally so straightforward and open.

'I've got to pick up the kids now,' Becky said.

'OK, see you later,' Peter said. Becky's behaviour was strange, he thought. He determined to find out more.

Jim and Isabelle had set off for Cambridge in the inappropriately named Passion Wagon. Jim's old Triumph Stag had been traded in for a red MGB Roadster that he had picked up from an acquaintance in the antiques trade. Isabelle could see that it might have held some appeal when it was new, fifteen years ago, but Jim's business side-line, trading on eBay and picking up stock at car boot sales across East Anglia, had left the car battered and in need of the attentions of Mike and Edd from Wheeler Dealers. The registration JL 69 was its only remaining striking feature—apart from the strong odour of Jim's pheromones that hit Isabelle as she got in on the passenger side, removing Jim's scarf and sunglasses from the seat in order to be able to sit down.

'What d'you think, then?' Jim said, expecting Isabelle to be full of admiration for his 'ride'.

'It's just you, Jim. I can't think of anything more appropriate,' she said.

'Yeah, well,' Jim said, 'it does go down rather well with the young ladies. Only problem, it's a bit of a squeeze in the amorous activity department.'

Isabelle smiled as Jim managed to get the speed up to 70 on the dual carriageway and the Passion Wagon began to vibrate.

'Feel that!' Jim said. 'It goes right through your body. Many a young lady has been sent into ecstasies by those sensations.'

'Yes, Jim,' Isabelle said, thinking it might yet be in her best interests to flatter Jim's amatory ego. 'I can definitely feel something.'

Vicky was the first of the four to arrive home at her house overlooking the Cam. She found it cold on her arrival. She had turned down the central heating while she was away. The fridge was empty, too, save for a bottle of Croatian Riesling that she had been given by some undiscerning guests at a dinner party she had hosted two months previously. It was either a tin of corned beef on Ryvita or a trip to the local takeaway. She opted for the former and opened the wine. So this was what was left of her life, she thought, but did she really envy those with seemingly happy family lives? There was so much unhappiness in the world, much of it masked by human relationships. Yes, Peter was happily married. That was the impression he gave, but she had seen beneath the veneer an insecure man, looking for a new relationship. She had seen the way he looked at Beebee and how he interacted with her. She had noticed how he chatted nervously to her on the train, felt sorry for his pathetic chat-up lines and realized he was desperate for a new meeting but couldn't bring himself to admit it. Then there was Beebee, divorced and on the lookout. She obviously showed interest in

Peter, but that could only ever be temporary. Did she want an affair? No, with Beebee it would only be a couple of casual encounters to keep her hand in until she found the right new partner. As for Jim, she thought he was probably beyond redemption. Still chasing after dolly birds at his age, he apparently hadn't held down a relationship for longer than a few months. He might or might not have slept with Isabelle, but didn't he see that she was using him, that nothing could ever come of it? How would he feel in his sixties? Sad and lonely like her, she supposed. She had got married to an Irishman when she was twenty-one; she had even converted to his religion, but the marriage was short-lived. Divorced six years later, she had met Susan in the IT Department at RARE, and they bought a house—this house—together. Susan wanted a civil partnership, she didn't, and they parted. Vicky bought her out. Yes, that was why she said to Peter she wished she could say she was going back to the wife and kids. She nearly had a wife, but there were no kids. She missed having them, and now, at forty-one, she probably never would have. Should she give it one last chance? A sperm donor perhaps? That would be so complicated, though. Pick the right man and have sex with him a few times. She'd even sacrifice her career for the sake of the child. After all, on her £80k salary, she had been able to save a substantial amount. She had no mortgage, and her share portfolio had yielded some very impressive profits. Jim or Peter? She could have Jim for the asking, she supposed. It might even turn into something more—they were not so far apart in age, and Jim needed to settle down sooner or later. But Mrs Lubbins? No, of course not. She would always remain Ms Atherton. She hadn't taken her husband's name previously. Mrs Kelly wouldn't have fitted the image for a smart, thrusting businesswoman. Insemination without the rigmarole and without the emotional turmoil. Another meeting or two with Peter, and she would see a return on her investment.

2. A NEW ACADEMIC YEAR

Friday, 19 September

Peter set out for London Bridge the following morning. As Head of Department, it was his job to ensure everything was in place for the start of term on Monday. The commute was something he had got used to over the years, but every time he did it, he sighed and wished he had had Jim's luck in landing a job at the University of the Fens, a term with which he consoled himself when his nostalgia for Needham College got the better of him. The final leg of his journey was a tube ride to London Bridge Underground station and a ten-minute walk to the University. When he had arrived, he often felt like turning round and going back home again. He had managed to arrange his timetable so that he need only be in on three days in a good week, but most weeks weren't good. As a senior academic, he was also required to sit on university committees and the like, so he was lucky if he got one day off for research during term time, usually a Thursday. He had scheduled a meeting with the Departmental Secretary, Ms Johanna Grunewald, who was originally from Germany. The *Ms* disguised the fact that she had reached her fifties without marrying. Most other details of her life were kept well hidden from the academic staff. Maybe she divulged more to her secretarial colleagues. Peter never enquired. Johanna had been transferred, along with the students, to Other Languages when the Department of German was shut down and most of the staff pensioned off or moved to Other Languages, which was referred to disparagingly as the Linguistic Ragbag or the Odd Bods. It was this department of which Peter had the honour to be head, and this department that was served by possibly the worst secretary in the University. She was distinguished by one thing only—her length of service. Appointed twenty years ago under a different head, she had managed to cling onto her post by various dubious means, doing the minimum required by her contract. When the university support staff staged a work-to-rule, it was business as usual with Johanna. With her, Peter had scheduled a meeting at 11:00.

When Peter arrived in the Department, he found Johanna sitting at her desk, attending to her coiffure.

'Have there been any messages in the last few days?' he asked.

'No, nothing at all,' Johanna said. 'It's been very quiet.'

'I'll see you at 11:00 to go through the agenda for the staff meeting at 3:00, then. And please bring the lists of students with you. We need to sort out tutorial groups, etc.'

'I might be a few minutes late,' Johanna said.

'Oh, why's that?' Peter asked.

'I'm meeting the French secretary for coffee.'

Peter's spirits sank. *Oh no!* he thought. Not another year of Johanna's truculence, constantly battling against his attempts to raise standards in the Department. He was about to upbraid her, but what would be the use? He was stuck with her until she retired, unless … Peter's thoughts ran away with him. No, that might land him in prison.

At 11:30, there was a knock at his door.

'Come in,' he said, expecting to see Johanna, but it was Michael Harrison, a postgraduate student, come to enquire about grants for study abroad. Peter got out a few leaflets and discussed the possibilities. At 11:40, Johanna knocked and burst into the room.

'I'm with a student now,' Peter said. 'Come back in ten minutes.'

Johanna gave him a glare and left without saying anything. Twenty minutes later, she returned.

'I'm sorry, Johanna, but this really isn't good enough. You were meant to come at 11, and it's now 12. Please see that it doesn't happen again.'

She gave him another glare and shoved a pile of papers under his nose.

'That's the agenda,' she said.

'Thanks,' Peter said, 'but that's only half of what we need to discuss. You know we always discuss timetable and tutorial groups at the beginning of the year. Can you add those, please.'

Johanna looked sullen.

'I'll do it after lunch,' she said.

Peter was about to explode, but he managed to contain his anger.

'Well, let's quickly look at the tutorial groups for the First Year.'

Peter read through the new students that were assigned to his group:

Amanda Atherton
David Beddington
Bebra Bevington
Nicholas Drown
Celia Crouch

The first name stopped him in his tracks. That sounds familiar, he thought, but Vicky said she didn't have any kids. Or did she? If she had had an illegitimate child, it would bear her surname. He thought no more of it.

'These names are meant to be in alphabetical order,' he said to Johanna.

'They are,' she replied truculently.

'They aren't,' Peter insisted. 'Drown comes after Crouch. And anyway, who on earth is Bebra Bevington? I've never heard the name Bebra before.'

'I'll amend the list after lunch,' Johanna said.

The revised list came back with Johanna at 2:15. *Bebra* had been changed to *Debra* and *Drown* to *Brown*. The order remained the same.

'Have you put Constitution of the Board of Examiners on the agenda?' he asked.

'No, I'll add it by hand,' Johanna said.

'I'd like you to type it and print it out again,' Peter said.

The agenda returned at 3:00 with Johanna in time for the start of the meeting. Johanna tried to absent herself from the meeting with the excuse that she had a great deal of work to catch up on, but for once, Peter was firm with her and made her take minutes.

Vicky had got back into her routine at RARE. She had started to contemplate further her plans for getting pregnant. Peter would provide a most satisfactory sperm donor, she supposed. She needed to arrange a meeting and test the waters. On Friday afternoon, in a lull in streamlining, when she had got tired of restructuring, she took a coffee break. She went to the vending machine and fetched herself a caffè latte. Where was her life going? she wondered. The Subpanel Z meeting of the RRE had a dream, quite the best of the various RRE meetings she had experienced. She could capitalize on the experience, leverage her assets. That meant a loan from Peter. She began to type an email:

Hi Peter,

I hope you got back safely yesterday. I did, but the house was cold and lonely and only a bottle of Riesling for comfort. I'm missing the fun of the RRE. I was wondering if you're up for a Chelsea bun soon. Anytime next week would suit me.

Hope to see you soon.

Love,

Vicky x

Peter was in the middle of the departmental meeting when the email arrived. He felt his phone vibrate in his pocket to announce a new email.

'We're all agreed then, Alan for Chairman and Will for Secretary. Now we need to fix a date for the production of draft papers and the first meeting of the Exam Board. Over to you, Alan.'

While Alan was speaking, Peter took out his phone and looked at the email. He smiled and put it back. Johanna was looking out of the window and had stopped writing.

'Did you get all that down, Johanna?' Peter asked.

'Yes,' she said in a voice that betrayed uncertainty.

After the meeting, Peter went back to his office and turned on his computer to read the emails properly. The first that he read was from Harrison, asking him to write a reference for a scholarship in Germany. He next turned to Vicky's, which he found flattering. Yes, he'd love to meet her, he thought. He began to compose:

Dear Vicky,

I should love to meet up for a bun and a chat. Would teatime on Thursday suit you, as I'm in Cambridge on that day? I'll be working in the University Library. How about meeting at Fitz-billies at 4:30?

Love,

Peter x

An email came back from Vicky by return:

Hi Peter,

Let's make it 4 at the UL. We can go on to Fitzbillies from there. See you in North Wing 5 at 4 on Thursday. Let me know if there are any problems: 07700 900243.

Can't wait!

Lots of love,

Vicky xxxx

Strewth! Peter thought when he saw the way she ended her email. *Lots of love and four kisses!* She *was* coming on to him. Peter had seldom been in such an enviable position where three women were showing interest at the same time. Then he thought, *Only two, actually.* Becky had long since lost anything other than a historical interest, dependent on marriage vows made twenty-six years previously and the need for a secure home. And then there were the unexpected absences of the last few days. He hadn't yet had a chance to probe further. Moreover, he found Beebee by far the sexiest of the three, with Vicky in second place. Was the order about to be reversed? Pangs of guilt seized his thoughts and killed his erotic aspirations stone dead. Becky was his wife. He must be faithful. But at all costs? He was weak. Look at the way he let Johanna get away with things in the Department, walk all over him and be cheeky, too. She had corrected Bebra on the list of tutorial groups, but the name was uncorrected on two other lists. He had asked her before the meeting to correct them and print them out again, but they were distributed with ugly handwritten corrections. Peter apologized to the meeting but was afraid to upbraid Johanna. He was weak with students, too. He felt sorry for those accused of wrongdoing when only minor foibles were at stake. He stuck up for Emily Boyd when she had posted a defamatory message about an incompetent administrator on Facebook and was facing a disciplinary hearing. It wasn't really weakness in this case but his sense of right and wrong—weighing things in the balance. There was right and wrong on both sides, but Emily was a good student, and she didn't deserve to have her career sacrificed on the altar of hypocrisy. The administrator was useless, but Emily might have been less forceful in her use of f***ing language. Anyway, he thought, what does this have to do with his moral weakness? He could be like Derek, who didn't care a jot whether people liked him and who rode roughshod over all and sundry. There was no weakness there, and he had no moral constraints when it came to sexual relationships. Hey! What was he doing, letting his imagination run away with him? He wasn't planning to jump into bed with anyone yet, least of all Becky! 4 p.m., Thursday, North Wing 5.

Peter stayed until 6:30, then began the trudge back home. On the train, he turned his mind to exam questions he might set—*The glottal stop is a frequently misused obstruent. Discuss.* He would need to write that down when he got home—and his pitiful life. How many more years would he stick this for? Was there no means of escape? The RRE had been fun and had opened up new possibilities. Should he pursue them? Did he even have time? *Examine the role of affricates in AT LEAST TWO modern European languages.* With this, he came back with a bang. *Oh no!* The train had arrived at his station. He gathered up his things with the utmost haste and ran for the exit, jumping off the train just as the doors had begun to close. Becky was in a better mood than yesterday when he got back home. He was in a worse one. Ben and Richard had eaten early. Peter ate with Becky in the kitchen and went to his study afterwards to enter the exam questions into his computer.

Peter was counting the days until Thursday. It would be his only non-departmental day that week, and he needed to check a few references for his magnum opus, which, after such an elephantine gestation period, was nearing completion. He would take his laptop into the library and look up the references in the stacks. That way, he wouldn't need to carry armfuls of books down to the Reading Room, a practice he was used to from when he was a PhD student but which, with increasing age, he had found less than satisfactory. He almost pined for the Reading Room of the British Museum, in which he had written one of his most brilliant articles on the incipient tendencies towards glottalization in early English. A two-hour wait for books had seemed monstrous to him then, but he'd take it in his stride now. Actually, he hated working in the stacks at the UL. It was cold and draughty, and the temptation to look out of the long, narrow windows and speculate about the business of the tiny figures below, walking or cycling along Burrell's Walk, was too much of a distraction from the liquids and sonorants, to say nothing of the glottalics in Indo-European. But on Thursday, he would make the sacrifice and work in North Wing 5 all day. That way, he would see Vicky as soon as she arrived and could forget about the tedium of his daily grind.

Jim had spent the days before the start of full term, working in the UL, too, preparing his lectures on Imprecations and Vulgarisms in old European Languages, which he had scheduled in the Lecture List with an eye-catching title, hoping thereby to attract a sizeable number of students, preferably young ladies, to his unique style of teaching:

OTHER LANGUAGES TRIPOS

> Advanced Old European Dialects Th. 11
> DR J. LUBBINS
> *Guanna sarden ger? quot vices fotisti?*
> Fucking in Old Bavarian Dialects.

> German Literary Texts Th. 12
> DR P. HITCHINSON
> *Woyzeck.* (weeks 1–2)
> Heine, Poems. (weeks 3–4)

Jim had taken Isabelle back to Cambridge in his Passion Wagon and had dropped her at her flat in Rustat Road after failing to entice her into Jim's Pad, as he called his bachelor residence, a Victorian house in Ainsworth Street, that had as much charm and suitability for wooing females as the man himself.

'Yeah, well, you had your chance,' he said to Isabelle, as he said goodbye to her. 'You can always ring me if you want to come round and discuss jobs. Or better still, meet me after my lectures on fucking on Thursday at 1 p.m. for a spot of lunch and who knows what.'

Beebee was missing the heady days of the RRE, too, as she settled back into term at Essex. Her classes on practical Swedish language were well attended, but together with responsibilities for all the foreign exchange programmes in the humanities, which necessitated frequent trips to far-flung places, she was finding term a pain as soon as it got underway. Unlike Peter, she didn't even get one day a week for research. Weekends in summer were her only consolation. On such occasions, she would get into her Golf Cabriolet and allow her blonde flowing hair to be blown by the wind and her cares to be blown away. But it was October, and the soft top had to be kept almost permanently in place now. She wondered about getting in touch with some of the conspirators, who had in the short space of three days, become firm friends. Which one should she choose?

3.   WEEK 1

Monday, 22 September

After a weekend of writing exam questions and obsessing about lists of students, Peter slogged into work on the early train on Monday morning and was in the Department by 9:00. That was a good time to nose about Johanna's room and see what horrors she had been up to, particularly while he had been away. He didn't believe her when she said that there hadn't been any messages. At least she could be trusted to jot down notes on a reporter's pad, which she always left lying beside her computer screen. Peter determined to read through her jottings, going back a week or so. On the previous Monday, she had noted down a message from the Professor of French, René Delacroix. *Ring Prof. Dela. asap about Combined Studies cooperation.* Tuesday's messages included a call from the German Embassy, regarding a proposal to award him an honour—please call back before Friday on *021 675 30??* Wednesday had jottings about various new students who needed information before the start of term. Peter wondered whether it might not have been better if he hadn't actually discovered this information. When Johanna came in at 10:10, he confronted her.

'I can't believe that there were no messages while I was away. Will you please go through your notes again,' Peter said.

Johanna had no option other than to go through her jottings while he stood beside her.

'No, nothing of importance,' she said.

'Are you sure?' Peter asked. 'Let me look.'

He decided not to make a fuss about René's request and would deal with that anyway, but when he came to the German Embassy, he decided to probe deeper.

'That looks important,' he said. 'Call the German Embassy before Friday. Why didn't you tell me? I could have called from Scotland.'

'I didn't get the number down properly.'

'That's really no excuse.'

'Well, if it's important, they will ring again.'

Peter left the room, angry. He met Harrison in the corridor.

'Good morning, Professor Lampton,' Harrison said. 'Can I come and see you, please?'

'What is it?' Peter said brusquely.

'It's personal.'

'I'm afraid I don't have time now,' Peter said. 'Can you come at lunchtime?'

'OK,' Harrison said disconcertedly.

Peter went back to his room, already exhausted from the morning's events, and he hadn't even yet had coffee. 'Damn! Damn! Damn!' he exclaimed with increasing volume. A student who was passing his door heard the last *Damn!* and looked in through the window in the door. Peter hastily removed himself from view and began typing.

Whenever he sat at his computer, he always checked his emails first. One flashed up on the screen from Dr Beatrice Frensham:

Hi Peter,

I got an email yesterday from your Exams Board Secretary, notifying me when the draft papers would be available for scrutiny and when I should be needed for oralling. I was surprised that you don't want to see me in person until the summer. Anyway, I'm missing my favourite phonetician and would like to relive some of the excitement of the RRE before the next meeting. We could meet up one weekend for a ride in the cabriolet before it gets too cold. I thought it would also be nice if you gave a lecture in Essex. How about "Where is your glottis and what can you do with it?"? That's suggestive enough, don't you think? It should pack them in. A bit like that inaugural on oversexed German nouns! Whoever thought that one up?

Looking forward to seeing you soon!

Love,

Beebee x

Wow! Peter thought. He couldn't believe his luck. Whoever would have thought that glottalization could be such a turn-on for women? Beebee, Vicky, Becky—he'd got the order clear in his head now, but then, he was meeting Vicky on Thursday, and the odds looked favourable. She was the favourite. *Oh damn!* Becky, Becky, Becky was the only possibility. He'd give her a quick call to ask about the lecture and to show his affection. At least, that way, she might cook him a nice roast dinner! He pressed the speed dial, but the call was rejected. He tried again; it went to voicemail. He couldn't waste more time on private matters, so he gave up. He'd ask her tonight. He needed to reply to Beebee. Strike while the iron is hot! he thought. Was that /hɒt/ or /hɒʔ/? His head was in a spin. 'Damn the glottis!' he said sotto voce. He began to type:

Hi Beebee,

Lovely to hear from you! All that you say is great. I'd love to give a lecture, and a ride in the cabriolet would be heavenly. We'd have to choose a time when the weather's nice and when Becky and the kids are away.

I'm sure you'll be needed for some special orals before the summer. I'll keep you posted.

Oversexed nouns! We could all do with some of those …

Be in touch.

Love,

Peter x

Peter was somewhat surprised at Beebee's eagerness and turned it over in his mind. He knew she was divorced and lonely, but he'd always assumed that she was on the lookout for a long-term relationship and would realize that that was not possible with him. Maybe he'd been right all along—keep women at arm's length. But he'd begun to review his thinking. It had taken him long enough to meet a mate, and he'd given up looking after that. But there comes a time with every man, he thought, when he begins to wonder if he's done the right thing. Time is running out. Soon it would be too late. But the consequences!

By now, it was nearly lunchtime. He espied Johanna slinking out of the Department at 12:55, before students emerged from lectures, so that she would not have to deal with any enquiries and they would find the departmental office firmly shut until 2:05, by which time they would be in lectures again. She was oblivious to the students' satire in calling her *Johanna of the Long Lunchbreak*. Peter called her *Johanna of the Stockyards* without the *Saint. Damn Johanna!* was his constant imprecation. He wondered if Jim had an Old Bavarian one appropriate to her. Here was one lady in whom he would surely show no interest. Was his department one big stockyard? he wondered.

On the stroke of one, Harrison knocked and entered Peter's room.

'Have you come about the reference?' Peter asked. 'I haven't quite finished it yet,' he said half truthfully, meaning he hadn't even started it. 'I'll have it ready tomorrow. You can pick it up at lunchtime.'

'Well, it's to do with that in a way,' Harrison said. 'I need to get away from the Department until the end of the academic year.'

'Oh, how come?' Peter said. 'It's only just started.'

'I believe Frau Schmidt is leaving in June,' he said. 'I can't be around while she's a language assistant.'

'Why ever not?' Peter asked naively.

'She thinks she's pregnant,' Harrison said, 'and that I'm the father.'

Oh damn! Peter thought. *Not another unwanted pregnancy in the Department!* 'Why didn't you take precautions?'

'We sort of did,' Harrison said, 'but she's a Catholic from Bavaria.'

'Vatican roulette?' Peter asked.

''Fraid so,' Harrison replied.

'Have you tried the University counselling service?' Peter said.

'No, not yet,' Harrison said. 'Gisela has only spoken to the Catholic chaplain so far.'

'Oh damn!' Peter said, forgetting to keep his reactions to himself. 'I'm not sure it's a matter I can help with,' he said, 'but I'll write you that reference, anyway. Do you want me to mention the circumstances?'

'No, better not. Thank you, anyway, Professor Lampton; you've been a great help.'

After they had said goodbye, Peter felt emotional. He always empathized with students who were in a fix and did his very best to help. He so hoped that things would turn out right for Harrison. Frau Schmidt was less of a concern. Of course he felt sorry for her and responsible to a degree, but why did the silly woman go and get pregnant when she could have been on the pill or when a cheap packet of Durex would have saved years of complications? Maybe she wanted a child ... Women—he would never understand them. Of course, he wouldn't say anything to her; he'd have to go on as if he knew nothing and wait to see if she said anything. *Oh damn!* Term had begun with a vengeance. *Oh damn!*

Peter went out and bought himself a couple of sandwiches then returned to his room to eat them. He was unable to relax and woke up the computer, whose screen saver had kicked in. One of his postgraduate students, who was skilled in IT, had made a special screen saver for him where the IPA sign for the glottal stop coursed about the screen and eventually disappeared, repeating itself every few minutes. It amused Peter amidst all his woes. *Evaluate the complementary distribution of allophones in TWO OR MORE modern European languages.* His Phonetics I paper was nearly complete. In the afternoon, he would contact the German Embassy and the Professor of French. He supposed that those students who wanted to find out things in advance from Johanna had either now given up or had found out from other students.

Damn! he thought as he remembered the cheese and wine party for new students. He had promised Becky he'd be home at 6:30. The party started at 6:00. *Damn!* He called her number and got voicemail. *Anyone would think she was avoiding me*, he thought and left a message. At 3:00, he phoned the German Embassy and was put through to a cultural attaché in charge of academic relations. Peter explained who he was and that he had had a message while he was away. He wondered if it had been directed at the right person, since he had never expected to be in contention for any kind of honour. Johannes von Streibnitz, the young attaché, explained that the embassy had a number of awards each year to allot and that he had been nominated by a colleague for his contribution to European linguistic integration and especially for his pioneering work on glottalization. Von Streibnitz explained that the Verdienstkreuz dritter Klasse was thought to be appropriate. Peter, whose knowledge of German honours was not the best, didn't like to ask what that honour was but noted it down carefully and thought he would ask Johanna later. She was a native German after all, and he had an inkling that her father had received some kind of honour once. He explained how honoured he was and looked forward to receiving further details. He next sent an email to René about collaboration and suggested he might like to pop in to the First-Year party that evening.

Peter went to look for Johanna but found the departmental office shut. There was a handwritten note on the door: *Closed for party preparations.* He popped along to Room OL 5 and found Johanna setting out wine glasses and cutting blocks of cheese into bite-sized chunks, which she speared with cocktail sticks. Disposable plates and bowls were arranged around the room with crisps and other nibbles, which by 6 p.m. would be soggy or otherwise unpalatable. Peter despaired. Now was not the time to ask Johanna about the Verdienstkreuz. He checked with her that everything was in order for the party and if Dr Herbert was prepared with a few jokes to kick off the evening with a wine tasting. Yes, in his state of distraction, he actually said *kick off!*

'I think so,' Johanna said. 'We have Riesling, Mosel, a Spät-burgunder, a Chardonnay, and a Rioja from Aldi.'

'Hardly a European cross-section,' Peter said. 'But I expect he will put on a fine performance.'

Peter left Johanna in the room folding paper napkins and avoiding the need to do any clerical work. He returned to his room, satisfied that everything was in place. He felt he could now relax and phoned Becky again. Her phone went straight to voicemail. *Damn her!* Peter thought. *It could be a bloody emergency! Can't she ever pick up?*

At 6 p.m., he went over to OL 5, where the first students were gathering, looking sheepish and out of place in this new environment. Johanna did her best to encourage them to eat soggy crisps. James Belfield, a confident-looking student, pointed to the bottles of wine and asked when they were going to get some.

'You will have to wait until Dr Herbert's here for his wine tasting,' Johanna said.

Five minutes later, Dr Herbert turned up with a red face. He could speak three European languages passably and had a penchant for wine—indeed, the students in the know called him Druncan Duncan. Most of the First-Years and staff had by now arrived, so he began.

'Mesdames, messieurs, meine Damen und Herren, ladies and gentlemen, Señoras y señores. Je voudrais vous présenter des vins délicieux de toute l'Europe.' Eyes were raised heavenward by the more savvy students. He repeated the introduction in the remaining languages while everyone looked on embarrassed at Druncan Duncan making an exhibition of himself.

'I think I'd better continue in English only now,' he said, 'even though I can talk about wine in ten different languages … Only joking.'

Students groaned.

'I'm going to ask Ms Grunewald to hand round a glass of wine number 1 for tasting. Let's see if any of you can guess where it's from.'

Johanna went to the bottles.

'We do not have a screw,' she said in her strong German accent.

Peter covered his eyes in disbelief.

'I've got one in my room,' he said. 'Can you go and fetch it, please, Johanna?'

'No, I do not know where it is,' she said.

Peter wanted to disappear through the floor in embarrassment.

'In the top drawer of my desk,' he said.

He left the room to fetch it himself.

When he returned, Belfield had already opened two bottles with his Swiss Army Knife.

Damn it all! he thought and gave his corkscrew to Amanda Atherton, who smiled sweetly at him and began opening a few more bottles.

After the Riesling tasting, Peter got talking to a small group, amongst whom was Frau Schmidt. The group gradually dispersed, and he was left talking to her alone. Was she going to say anything? he wondered. No, probably not; this wasn't the time or place. An innocuous question maybe? Perhaps that would prompt her to come and see him privately later.

'Have you made any plans for when you leave us?' he asked.

'No, I am going back to Bavaria and will wait to see what turns up.'

The Rioja was next, and the students were already in high spirits after a full glass of cheap Riesling, albeit a German one.

'Señores, señoras y señoritas,' Duncan said, 'ahora tememos un vino español exquisito.' Spanish was his favourite language, and he wasn't going to let the occasion for showing off his command of it slip. Juan, an Exchange student, launched into a long, complex, and fast question about wine, which Duncan only partially understood, stuttering, 'Vamos a ver.'

Peter suggested that only half a glass should be given for the remaining tastings. Johanna ignored the request and served the cheese on sticks. By the fourth glass, the level of conversation had risen to extreme levels, so much so that a messenger was sent over from the departmental library to tell them to keep the noise down. Peter made an announcement, and the noise dropped temporarily to normal levels. Duncan was dissuaded from tasting the Spätburgunder. Peter found himself in conversation with Johanna, so he was able to put his question to her.

'Have you come across the German Verdienstkreuz dritter Klasse?'

Johanna burst out laughing so that everyone looked round.

'That's what they give to people who are useless,' she said. 'They haven't offered you one, have they?'

Peter smiled and walked away. He fetched himself another glass and went to chat with Amanda Atherton and a group of pretty young First Years.

'I don't suppose you know a Vicky Atherton, do you?' Peter said.

'Yes, of course; she's my aunt,' Amanda said.

Peter mumbled something about it being a small world and wondered whether he should be pleased or worried.

At 7:30, the party came to an end. Students helped Johanna clear up and put things into a corner of the room. It was too much to ask her to remove the empty glasses and remaining food, which he offered to the student helpers, together with a couple of bottles of wine.

He trudged back up to his room and sank, exhausted, into his chair. *For heaven's sake!* he thought. How much longer would he put up with this? He caught the tube back to Kings Cross and got on the 21:07 train. *Damn Jim in his Passion Wagon with his young ladies*, he thought. He would have tried to score at a departmental party in Cambridge, he supposed. *Damn him!* There would not be much passion on the 21:07 from Kings Cross, arriving at 21:51, or indeed when he got home to Becky. *Oh damn!*

When Peter eventually arrived home, it was 10:30. The boys were upstairs and theoretically on their way to bed. Peter was exhausted and hoped for a plate of something substantial that would both satisfy his hunger and sop up the excess of cheap wine that he had imbibed in the Department.

'What's for dinner?' he enquired of Becky.

'Bread and cheese,' she said.

'Oh no!' Peter said. 'I've had enough bits of cheddar on a stick in London. I tried to ring you about dinner but only ever got your voicemail.'

'Yeah, I've been out a lot,' Becky said.

'Not doing anything you shouldn't, I hope,' Peter said.

Becky looked sheepish.

'The kids had another rehearsal,' she said.

'At 3:30, too?' he asked.

Becky made some excuse. Peter began to put two and two together, but he was too tired to pursue the matter, and even if she were having an affair, he would grant her that pleasure as long as she didn't desert him. He wouldn't probe deeper but might discuss it rationally with her sometime when he was less exhausted.

Having now finished his exam papers for the scrutiny meeting in November, he passed a pen drive with the questions to Johanna on Wednesday so that she could co-ordinate the collaborative papers and add headings and times from information provided by the Exams Registry.

'Please ensure that your door is locked at all times when you're working on exam papers, Johanna,' he said sternly.

She laughed.

'I'm not joking,' Peter said.

'Of course not,' Johanna said.

'You'll have all day Thursday to work on them, as I shan't be in then, and probably no-one much else will.'

Johanna had already made plans for Thursday in anticipation of Peter's absence—coffee with the French secretary in Lantana and a traditionally extra-long Thursday lunchbreak from 1 till 3. Such occasions sometimes had to be cancelled at short notice if Johanna knew that Peter would be in the Department, but tomorrow, she had the all-clear.

Peter went home on the early train, satisfied that the term had begun well and that he could enjoy the first day off of the new academic year on Thursday, safe in the knowledge that his exam papers were complete, the new students satisfactorily welcomed to the Department, and that there were no outstanding problems. He had forgotten Harrison and Frau Schmidt, and while his honour wasn't a problem, it would need some further investigation. Would he have to write a speech? Would he need a new suit?

Thursday, 25 September

Peter had a leisurely start to the day on Thursday. He got up at 7:30 and checked his emails in his study. One from Vicky had been sent at 12:10 a.m. after he had gone to bed:

Hi Peter,

I'm burning the midnight oil, working on papers for Subpanel X meeting on Wednesday in London. Yawn! What a boring bunch they are! No-one at all for a girl to show interest in. To hell with streamlining. I need to restructure my life. Concerning which, I have a proposition to make.

See you later in NW5 … 4 p.m. Don't be late!

Vicky xx

Peter was excited at the prospect of the meeting and doubly excited at this latest twist in the plot. What could this proposition be? He would be on tenterhooks until 4. He wrote a quick email to Johanna and went to meet Becky at breakfast. She was normally a late riser but had taken the boys to the school bus that morning so that she and Peter could share breakfast at 8:30ish.

Peter thought he would surprise her with freshly made toast and freshly ground coffee.

'To what do I owe this surprise, then?' Becky asked when she was presented with this unwonted pampering.

'Is it so strange?' Peter asked, somewhat annoyed.

'It's not normal,' Becky said.

'What *is* normal?' Peter asked in philosophical mode. 'Shall I butter your toast?'

'Shall you butter me up?' Becky retorted.

'Fowler!' Peter said.

'Foul enough,' Becky said.

'Very droll,' Peter said. 'H. W.'

'Are you messing with me?' Becky said.

'No, deadly serious,' Peter replied. 'Use the form of the auxiliary verb in the question that you would use in the answer—*The King's English*; at least I think it is.'

He would look it up later.

'I'll stick to what I know,' Becky said.

'Will or shall? It's not so simple.'

'Will you shut up.'

'Was that with a question mark?'

'Shut the fuck up—Exclamation mark!'

'I blame the Americans,' Peter said.

'You usually do.'

'Except for the glottal stops—they're much less common in American English.'

'Well, that's a blessing,' Becky said. 'Is this the sort of thing that you've been talking about in Scotland?' she asked.

'No, 'fraid not,' Peter said, 'but it was great fun.'

'The toast has gone cold now.'

'It's not the only thing.'

'Screw you!'

'I don't mind you having an affair.'

'That's very magnanimous of you.'

'As long as I can have one.'

With that, they parted. Peter got into his car and set off for Cambridge. He turned the radio on, which was normally tuned to BBC Radio 3.

'Not bloody Stockhausen!' he said when he heard the announcement. It turned out to be Chausson, which he quite liked. He'd never heard of him before. At the end of the piece, he made an effort to remember the name, *Poème symphonique,* Op. 5. It might calm his nerves when they were under attack from Johanna or Becky. He parked his car at the University Library and counted himself lucky to have found a space. That was often a problem later in the day. He trudged up the steps and through the revolving door. Where was his youthful enthusiasm now? he wondered. He had bounded up the steps as a research student after parking his bike on the north side. He sighed. The once cherished building, which he had revered as the greatest temple of learning in the world almost, now no longer held the same fascination for him. His visits were now few and far between. A quick in and out to borrow a couple of volumes and take them away in one of those distinctive see-through carrier bags with the imposing building and its almost too obviously phallic tower imprinted thereon, the repository of reserved and restricted items not open to public view. The building would not have looked out of place in Nuremberg or

Berlin, and Peter wondered whether the Librarian was ever tempted from his fourth-floor office to imagine he was addressing adulatory crowds below, stretching far beyond Clare Memorial Court.

Oh no! He was getting like Derek, Peter thought, always working at home now. Occasionally, he would make a detour to the Tea Room to savour one of the cheese scones that tasted better than any he knew. He imagined that some underpaid servant, who had worked there all her life, got up early in the morning to stir the mixture and bake the delicious savouries according to a recipe known only to her. He dared not enquire, since to know the truth would probably destroy the illusion, after which they would never taste the same.

He went into the Catalogue Room and entered glottal stop into the computer to see whether anything new had been published on the subject. He noted down some titles about Tibetan and Chinese but thought he wouldn't bother to look these up. Next, he checked a few references that he had printed out at home but for which he had not yet checked the Library's holdings. He looked up the classmark for Fowler's *King's English* and was pleased to find that the book was located in North Wing 6. That would provide a proximate distraction from the glottal stops.

After gazing nostalgically through the doors of the Reading Room, where he had written the greater part of his PhD thesis, he passed by the new books display and looked at the titles on linguistics. He could delay the ascent to North Wing 5 no longer. It was now 10:00. He had made it a rule never to go to coffee before 11:00, when in the heady days as a research student he would join a happy band of researchers and bibliographers in the old Tea Room, located off the Catalogue Room, down the stairs. How many happy hours he had spent in that room, most unattractive in itself, with its glass-partitioned smoking room, thick with blue haze and marked out with a sign that somehow seemed to express disapproval of its purpose, but what intellectual delights! It was here that he had made academic contacts that would help him progress in his career, here that he had made new friends after his undergraduate friends had left and moved on. The new Tea Room had nothing of the attraction of the old, cramped one where often seven or more people would end up sitting round a table designed for four. He wondered whether their ghosts haunted the old room. Indeed, some of these friends were long since dead; with others, he had long since lost contact. These days, Peter was lucky if he saw anyone he knew at all, and that, too, contributed to his aversion to working in the Library nowadays. There was actually no reason why he should spend the whole day working in the narrow, prison-like thoroughfares of the North Wing stacks, the sense of incarceration of which was enhanced by the bare painted walls and metal bars of the windowpanes. He could go and work in the Reading Room or the West Room, where the latest periodicals were kept and where in those days, he had been given privileged access to restricted material by the kindly superintendent. That, too, would be unthinkable nowadays. Peter was almost overcome with nostalgia. He had spent every working hour in there for two years, and all for what?

No, the stacks could wait. He would delay going there until after lunch. He swung open the heavy doors of the Reading Room and turned right, intending to reclaim his old seat on the far left-hand side of the middle table nearest the east wall looking east.

Damn! There was a scruffy student sitting in it writing, with hardly a book in sight. Should he try to edge him out? No, he had not lost all sense of decorum in his long absence from the intellectual mecca. He would take the seat at the other end in the hope no-one would sit opposite him, since he liked to arrange his books upright in front of him and to one side, leaning the books against the lighting supports. Here he was, thirty years later—everything was the same, and yet nothing was. You can never relive happiness, he mused. Nostalgia was the sad realization of this.

Peter left his seat and made his way to the Tea Room. He had to think hard how to get there, whereas he would find his way daily to the old one on autopilot. He selected a cheese scone with the tongs provided and ordered his coffee.

'White coffee, please,' had become a habit in those days to distinguish it from dark coffee, which was the choice of several of his friends, something he had never encountered before or since. He scoured the room for anyone he might know but found no-one and ended up sitting at a table alone. Occasionally, people got into conversation with other strangers at tables when there were no free solitary tables, but this was an exception. The rule was to smile at the other person, who might even deign to acknowledge the newcomer, and sit down, not even to ask if the seat was free. If it wasn't, there would be an objection. Strange people, academics, he thought. Did they eschew company? He drank his coffee and ate his scone in silence. Maybe he wouldn't return for lunch after all. That might be too much of a good thing, bearing in mind the planned teatime Chelsea bun. He returned to the Reading Room and tried to concentrate on his references from the few books he had already fetched. He worked through the lunch hour and went up to the stacks at 3:00.

The stacks were sparsely populated since term had not yet started in Cambridge. Peter found a space in front of a window at a convenient distance from the other readers. First, he climbed the stairs to North Wing 6, that desolate part of the library where there were no longer any windows to look out of but merely oblong slits at head height, which provided minimal illumination and kept that part of the building in almost perpetual semi-darkness. It was here that many of the linguistics books were kept, but to access them, it was necessary to venture into the long, narrow, and even darker stacks that could be temporarily illuminated by the turn of a knob for a minute or so while one searched for one's book. Peter located the position of *The King's English*, classmark 768.d.90.37. It was round a corner behind the stairs, almost as if in a maze. He stayed too long in the stack, and the light went out. He half groped his way to the gloom of the corridor and descended the stairs to the daylight of North Wing 5. There he began to check the book for confirmation of what he had been arguing about at breakfast with Becky, which he found on pp. 139f. He noted down, 'Second-person questions invariably have Sh. or W. by assimilation to the answer expected.' Would he tell Becky? Should he? he chuckled. Not the same at all!

Vicky arrived a few minutes before 4:00. Typical business-woman, Peter thought, always on time. She came up to him and gave him a peck on the cheek. A good start, he thought. He smiled.

'What did you want to meet me here for?' he asked.

'I want to show you something,' Vicky said. 'Remember those oversexed nouns? I need to borrow that for the German Subpanel X meeting next week. Do you know the author? He sounds a rum chap.'

'What's his name?'

'David Yeandle.'

'Yes, he's at King's. I met him once. Nice chap, but I don't think I would—I mean should—have dared call my inaugural lecture *Are German nouns oversexed?* Takes all sorts, I suppose.'

'Come and help me find it: 775.c.98.877.'

'That's upstairs.'

'I know.'

They climbed up to North Wing 6, and Vicky went to the location on the otherwise deserted floor. Follow me, she said. She turned the knob a minimal amount, and they both entered the temporary illumination of the narrow bookstack. Vicky bent down to get the book. The faint whirring of the timer stopped, the knob went click, plunging them into darkness. Vicky raised herself up and held on tightly to Peter for support. *What is she doing?* he thought, taken aback. He wasn't going to resist, however. Their mouths met in a passionate kiss. They heard footsteps approaching.

'Shall we relocate to behind the staircase?' Peter asked.

'Are you oversexed?' Vicky joked. 'You go first, and I'll follow.'

After several minutes of oral exploration, Peter stuttered, 'Chelsea buns.' They composed themselves and left the library after each borrowing the books they needed. On the walk to Fitzbillies, Peter asked Vicky why she had suggested meeting at the UL.

'Isn't it obvious?' she said. 'I needed to test your reactions, and there was no better place. We could hardly have done it in Fitzbillies.'

'No, but there are a hundred and one places where people can have a snog,' Peter said.

'Yes, but not academics,' Vicky said. 'Excitement, thrill, danger, erudition, all together. There's the difference. Knowledge of good and evil.'

'Don't go getting religious on me,' Peter said.

'I *am* a Catholic,' Vicky said. 'What do you expect?'

'I'm still a bit puzzled by all this,' Peter said. 'There must be a catch somewhere.'

'No, not really,' Vicky said, 'just a proposition.'

'You don't mean a proposal?' Peter said jokingly.

'I might do,' Vicky said.

They strolled along the Backs and on towards Fitzbillies.

'Well, aren't you going to tell me?' Peter said.

'When we get there,' Vicky said.

They ordered their Chelsea buns and tea and sat at a table away from the other customers.

'Right, now you can tell me,' Peter said.

'I want you to fuck me,' Vicky said.

Peter didn't know what to make of Vicky's forthrightness.

'You must be having me on.'

'No, deadly serious. I want to get pregnant,' she said.

Peter mopped his brow.

'Well, the first bit's OK, although I'm not sure what Becky would say, but I'm not sure I want to be a father again, especially at my age.'

106

'No-one need ever know.'

'Oh no! I don't know that I can eat my Chelsea bun now. I keep thinking of a bun in your oven.'

'You'd be doing me a great favour.'

'Have you thought of anyone else—Jim for example?'

'Bavarian vulgarity versus phonetic subtlety. There's no contest.'

'I'll think about it.'

Peter wasn't sure how he found his way back to his car after the bombshell. Did he stumble along Silver Street, past the elegant balustrading of Lutyens's white stone bridge? Did he even notice the Mathematical Bridge and the mock-Elizabethan contours of the Fisher Building or the brutalist horrors of the Cripps Building? No, he would not have let his eye alight for long on those, anyway. But this afternoon, he took in nothing, not even the odd punters on the Cam, the classical glories of the Gibbs Building and the perpendicular perfection of the more distant King's Chapel. He crossed the road and walked through Memorial Court, now spoiled, in his estimation, by the addition of the Forbes Mellon Library, which not only detracted from the original aesthetics of the open court but more importantly blocked the emerging sight of the prodigious phallus rising from that great temple of learning, in which he had indulged in amorous activity with Vicky not two hours previously.

Peter's mood was a mixture—elation on the one hand—elation that, after all the years of faithfulness to Becky and the tedium of his marriage and career, he had the chance to break free at last, but terror on the other hand—terror and fear of the consequences. What if the whole enterprise—the proposition—went disastrously wrong? What if he ended up falling in love with Vicky, divorcing Becky and marrying her? And what of the child? What would his feelings towards it be? What would be the reaction of Richard and Ben? What if … No, it couldn't be. He could not inseminate Vicky under the circumstances, but how to break it to her gently?

He got into his car. An announcement for the evening concert came on the radio. *Damn! Scriabin* … At least the stress was on the right syllable, but definitely not his favourite. Should he switch to the classical muzak of Classic FM? *No!*—That was unfair. What if it was the Radio One of the classical world? What if most of the music they played wasn't even classical? There was plenty of Bach and Handel beside the Boccherini and Karl Jenkins. No, he would resist the temptation of easy listening and persevere with Scriabin. As the music progressed, he realized it suited his troubled mood perfectly. The mixture of sonorities—the comforting horns, the jumpy strings, the shrill trilling of the flutes all seemed to signal something to him. And what of the enigmatic questioning of the final three notes? Should he, or shouldn't he? Would he, or wouldn't he? Damn Vicky! She was so alluring. He turned the radio off. The remainder of the journey passed in silent contemplation. He almost missed the turning to Bluntingham.

It was 7:30 when he arrived back home to domesticity—another world. Becky's mood had improved since her tetchiness in the morning.

'Did you have a good day?' she said. 'You've been gone a long time.'

'Yes, thanks. Lots of references. A lot of nostalgia. The UL brought back memories.'

'Did you see anyone you know?'

'No—not really.'

Peter excused this untruth by the addition of 'not really'. If she probed further, he could mention library staff he vaguely knew from thirty years ago. There was no need to mention Vicky—at least, not at this stage. Becky did not probe; Peter had half-assuaged his conscience.

'What was *your* day like?'

'So-so. Shopping, kids, housework. You know …'

Peter didn't know; he didn't care. They each acquiesced in the knowledge that any affair either of them was having would probably have no serious implications for their marriage.

Peter's hadn't even started properly. He didn't know if it *was* an affair or if he wanted it to be. He wanted to know the name of Becky's lover, though. All he had to go on was an R pencilled in on the calendar next to the entry for flower arranging with Bridget.

The evening meal was eaten largely in silence. The kids had already eaten, joined half-heartedly by Becky. Now she was prepared to eat a much lighter second meal, to share a portion of microwaved pizza with Peter, who had noticed the deterioration in the culinary offerings of the last few days, despite the alleged frequency of grocery shopping, but he said nothing. Neither did he inspect the supplies.

'D'you fancy a glass of wine?' he said.

'That'd be nice,' Vicky responded joyfully.

Peter thought he had made a breakthrough. He opened a château-bottled claret, and they both sipped at it.

'Hm, better than the crap we got in the Department on Monday,' he said. 'That all seems a world away now. In fact, I feel as if I inhabit multiple different worlds, all interconnected but so very distinct.'

He did not elaborate further. Becky smiled but said nothing. Peter's worlds no longer interested her. She had met R— and was being sucked into his world. Could she cope with it?

After only one glass of wine, Peter went to his study to check emails. The allure of instant communication was too great for him. He had been away from his computer for a whole day and had resisted the temptation to look at his phone while he was with Vicky. Another email from Beebee ... What did she want?

Hi Peter,

You were right about those orals. Alan emailed to say I'm required for an extraordinary oral for a student accused of plagiarism. Do you know Fiona Stanhope?

It doesn't sound very romantic, but we might get a chance for a coffee—next Thursday. Will you be around then?

Love,

Beebee x

'Shall you be?' don't you mean? Peter thought. *I will be, but I don't know whether I shall be. Damn Fowler!*—He would have preferred an alliterating word but opted for a less offensive one.—*Who says 'Shall you be?', anyway, nowadays?* Thursday was the only day for another meeting with Vicky. Should he try to get out of meeting Beebee? Would he? He would ponder it. He returned to Becky and his Château Roquegrave.

Friday, 26 September

On Friday morning, Peter prepared to re-enter his possibly least favourite, but most important, world—the Department of Other Languages, with all its woes. What had it, or for that matter he, brought into this world? Cambridge was his Eden, London Bridge his dungeon horrible. And yet, he owed his very existence to these doleful shades. Was this to be his torment without end, or would hope supersede the pandemonium of Johanna and the torture of his existence? *Don't be silly, Peter! You don't know how lucky you are! Isabelle would even sleep with Jim to get a job like yours. There's always a way out. Vicky … Beebee. Oh no! Only complications … Becky, the kids.*

Peter pulled himself together and dug out his lecture notes for Phonetics I. He was going to teach the First Years the International Phonetic Alphabet, not forgetting, of course, the glottal stop. Could he resist citing his own work on the bibliography? It was only partially relevant … far too advanced for First Years. He resisted the temptation to add Lampton to his PowerPoint presentation. He would mention it *en passant*, though, to show the students that they were dealing with a serious scholar here. He traipsed into OL 5, which still had a faint odour of cheap wine and soggy crisps. Should he make a joke?

110

He wanted to make a good impression. The students didn't know he was nervous—although Belfield might. He seemed to pick these things up.

'Hello, everyone, and welcome to possibly the most important part of your whole course,' he began. The group was divided into those—mainly innocent young ladies—who believed him, and those like Belfield who realized this was a joke. Peter struggled to attract students to the intricacies of glottalization, affricates, plosives, phonemes, and allophones. This term, his ploy was to present his course as fun and himself as a jolly good bloke—one of the lads even, but he knew he couldn't keep it up. He was Peter the Pedant, albeit a thoroughly decent chap.

Start as you hope to go on, he thought. *Get them on your side.*

'How do you pronounce your names? Does anyone have a glottal stop?'

Damn! he thought. *I hope that doesn't sound too suggestive.*

Most of the students looked blank. Belfield piped up.

'He does,' he said, pointing to his neighbour.

'Great,' Peter said. 'Tell us your name, please.'

'Peter Betteridge,' he said without a hint of a glottal stop.

'Great potential for glottalization, but you obviously don't go for it,' Peter said. 'How about ˈpiːʔə ˈbɛʔərɪdʒ?'

Betteridge recoiled in horror at the uncouth pronunciation of his name.

'We don't drop our *t*s in our family,' he said with an air of haughtiness.

'Quite right, too,' Peter said, accentuating the alveolar stops. 'But you'd be surprised; even Her Majesty does in certain linguistic environments, and *she* speaks the Queen's English! It's just, you don't notice them all. Did you notice how I pronounced *don't*? Where was the *t*?'

The students began to smile.

'By the way, my name's ˈpiːtə, but you can call me ˈpiːʔə if you must. Or Professor Lampton if you insist.'

The students chuckled. Peter had won them over.

111

After the lecture, Peter returned to his room, as pleased as Punch. Maybe London Bridge wasn't so hellish after all. He fetched himself a coffee and sat down to enjoy it. There was a knock at the door. Johanna came in.

'Gisela has called in sick,' she said.

'Oh, yes?' Peter said. 'Did she say what was the matter?'

'Morning sickness, she said,' Johanna reported innocently.

For Chrissake! Peter thought. *What do* you *know about that? What does anyone know?* He'd ask Becky.

'See if one of the research students can cover. How about Ursula?'

Beebee had settled back into the routine of teaching at Essex, but she felt isolated in terms of her subject in a department where emphasis was on practical language teaching over a wide range of languages. She longed for the contact of likeminded colleagues on the RRE subpanel and of Peter in particular. She was concerned that he had not responded to her email about Thursday. Of course, she knew nothing of the circumstances. She realized that Peter was in something of a cleft-stick situation. From what he had said, however, she knew that Becky was the least favourite female for a romantic involvement. She imagined he was stuck with her for better, for worse, for richer, for poorer … but till death do us part? That remained to be seen. It was between her and Vicky. She would send another email.

Hi Peter,

I was wondering why I haven't heard anything from you. Did you get my email about next Thursday? I shall be in London Bridge most of the afternoon. I'm having lunch with Alan at 1:00, and we're doing the oral at 2:30. We could meet at about teatime. Shall I come to your room about 4:00?

Beebee x

Vicky was also concerned that she hadn't heard any more from Peter, but it was still early days. He would respond over the weekend, she supposed. Nevertheless, a reminder might be in order, she thought.

Hi Peter,

Have you thought any more about my proposition? I'm sad and lonely. The house is cold and comfortless. I know you can't offer anything permanent (?), but I need that loan from you. Non-repayable, of course, but I'll make it worth your while. There's a snuggly corner in Water Street waiting for you.

How about Thursday after work at my place?

Vicky x

Oh no! Peter thought when he read Vicky's email. He had tried to put yesterday's events out of his mind in the hope that the situation would somehow resolve itself. *These women! Why were they so eager? Damn them!* Eager one minute and screaming blue murder the next … He had been wise in the past to steer clear of them and their wiles, he thought. Could he trust either of them? How would he decide? He thought of the practicalities. Vicky was tricky … He chuckled at the rhyme and wondered if he should call her Tricky Vicky. No … she seemed genuine enough, but once inseminated, how would she react? What did that question mark in brackets mean? It wasn't as innocuous as a glottal stop symbol, he thought. And a 'loan' of that nature was a serious business. He might not have enough in his account to satisfy her. What if he failed to withdraw anything? That would be most embarrassing. It had been a long time since Becky had demanded any withdrawals. He had almost forgotten how …

Then there was the availability aspect. Beebee was only rarely available—specifically now only on Thursday next. He thought she was the favourite, too, but he wasn't sure. Vicky, on the other hand, was on his doorstep and readily available, but at what cost?—emotional, moral, and marital … He had made up his mind. A fabricated reason for having to be in the

Department on Thursday would satisfy the present needs. He wouldn't disappoint either woman. He would reply to Vicky first and see her reaction, depending on which, he would reply to Beebee.

Hi Vicky,

I've been thinking about your proposal. There's a lot to clarify first, not least with Becky. She's been rather touchy lately, and I need to sound her out gently. I think, if I approach it in the right way, the loan could be made. I'm afraid I can't make next Thursday, though, as I shall be in London on exams business.

Peter x

Not quite a lie, he thought. *Not quite the truth. That oath that people swear in court was damn tricky, Vicky,* he chuckled inwardly. He was glad he wasn't on oath. He did have a conscience …

A few minutes later, an email came back:

Hi Peter,

I'm very disappointed. I can't wait forever. How about the weekend? Or I might try Jim.

Vicky

Peter noted the change of tone and the absence of a kiss. Should he pack it in and give up the whole enterprise? he mused. Maybe, but he'd write to Beebee first. She wasn't actually demanding anything, but was she even offering anything? And the practicalities in future if she was …? *Oh f…fudge!*

Hi Beebee,

Thanks for the reminder. I can be in the Department on Thursday. I've got plenty of admin to do, departmental problems to solve, etc.

Come along to OL 15 when you're finished with Alan, and we'll take it from there.

Looking forward to seeing you.

Peter x

After writing to Beebee, Peter thought about what to say to Vicky. Was she too keen? Should *he* be? She was being difficult at best. He could let her stew, but that might be counterproductive. Her mention of Jim was undoubtedly a bluff. *A soft answer turneth away wrath: but grievous words stir up anger.* How often had he learned that to his disadvantage? *Softly, softly, Peter.*

Hi Vicky,

I'm very sorry to disappoint you. I didn't mean to upset you. It's just that I'm rather busy and stressed at the beginning of term and need time for reflection. By all means try Jim. I'd rather it was me, but I won't be offended.

Take care!

Peter x

He pressed 'send' and read through the copy to self. He was horrified. THREE grammatical errors in ONE email. *I'd rather it WERE I, but I SHAN'T be offended. But who on earth says that?* Should he send it again? *Yes,* but would he? *Yes and no! Damn the English language! Damn Vicky! Damn everything!*

He went home to dependable Becky. But she was no longer so dependable. He knew she now had a boyfriend. How serious was it? Had they done the deed? At least she wasn't troubled like he was. *AS, Peter!* he screamed silently. He ringed round *like* with his imaginary red pen. Maybe he could do some snooping over the weekend like Derek. That one's OK. *Damn it!* That was a world away. There was a substantial proportion of his life in need of some restructuring that showed a significant amount of utter crap and fucked-upness. Was that even a word? Had he coined a new one? He Googled it—26,100 with the hyphen, 35,500 without. *Bloody English language! You can't even coin anything new these days.*

Sunday, 28 September

On Sunday, he managed to get hold of Becky's phone, which she had left in the bedroom beside the marital bed. *Marital bed my foot! When was the last time it* served *that purpose? Screw Becky!* Sadly, he didn't want to anymore. He slipped the phone into his pocket and took it to his study. *Damn!* Password protected. He tried a few obvious possibilities until it was locked and would remain so for 24 hours. He replaced it carefully. How was he going to explain that one? Could it get lost—forgotten in the car? No, she was bound to look for it soon. Plausible denial was the only way out. He didn't even remember seeing her leave it anywhere. It must have reset itself after an update. He could check it on the internet. She might believe him. Damn her if she didn't. Who was R— anyway? Someone from the Flower Guild? But then, men don't arrange flowers. Or do they in Bluntingham? *Oh no!* She was a dyke. That would explain everything. *Don't be silly, Peter. Ask around … Try the kids.*

4. WEEK 2

Monday, 29 September

After the weekend's fraught musings and strained relations with Becky, who had grudgingly accepted Peter's utterly feeble attempts to convince her that her phone's being locked was a commonly occurring phenomenon, Peter felt relieved to be embarking on another week in the Department of Other Languages, albeit in London Bridge, where he would spend five working days, with no cheese and wine parties for entertainment, no female colleagues for fun—he discounted all the women in the Department: Johanna obviously, Frau Schmidt goes without saying (she wouldn't be interested at his age, and there was the Harrison problem additionally), Dr Compton, who was a year off retirement, and Dr Warham, a fifty-something antipodean, who was married to an eminent physician.

Despite this, he was in reasonably good spirits for the ensuing week. He had kept abreast of his emails over the weekend and had discovered nothing that needed dealing with urgently. Beebee was pleased he would meet her on Thursday. Vicky had been held at bay—at least he hoped so. If she became uppity, that was her loss. He hadn't set out to woo her.

He took his first language class of the term, since no classes scheduled for a Monday had taken place last week, owing to the introductory intensive days for First Years.

He reminded the Finalists of the new departmental naming policy—students were welcome to call teaching staff by their first names—except for Dr Warham—'Don't try it on with her,' he quipped and turned his attention to a passage of *Great Expectations* to be translated into German: 'Bentley Drummle, who was so sulky a fellow that he even took up a book as if its writer had done him an injury, did not take up an acquaintance in a more agreeable spirit.'

He explained the difficulty of translating take up in the two different contexts and how that didn't work with the same word in German. He pointed out how professional translators skated over problems, paraphrasing instead. The students looked bored, so, in jovial mood, he asked them, 'Does he remind you of anyone? I can certainly think of a colleague who comes into that category. Not here, of course.'

The hour passed agreeably, and Peter was satisfied that at least in his professional life he was a success, albeit a limited one. Of course, he would have rather been in Cambridge, but he would probably have stuck at lecturer grade there. It was indeed swings and roundabouts. He wouldn't swap his life for Jim's. He went back to his room for a coffee.

In walked Frau Schmidt, after timidly knocking. She burst into tears.

Jim's first lecture of term was scheduled for a smallish room in the Raised Faculty Building. He was disappointed when he saw the capacity of the room—only about twenty students. He had assumed that more students would have opted for his course in Part II of the Tripos and that it would also evidence the Lubbins effect, by which he meant it would attract students from other triposes and those taking other Other Languages papers, to which his lectures might be tangentially relevant. This would not do, he thought. On Monday morning, he went to Alec, the faculty administrator, to complain and was told to see how it went on the first Thursday. If need be, a larger room could be found.

'Haven't you heard of the Lubbins effect?' Jim asked the agitated administrator, who was new to the job.

'No,' he said curtly.

'Yeah, well,' Jim said, 'you'll find that that has a significant effect on the female population attending the lectures.'

'Wait and see, Dr Lubbins. And incidentally, the title has been changed to *Old Bavarian Dialects* on the instructions of the Head of Department.'

'Yeah,' Jim said, 'he's a stuck-up prick.'

'I'm sorry, Dr Lubbins.'

Jim went away, dejected. He would show them. The Lubbins effect would prove them wrong. Sod them!

Peter wasn't sure how to deal with Frau Schmidt. It is true that he had occasionally encountered the odd female under-graduate who had had a little weep over her misfortunes and even a couple of emotional men who had just managed to hold back tears, but he had never had a person for whom he was in any way professionally responsible weep loudly and uncontrollably in his presence. Should he put his arm round her? No! That might be misconstrued, but to sit behind a desk while she sobbed seemed to him heartless in the extreme. He got up and sat in a chair adjacent to hers, sufficiently far away to show appropriate distance but near enough—he hoped—to show compassion and empathy. Of course, he knew what was the matter, but he had to act as if he didn't. When the sobbing subsided a little, Peter felt able to speak, asking her whether there was anything he could do to help. Frau Schmidt poured out her woes, beginning with her strict Catholic upbringing in Bavaria, her being jilted in love while a student in Munich, and her consequent decision to begin a new life in England. She explained her predicament, her embarrassment, at which Peter smiled in view of its meaning in Spanish but hastily wiped the smile off his face in *his* embarrassment, her lack of support and her decision to return to Bavaria. She omitted to say who was the father or how far the pregnancy had progressed.

'Do you think you'll be able to continue until the end of the year?' Peter asked. She burst into tears again.

'Please understand I'm here to help,' Peter said. 'Come and see me at any time if there's anything I can do,' he said. 'Have you considered contacting the University counselling service?'

Frau Schmidt didn't answer. She shook her head and left with a brief 'thank you'.

'Damn!' Peter said under his breath as he returned to his desk. He began to compose an email to Harrison:

Dear Michael,

I apologize for troubling you with this, but I think you need to talk to Frau Schmidt and come to some kind of agreement.

I have just had a very tearful language assistant in my office. She seems unsure how she will cope with her difficult situation. Maybe you could pop by and have a chat soon.

Best wishes,

Peter

A few minutes later, an email came back:

Dear Professor Lampton,

I'm sorry to have caused problems for you. I have been unable to concentrate on my work this term and am considering giving up my PhD.

I hope to call in soon when I have sorted myself out a little.

Kind regards,

Michael

Johanna knocked at the door. It had locked itself after Frau Schmidt had turned the handle when exiting the room, so Peter had to get up to open it.

'Yes, what do you want, Johanna?' Peter said brusquely.

'The exam papers have disappeared,' she said.

'All of them?' Peter asked.

'Yes, all of them.'

'I can't be doing with this now,' Peter said. 'I'll have a chat with Alan and get back to you. Did you keep the door locked at all times like I said?' He didn't even wince at his own misuse of the word *like* but consoled himself that the OED now grudgingly recognized its use as a conjunction.

'Most of the time,' Johanna said.

'Get out, please,' Peter said, 'and don't come back.'

'You are very rude,' Johanna said and walked away.

'No! No!' Peter said with emphatic emotion.

Ten minutes were devoted to rumination, after which Peter got up and went to look for Alan. He was teaching, so Peter returned to his room and wrote to Beebee for her advice as External Examiner:

Dear Beebee,

Disaster has struck. Johanna has lost all the exam papers. I assume you never got yours. I don't know what to do. Any ideas? Has it ever happened in your Department?

See you on Thursday,

Peter

Alan emerged from his lecture at 1:00, cheerfully chatting to a group of students about nineteenth-century European drama.

'Can I see you for a moment?' Peter said.

Alan went into Peter's room and Peter explained the situation.

'Maybe something will turn up,' Peter said.

'Maybe,' Alan said. He couldn't think of anything light-hearted to alleviate the awfulness of the situation. He emerged from Peter's office, looking downcast.

Thursday, 2 October

Peter made his way into the Department on Thursday morning. Although he was looking forward to seeing Beebee, the journey provided him with no pleasure. Park the car at the far end of the station car park, where he would usually find three or four spaces remaining; feel aggrieved at the horrendous price of parking; trudge to the ticket office and buy an off-peak ticket to London from the cheeky chappie, an amateur football fan, behind the counter; feel aggrieved at the horrendous price of train travel; ponder about how other customers seemed to converse easily with the said cheeky chappie, which was something he could do only occasionally; regret his lack of social interaction skills in a context where he did not feel at ease; trudge up and down the footbridge and wait for the train usually for some ten minutes, weighing up the other passengers. He was shattered already. Was that Tom Emmerington, an old school mate of his, with whom he had lost contact? *Could be, couldn't be. No, probably not.* He wouldn't ask. He'd feel a fool. Ah! There was someone he did recognize—Charles Burnham, a local composer, under whose baton he had occasionally sung years ago. He looked him up and down. No recognition. He didn't know him well, so why should he bother? No contact. He got into the train and tried to find a pleasant seat away from the day trippers—the East Anglians up from the country, for whom a trip to London was a rare event, a treat even. *Yeah, well*, it certainly wasn't for him. *Poor Jim*, he chuckled—*yeah, well*—did he, too, have a catch phrase with which he introduced his utterances? He thought not. *I think you'll find I don't, Derek. Damn you! Damn London! Damn Jim! Damn Becky! Damn Johanna! Damn …* his life! He got out his Sony Walkman or was it a Diskman, or had he progressed to an iPod? Whatever it was, he listened to music, always something classical. Well, nearly always. With some, he wasn't sure. His penchant for choral music, going back to his undergraduate days as a choral scholar at Needham, which extended over several centuries, stretching even into the twentieth, made him disregard the distinction between classical and romantic—he didn't go beyond. Can church music ever be romantic, though? Doesn't the Church hate sex and romance? He was not really religious but had been in his youth. He was old and jaded now—actually not really old, just jaded. His life had been a disappointment to him, despite its successes. *Snap out of it, Peter, you don't know how lucky you are.* But you always want something better. The grass is always greener, but actually, the people whom you envy are probably even more miserable than you are, dare he say fucked up? He had begun to allow himself the use of the *f*-word increasingly in middle age. What was so problematic about it? Why did hypocritical people recoil in horror at it? It was harmless etymologically, had a very definite meaning, but the associations … I think you'll find we're all fucked up, Lampton. Yeah, well, you certainly are, Brown. Perhaps the most of all, but you'd never admit it. He envied the way Vicky just came out with it, 'I want you to fuck me.' I think you'll find that that's the best way, Brown. Yeah, well, Jim, I envy you, but your life isn't so very rosy. Was there anyone he knew who had the perfect life? Perfection could never exist in a fallen world. Should we strive for it? He strove for perfection in his research, less so in his teaching. He wanted to eliminate glottal stops from the English language, but he used them all the time, like the Queen in certain linguistic contexts. He was a hypocrite. He hated hypocrites! Ergo … Did he really hate himself?

On the journey, he weighed up recent events. He needed to compartmentalize—there was home life with all its difficulties, Becky having an affair, but who with? Shouldn't that be *with whom*, Peter? Damn Churchill and his *up with which I will not put*. He was right in his use of *will*, though, if he ever said this. A gentleman's degree but look where it got him. Maybe he would have better luck snooping next Sunday. Did the young goats know? He knew he was in a particularly bad mood when he resorted to such unnecessary pedantries. Was that even a count noun? He would have to check. Yes, OK. Really *orl korrect*? Okay? WTF! Who gives a toss? Exclamation mark, question mark? Excuse me, Mr Chairman, but I think you need a comma there. Indeed, Dr Compton, an Oxford comma; thank you for pointing that out.

He had so far only populated one compartment. Shouldn't that be *populated only one*, Mr Chairman? He quite liked those old-style trains with six seats to a compartment, or was it eight? They had got rid of them on Southern Region because of women's safety. A terrible business. Rape, attacks. Late at night, he supposed. Back to your metaphorical compartments, Peter.

Number 2—the Department of Other Languages. You know enough about that, whoever you are. Only problems there. No not only. Some joy, too. That's why he was going in today—to see Beebee. What would that bring? What did he want? What did Beebee want?

Number 3—Vicky and her needs. At least that was straightforward. He knew what she wanted. Did he know what he wanted? Yes and no.

Number 4—the RRE. That was quite simple by comparison with everything else. Nothing was intractable. There was no problem that a bit of espionage and trickery couldn't sort out. Maybe he should mould his life as a perpetual RRE—constant restructuring. A kind of cycle of death and rebirth until he reached his nirvana.

Kings Cross. Shouldn't that have an apostrophe, Mr Chairman? Yes, Dr Compton. Please add an apostrophe in Question 3.

Peter had spent a whole train journey in fruitless internal debate. Had he sorted anything? — No! Sorted out, Peter. A phrasal verb, you know. No, you haven't sorted anything. He was now rebelling. He might even soon have the bottle to use an intervocalic glottal stop. That would show them, but not in front of the students. He had to keep up appearances there. Poor Fiona Stanhope … What did she think she was doing when she plagiarized an essay on Brecht? Did she think the examiners were too stupid to recognize the polished style of large chunks as opposed to her clumsy undergraduate prose? A quick Google search, and the case was proved. Why had she appealed? Would her case be furthered by the need to convene a special viva with the External? What did she think? Would it destroy her chances of a II.1? Half the students who got one these days didn't deserve it. It was very difficult to get less. Grade inflation? Of course. How could the Government be so naïve or dishonest as to pretend otherwise? Such a thing would never happen in the RRE … or would it?

Peter emerged from his tube train and walked the remaining few hundred metres to the Department. The last person he wanted to see was Johanna. The first person he saw was Johanna. She ignored him. He ignored her. He would sort her out today. Fire her if necessary. Wouldn't that require a tribunal? He would give her a stern talking to anyway. *It's now or never, Johanna. Either you wake your ideas up or you can collect your cards.* What a silly expression. There were no cards—at least, not nowadays. And would they even get a replacement? No, he would wait until the afternoon, ask Beebee's advice and come to some kind of decision in conjunction with her and Alan. They could settle it over lunch. He went along to Alan's room.

'Do you mind if I join you for lunch?'

Alan looked less than pleased. Did he, too, have designs on Beebee? He should be so lucky. Beebee was Peter's prerogative. He was Head of Department and outranked a mere Chairman of Examiners. He was a member of Subpanel Z of the RRE. Alan should be pleased that his work was even being considered for restructuring.

'Yes, OK. We're going down to the staff dining room at 1:00,' Alan said.

'See you later.'

Over lunch, they agreed that Fiona's mark for the paper be rescinded and that a resit, pegged at 40%, would be allowed as a gesture of kindness. They would still have to go through the motions of an oral, though.

'What are we going to do about the lost papers, then?' Peter asked despondently.

'I'm afraid you'll need to set a whole new set,' Beebee said. 'They'll probably be for sale on the internet or somewhere by now.'

Alan agreed reluctantly.

'That won't go down well, especially with Dr Warham,' Peter said. Even he hadn't got used to calling her Maralyn. The name didn't suit anyway.

Peter left Alan and Beebee to take coffee together. Perhaps that would satisfy Alan's sense of importance and his need to assert himself.

'See you later, Beebee,' he said and went back to the Department.

Poor Fiona Stanhope was waiting in the corridor, clutching a copy of her plagiarized essay. Peter wanted to avoid her, but he had to speak to her.

'Dr Jameson will be along soon. You can wait in OL 5 if you like. I hope all goes well.'

Why was he doing this? Did he really hope all went well? Did he give a fig? A euphemism, eh? Wasn't life one big euphemism? He must look it up. It wasn't what he thought but obscene nonetheless like so much else. Wasn't language a wonderful thing? A rhetorical question, should it have a question mark? It didn't seem appropriate here. He would bottle out of it, glottal stop and all. He was looking forward to seeing Beebee.

At 3:00, a tearful Fiona emerged from OL 5. She looked through Peter's window as if to evoke his pity and compassion. He gave her one of those inscrutable smiles that says hard luck, but we mean well—you know how it is. She went away again. She'd get over it, he supposed. A few minutes later, along came Beebee.

Peter showed her to one of the comfortable seats, which was round a corner, out of view of the window in the door. He went to the door and discreetly ensured it was locked. Johanna

126

was the only other person in the Department with a key. She could be relied on not to enter. At this time in the afternoon, she usually went for a tea break with the French secretary. Peter and Beebee were alone.

Peter was edgy. His feelings for Beebee were strong, but he never made the first move. Come on, Peter. This is what you've come in for. — Shouldn't that be *that for which you have come in*? — Shut up, Winston. That's a preposition at the end, too. — But it's a phrasal verb. — Point taken. Gentleman's degree.

'Did you have a good trip, Beebee?' *Come on, Peter, you can do better than that.*

'I haven't come for idle chitchat.'

'No, I suppose not.' Oral exploration? No, that was Vicky. For Goodness' sake, Peter, show a bit of manliness.

Beebee got up and went over to two armless chairs that were positioned side by side.

'Come and sit here. Show me your glottis.'

'The storeroom,' Peter stuttered.

'All right. You lead the way,' Beebee said.

They emerged, after exploration of the departmental detritus of ten years—bundles of past exam scripts, books donated by the relatives of deceased members of the Department, old computers, fit only for a museum of ancient technology—to an empty Department. There was no-one to witness their collaboration, no-one to suspect their shared interest.

'We've got to find a better place next time,' Beebee said. 'The cabriolet?'

Peter looked uneasy. He had never done it in a cupboard before, let alone standing up and certainly not in the Department. His face turned into a broad grin.

'The cabriolet next time,' he said.

They left the Department, looking demure and very business-like. A most successful oral.

For the entire journey home, Peter wrestled with his conscience. Was that really what he wanted out of life? he asked himself. He couldn't answer this. A smile, discreet and scarcely noticeable at first, spread over his face in the fully populated railway carriage until it began to attract stares from his fellow passengers. Peter smiled back at them as if they wished to communicate with him. They hastily looked away. His sense of satisfaction at having done something that was ever so naughty increased. He had scored in a store cupboard in the Department of Other Languages at the University of London Bridge no less—they hadn't.

The train arrived at Peter's home station. Peter was one of the first up the stairs and over the footbridge. He made it to his car in record time and was one of the first to leave the car park. He wasn't sure what had propelled him, whence his eagerness came. It certainly couldn't be to get home to Becky, could it? Would there be an interrogation? Why should there be? Would she suspect anything? Would his demeanour betray anything? Can't women always tell?

He drove home at a steady pace and walked nonchalantly into the house.

'Did you have a good day, dear?' Becky asked Peter when he got inside the house.

Peter was suspicious. She didn't normally ask. Did he ever have a good day? He supposed there was the odd one, but what did it interest her? *Don't sound too enthusiastic, Peter.*

'So-so,' he said. 'We had a special viva because of a plagiarism case.'

Becky's eyes had already glazed over. She suspected nothing.

'How about you?'

'Not bad—the usual.'

'More grocery shopping?' Peter asked, tongue in cheek.

'You got it.'

'Are you sure? Where did you pick that up from?'

'Don't you mean, "From whence did you pick that up?"' Becky retorted.

'Very funny! I meant the Americanism.'

128

'The Flower Guild. I did the arrangement for Sunday.'

As improbable as it seemed, there might be some truth in it, Peter thought.

'Who were you doing the flowers with?'

'With whom?'

'Very droll!'

'Bridget.'

'Is she into Americanisms?'

'No.'

Peter could see that the conversation was going nowhere. Becky was getting tetchy again. Was it just a red herring? A deliberate deflection? A false trail? Would he ever be able to find out? He might see Bridget over the weekend and casually ask about Thursday morning. After supper, he went to his study for the obligatory checking of emails before settling down to an evening of TV and humouring Becky. Four emails of note had arrived since he left the Department. The first had a date stamp of Thursday, 2 October, at 19:13. It was from Frau Schmidt:

Dear Peter,

I'm very sorry to let you down, but I'm finding teaching both physically and emotionally draining.

After long consideration, I have decided to tender my resignation from Monday, 6 October. I will, of course, work out my one month's notice. I hope this will give you sufficient time to find a replacement and apologize again for disappointing you and the Department.

Kind regards,

Gisela

The second had a date stamp of Thursday, 2 October, at 19:25. It was from Vicky:

Dear Peter,

I wasn't joking about the proposition I made to you last Thursday. A whole week has passed now, and this has strengthened my resolve still further. It's now or never.

Patrick was never able to give me the child I wanted. I know you can. When can we meet up? This weekend?

Love, Vicky xxx

The third had a date stamp of Thursday, 2 October, at 19:27:

Dear Professor Lampton,

I regret to say that I have decided to give up my PhD studies. I couldn't stay in the Department with Gisela in it, but now she is leaving, I realize that it's my duty to support her and the baby. I may be able to resume registration at some stage in the future, but for now, I should like to thank you for being a kind and sympathetic supervisor and a great Head of Department.

Glottal stops will always have a place in my heart.

Best wishes,

Michael

The fourth had a date stamp of Thursday, 2 October, at 20:01:

Dear PL,

I hope you got home safely after today's excitement.

I wonder what further treats are in 'store' for me. I'm taking the cabriolet for a spin on Sunday. Any interest?

BB x

Friday, 3 October

Jim was gearing up for Fucking in Old Bavarian. He had decided to rewrite his sixteen-page article as lecture notes, with plenty of jokes aimed at the young ladies, and was already

130

regretting his choice of title. He was concerned that it might put the young ladies off rather than encourage them and was rather taken aback by a complaint to the Head of the German Department by a sensitive undergraduette from Girton.

He pondered how he might best entice Isabelle into Jim's Pad. He could ask her opinion then; maybe she would even help him with the typing, but that was a feeble excuse, he thought. He would have to come up with something better. If only there were a job going! Not only could he help with a reference, but he would also make practical suggestions for her application—up close and personal if need be. He knew colleges would soon be advertising for research fellowships. If she got in ahead of the competition, that might be to their advantage. He would ring his buddy Philip at Needham College. The phone was answered speedily.

'Hitchinson speaking.'

'Yeah, Jim here. Fancy a pint sometime soon?'

'To what do I owe the pleasure? Not to discuss *Woyzeck* or Heine, I presume.'

'No, none of your namby-pamby stuff. I've got a proposition to make.'

'I'm all ears.'

'Not over the phone.'

They agreed to meet at the Champion of the Thames in King Street on Thursday evening.

'We can have a few bevvies and go for a curry afterwards at the Bombay,' Jim said. 'I'm heavily into vindaloo.'

'It's in the wrong direction for me,' Philip said. 'I was planning to eat in college.'

'Yeah, well, you'll be wanting to forgo your posh pleasures for Jim this time, won't you?'

'See you on Thursday,' Philip said. He wondered what it was Jim wanted but thought no more about it. Most of his schemes were hare-brained anyway.

5.   WEEK 3

Thursday, 9 October

On the first Thursday of Full Term, Jim went along, full of anticipation, to his lecture. There were ten students, mainly male, leaving the room half empty. Even a few risqué jokes that caused a ripple of laughter among his listeners did little to cheer him up. He finished on time at 12:55 and walked dejectedly towards the exit. The Lubbins effect had failed to materialize. *Yeah, well,* Jim thought to himself, *better luck next time. Perhaps not all students have made their course choices yet.* As he left the building, a voice calling his name lifted his spirits. Isabelle was waiting to one side of the doorway.

'Come on, Dr Lubbins,' she said, 'let's go and have lunch. Did you expect to see me? I didn't want to embarrass you by coming to your lecture.'

They decided to walk over and get a cafeteria lunch at the Grad Pad in Mill Lane.

'It's probably just as well you didn't come to the lecture,' Jim said. 'There wasn't a spare seat in the house, but I'd have fitted you in somewhere,' he said with a wink. 'How've you been keeping?'

'I've been at a bit of a loss,' Isabelle said. After I got everything typed up and sent off to Niamh, I had time on my hands until yesterday's meeting of Subpanel X … Boring Germans, but it was only in London. Maybe they get up to hijinks when they're away for an extended restructuring session like we had in Ayr.'

'Yeah, it was fun,' Jim said. 'Have you heard anything on the job front?'

'No, not really. Niamh might have something coming up at Bristol, but it would only be temporary and more in admin than academic.'

'Yeah, well,' Jim said. 'I might just be able to help there. Things have progressed since I last saw you—I'm having a drink with a mate tonight who might be able to pull a few strings. You'll need a new research project, though. I might be able to help there, too. I've got a joint project in mind. Why don't we go to Jim's Pad after lunch and do a bit of research?'

Isabelle was concerned by the way Jim stressed the word research. She had never experienced Jim's Pad before and was feeling apprehensive. They had had a fun time flirting in Scotland, but so far, she had managed to avoid Jim's attempts to bed her. He was, after all, old enough to be her father.

'Tell me a bit more about this joint research project,' Isabelle said. 'There's no need to go over to Jim's Pad now. Things might change after your drink tonight, though. I'll see how I'm placed after that.'

Jim was disappointed. He hastily thought up how they might apply for funding for a collaborative project on imprecations in old European languages and their relationship to Latin.

'Sounds great, don't you think?' Jim said.

Isabelle had to agree.

'Canis culum in tuo naso,' she said.

'Pheromones up yours,' Jim said. 'I'll be in touch.'

Was that a double entendre? Isabelle wondered. 'Thanks for the lunch,' she said and blew him a kiss.

When he got home, Jim decided to give Isabelle a ring, with an eye to arranging a get-together. Maybe he had seemed a little too eager, he thought. She had shown a reluctance to be enticed into Jim's Pad, but an excursion at the weekend to an antiques fair in Newark might prove the perfect opportunity.

'Yeah, Jim here,' he said. 'I've got to go to Newark on Saturday to an antiques fair. D'you fancy a day out? You like antiques, don't you?'

'Come off it, Jim, you're still quite young even if you could be my dad.'

'Yeah, well. I'll treat you to lunch at the Lord Nelson, and we can look round the fair together.'

'I don't think so, thank you, Jim,' Isabelle said.

'Pity. If things go well tonight, I thought I'd persuade my mate Philip to come for a curry again on Sunday, when I hope to iron things out. It would help if you were there. Only, I may be too tired to negotiate with him if I don't have help carrying my purchases on Saturday. If we make a good profit on eBay, I'll cut you in.'

'In that case, how could I possibly refuse, Jim?'

'Yeah, well. I'll pick you up on Saturday at 10:00.'

Jim arrived at the Champion of the Thames shortly after 6:30 on Thursday to find Philip sitting at a table, supping a pint.

'What can I get you, Jim?' Philip asked.

'I'll have a pint of what you're having, thanks.'

'A pint of lager, then,' Philip said to tease him.

'Lager's for wimps. I want none of your namby-pamby foreign muck. A pint of Abbot, please.'

'I thought you would like Löwenbräu, Jim. Isn't Bavaria your thing?'

'Yeah, well, when in Rome.'

'It's lovely to meet up—quite an unexpected pleasure. How's the new term going?'

'Yeah, that's what I wanted to see you about. I've met a young lady.'

'Aren't you always meeting young ladies, Jim?'

'This could be the one.'

Philip smiled.

134

'Pull the other one, eh, Jim?'

'I need to get her a job. That might lead to closer collaboration.'

Jim explained about the RRE and the successes of the Lubbins effect.

Philip smiled benevolently.

'It sounds as if you've already scored, Jim.'

'Yeah, well—in a manner of speaking, but there's work to be done still. That's where you come in.'

'How come? I'm not sure I want to get involved.'

'Isabelle needs a job that's appropriate to her academic status. She's just finished her PhD, and she wants to stay in Cambridge. That means a research fellowship. We're going to apply for joint funding from the Research Council for a project on imprecations in Old European languages.'

'Are you likely to get it? I've heard they're very competitive.'

'Bound to if we play it right.'

'I still don't see where I come in.'

'You play the stock market, don't you?'

Philip admitted that he had some competence and experience here.

'I've got a very good tip.'

Philip laughed.

'Buy shares in Lubbins plc, eh, Jim?'

'I'll trade you the tip for a research fellowship at Needham for Isabelle.'

'That wouldn't be ethical, Jim.'

'Yeah, well, what is? You scratch my back and all that. It's a start-up being floated on the London stock exchange in three weeks' time. Sure to double in price. My mate in the City says it's a sure-fire investment. Invest ten grand, and you've made twenty in a week.'

'Isn't that insider trading?'

'Yeah, well, not if *you* do it.'

'Do you fancy a game of bar billiards?' Philip asked.

'Yeah—I'll play you for a tip and a research fellowship. You can't lose.'

'I'm not quite sure I understand the logic, Jim.'

They had a couple more pints and a game of bar billiards then went on for a Jim's special at the Bombay.

'I need to know in the morning,' Jim said.

'I'll phone you after my supervision. I'll be in Needham and can sound out a mate beforehand, but no promises.'

Peter returned to Becky and settled down to an evening's TV. There was little need in the event to humour Becky. She seemed curiously content with her life at present. Peter thought he knew why, but how long would it last? All he knew was that his name began with an R—*Richard, Raymond, Robert, Rudolfus* …? He liked the last name, improbable though it was. He would forgive Becky for having an affair anyway. She knew the conditions of extramarital engagements that they had agreed upon. What's sauce for the goose is sauce for the gander. He was the gander and had already had a helping of very tasty sauce. But it was one of those niggling problems. As an academic, he always wanted to know how and why. Why was obvious—he was boring as a husband; she was bored with him even though she needed him and still wanted him—but she fervently desired something more from life. There comes a point in every marriage when the realization is made that this is the best that it can offer, not bad enough to jettison it—that was the last thing either of them wanted—but not good enough not to hope for a little supplementary excitement. Wife swapping was a rather sordid and distasteful affair, Peter thought. He imagined Becky would disapprove strongly on moral as well as hygienic grounds anyway. He couldn't imagine a swingers' party in Bluntingham where he might have to step over another fucking couple. That wouldn't be at all satisfying—sex for sex's sake. No, a discreet affair was what he wanted, what she apparently wanted—not discreet enough as to be deceitful and duplicitous, but the kind that a few people who were in the know would greet with a gentle, understanding smile and not deprecate. They knew the reasons and didn't disapprove. After this initial agreement, the matter was put to one side; it wouldn't be mentioned again unless it impinged upon the functioning of their marriage. Hence, Peter couldn't ask Becky who her lover was any more than she could ask him. Perhaps she didn't even care anyway. She supposed it was someone she knew—someone from Peter's work. She wasn't a fool—a three-day sojourn in Scotland in a hotel would be the logical place for such an affair to start up, but it might have been going on for months in London or Cambridge, or for that matter in Bluntingham. She didn't share Peter's need for sophisticated academic enquiry. She supposed it wasn't Johanna, but beyond that, it really didn't matter. She had heard Peter speak of Beebee and Niamh before. He always referred to the language assistant as Frau Schmidt, which she found strange—perhaps it was her. She was damned if she was going to say, 'perhaps it was she'. Peter could go and screw himself. Yes, she permitted that verb but usually not the *f*-word. No, why on earth was she even bothering to go through the possibilities? It would come out in the fullness of time anyway.

Peter had shelved the enquiry into Becky's lover. He would ask Bridget, pure and simple. If she mentioned anyone beginning with an R, he would have it. His immediate problems were, in order of importance, Vicky—she was demanding an answer speedily, Beebee—she was keen to take things further, and Frau Schmidt. He would have to speak to Human Resources and see how to proceed. Wasn't there a fourth? Harrison could wait until Monday.

Friday, 10 October

On Friday, he decided that the priorities had changed. He phoned HR as soon as he got into the Department and spoke to Mr Bulawayo. They arranged a meeting in Peter's office for 3:00 that afternoon. Peter was given permission to advertise for a new language assistant. He was able now to tick this off his to-do list. Next, he wrote to Harrison, who was in fourth position, lamenting the fact that he was leaving, but indicating that he could quite understand and extending his sympathy to him. Beebee came next. He would enjoy a ride in the cabriolet, but he wasn't sure if Sunday was the right time. He had promised to go out with Becky. Although this wasn't true, he could easily make it come true, so his conscience was assuaged. Finally, he wrote to Vicky. He was too busy on Sunday and couldn't get away. How about next weekend?

He received an email back almost immediately:

Dear Peter,

It's mean of you to keep me waiting. I have checked my cycle, and my most fertile days would be tomorrow, Sunday, and Tuesday. Are you sure you can't do one of these?

Vicky x

Peter was terrified. He hadn't anticipated being called upon to perform so soon, and then there was the problem of ED, which struck sometimes without warning when people were under pressure, and there's no doubt that he would be. There was no way he could give in to Vicky so soon. He needed to practise with her. That meant buying a supply of Viagra and preferably also some condoms. He wasn't sure why he needed the condoms—wouldn't they defeat the object of the exercise? On the other hand, he thought they would take the pressure off him. There was logic in there somewhere.

If he could put Vicky off until next weekend—for the practice session—he could prepare with the necessary equipment and also see if his own equipment was functioning satisfactorily. He went online and Googled *Viagra online*. The first that came up was Superdrug, which promised free delivery by Tuesday. There were three different strengths—25, 50, and 100mg. The pricing made the 100mg tablets the best buy by far. He could always buy a pill cutter and just take half or even a quarter. *Damn!* That might not even work, he thought. What if the strength were not evenly distributed in the tablet? He might

138

get the half where all the potency—or worse still, none of the potency—was concentrated. He began to get anxious. And what if his face turned red as a beetroot? He had heard that from a friend, who confessed that that was a major disadvantage. And what if it didn't work at all? It was said to be effective for 74% of men. That's a quarter of men who were left limp. That hadn't been a problem hitherto, but there was always a first time. They could build up to peak performance with practice. In the meantime, he would add a ten-function Bullet Vibrator and a ten-function Rabbit Love Ring to the order. He couldn't for the life of him think how they could get ten different functions out of each. He could think of only two. One or other love toy would be a consolation for Vicky in the event of a malfunction. *Strewth!* that little lot was going to set him back over £100. Becky must not know. He wondered whether he should have it sent to the Department but decided against. The risk of its going astray or being opened by Johanna was greater than the embarrassment of Becky's intercepting it. Although it might be embarrassing, he was not really ashamed to tell her, so he would let it be sent to Bluntingham.

He sent off the order and cleared all traces from his computer. Not for the first time his conscience had started nagging at him. He tried various ways to assuage it, none of which was even 74% effective. He would have to go to church on Sunday and square it with the Almighty.

When lunchtime came on Friday, Jim had still not heard anything from Philip, which he found disconcerting. He decided therefore to phone him.

'Yeah, Jim here. What's going on?'

'Hello, Jim, I was going to phone you after lunch. I had a meeting with the Senior Tutor, who deals with research fellowships. I mentioned the tip, and he mentioned it to the Bursar. If we invest, say, 100 grand in your start-up, we could fund a new research fellowship on the proceeds for three years. It wouldn't be open to competition but restricted to applicants working on certain subjects. We thought Old European

139

Dialects. The College could offer accommodation and free meals. There might even be the odd 20 grand left over for us that could be diverted to the wine committee. The successful candidate wouldn't be living in the lap of luxury, but we'd see she was all right. Of course, we would expect her to apply for research funding.'

'Yeah, well, let's hope the tip pays off,' Jim said.

'I thought you said it was a sure-fire one,' Philip said. 'Couldn't go wrong ...'

'Yeah, that's what my mate told me. I'll have to check.'

After lunch, Jim phoned his former colleague, Paddy, at Sligo Capital, plc.

'Yeah, Jim here.'

'Jim?'

'Lubbins.'

'Oh ... *Jim!* Great to hear from you. What, it must be at least ten years. How're you keeping, me old mate?'

'Yeah, well, I'm in a bit of a fix. I need a tip or two. Double or quits, preferably the former. What can you give me?'

'It's great you're doing so well in academia, Jim. How about meeting up sometime? It's always best face to face.'

'Yeah, well, I wasn't planning to come to London. I've got my lectures and supervisions, and then there's my new love interest.'

'Ah, same old Jim. I thought you'd have settled down by now. I got married a couple of years back.'

'Marriage is for wimps. Jim likes to play the field. *But*—I think this might be the one. She's very refined and great in bed.'

'What's her name?'

'Isabelle.'

'If you think I can be of assistance, we'll have to meet up. Bring Isabelle along, too.'

How about next Thursday, 1:00 at El Vino's? You'll love the spicy lamb and serrano meatballs.'

'Sounds like Jim's sort of thing. But—there's only one problem. I can't do Thursday. It's Fucking in Bavarian then, and I can't get out of it.'

'It sounds like you wouldn't want to, but that's the only time I can do. I'm tied up with a big IPO for the next couple of weeks. That one might interest you.'

'Yeah, well, just drop me a hint.'

'Sorry, Jim, no can do. El Vino's, Thursday at 1:00 if you want it. Lunch is on you. I'm really looking forward to meeting Isabelle.'

Jim was in a quandary. He put the phone down and thought it over. No tip, no research fellowship for Isabelle, ergo no fun in bed, ergo, Jim had to get out of Fucking in Old Bavarian. He might be able to rearrange it but probably not at short notice. He could get Alec to pin a notice on the door of his lecture room—'Fucking cancelled today. Will resume next week.' That appealed to the Lubbinsian sense of humour, but it might not appeal to the pompous pricks in the faculty and least of all to the arch-arsehole, Jim's Head of Department. He picked up the phone again.

'Hitchinson speaking.'

'It's Jim. What do you know about Old Bavarian?'

'Nothing, I'm afraid.'

'But you know about fucking.'

'I'd rather not comment.'

'Well, your lecture's just after mine on Thursday. You could cope with a bit of the old f-word stuff in Old Bavarian dialects. I'd give you the notes and take you through the details. I'm sure it would go without a hitch. Jim'll make it up to you. He may well have more than one tip as a result of Thursday's expedition.'

They agreed to meet on Sunday for another curry at the Bombay and then relocate to Jim's Pad for a hands-on session of FIOB, as Jim now referred to his lectures.

'You won't mind Isabelle being there, I hope,' Jim said.

'The more the merrier,' Philip said.

'See you on Sunday at 6:30,' Jim said.

Saturday, 11 October

Jim set out for Rustat Road in the Passion Wagon on Saturday at 9:30, having first cleared the seats of most of the junk. There wouldn't be room for anything bulky, but he might get a small corner cupboard or a couple of chairs on the back seat. He would keep the boot for the smaller purchases—medals, insignia, and especially silver. He had long been thinking of endowing a prize for the best undergraduate essay on an Old Bavarian theme on a topic to be decided annually by the Faculty Board in conjunction with the donor. The successful candidate would receive a modest cash prize, but the real honour would be in keeping the Lubbins Cup and Medal for a year. It was these that he would hope to purchase this Saturday. The cup, which he would have engraved, was paramount; the medal was not so important. Indeed, he doubted whether he would find a suitably unengraved one at an antiques fair.

Isabelle was waiting, dressed appropriately in jeans and a sweater with a padded jacket for warmth. She had looked at the forecast and discovered that rain was unlikely.

When she got in the car, she was met with the odour of what Jim called pheromones but which most people call BO. She did her best not to appear rude but after ten minutes asked if she might open a window.

'You've not been wearing the Eau Sauvage, then, Jim,' she said.

'Yeah, well, it's sitting in a drawer in Jim's Pad, unopened. I haven't yet felt the need to use it.'

'Ah, pity,' Isabelle said. 'It's one of those masculine fragrances that, I'm ashamed to say, rather turns me on.'

'Bloody 'ell,' Jim said. 'I wish I'd known.'

'Well, I did drop sufficient hints,' Isabelle said. 'It seems you didn't pick up on them. Pity.'

'Yeah, well, I'll remember another time,' Jim said.

They had an early lunch and walked round the huge fair. Jim got excited over a stall selling paintings and silver. Jim picked out a dark painting which had been so varnished over that much of the detail was lost. After haggling, he knocked the stallholder down to £150.

'Whatever did you buy that for, Jim? It's ghastly,' Isabelle said.

'Yeah, well, Jim has a nose for these things. It's a Salvator Rosa.'

'How do you know?'

'SR,' he said, pointing to the bottom right-hand corner.

'That could be anyone,' Isabelle said. 'Do you really think you'd find an original Salvator Rosa at an antiques fair?'

'I'll have it certified by Bonhams,' Jim said.

'Well, good luck there,' Isabelle said. 'They might certify you instead.'

They bought two silver cups and a German silver medal with an imperial eagle then went on to look for furniture. A chaise longue took Jim's fancy.

'Do you fancy trying it out in Jim's Pad?' he asked Isabelle.

She laughed politely and left Jim to fantasize. Jim went to feel how heavy it was.

'Bloody 'ell,' he said, clutching his chest. 'I don't think we can take that home today.'

'Are you sure you're all right, Jim?' Isabelle said.

'Yeah. Jim's no wimp,' he replied.

They drove back to Cambridge.

'Are you coming back to Jim's Pad?' he asked.

'No, I might see you tomorrow,' Isabelle said. 'Enjoy your purchases.'

'Yeah.'

Sunday, 12 October

On Sunday, after pondering his predicament all day Saturday, Peter cautiously approached Becky at breakfast.

'D'you feel like going to church today? I was thinking it's such a pity you don't go and see your flower arrangement in situ during a service. I don't even get to see them at all. Maybe I should go along. Any chance of you coming with me?'

Becky laughed.

'Since when have they interested you?' she said.

'Oh, I've always been one for red roses,' Peter said, embarrassed at such an inane reply. 'Are you going to come with me or not?'

'Or not,' Becky said. 'I must say, it's a bit suspicious, your going to church all of a sudden. It's not Christmas, you know.'

'No, but it soon will be—and All Saints' Day, too. I always remember that. It's when we have our scrutiny meeting.'

'Oh, yeah!' Becky said with heavy sarcasm. 'Are you scrutinizing your navels or is it your conscience?'

'Exam papers,' Peter said. 'It's all screwed up this year because Johanna's gone and lost them.'

'Very careless,' Becky said. 'You should be more hands-on with her,' she added tongue in cheek. 'Will your girlfriend be there?'

'Excuse me! What girlfriend?'

'What girlfriend my arse! Beebee or whatever she's called.'

'I don't suppose so. Girlfriends—I mean Externals—don't usually attend the scrutiny meeting unless there's a problem.'

'I'm safe, then, am I?'

'You're always safe.'

'I wonder if there'll be a problem by any chance.'

'It's unlikely, I think. Anyway, must be off. Don't want to miss the start of church.'

Peter went along to St Michael's, feeling a little sheepish. His appearance in church caused some head-turning. He smiled a nondescript kind of smile that might be interpreted as saying, 'Pleased to see you' or alternatively, 'What are you lot looking at?'

The organist was playing a piece of Bach. Peter was impressed by his skills—quite unlike the last time he had been to

144

church, when a little old lady had been at the console. Peter found a pew and looked towards the altar. Becky's flower arrangement looked splendid. He caught sight of Bridget out of the corner of his eye and gave her a friendly smile as if to indicate his approbation of the flowers. The service began, after the choir had processed in, with a welcome from the Vicar, a jovial lady with a Geraldine Granger-style smile. Peter wondered how genuine such overt friendliness was and whether friendliness was next to godliness.

'Welcome to St Michael's,' the Vicar said. 'And a special welcome if you are visiting or haven't been for a long time.'

She looked sideways at Peter, who sensed he was being observed and smiled agreeably.

'Today is a very special Sunday,' she said, 'because we welcome our new organist, Robert. Take a bow, Robert.'

The man at the console was a good-looking forty-something with horn-rimmed glasses and a check shirt. His bow-tie peeked out from above his academic surplice, which occasionally opened to display his rather pretentious attire. He raised himself slightly on the pedals and nodded towards the congregation with a warm, but embarrassed, smile.

'Robert's from California. He's on a year's exchange at the University. Of course, we'd love to hang on to him, but who knows whether he'll want to stay? He's been getting to know the organ in the past month. The old girl's action is a bit stiff— no, I don't mean the Vicar, but Robert's been softening her up, haven't you, Robert?'

Robert smiled.

Peter wasn't sure whether to be amused or repulsed by the Vicar's jokes. Church was not the place for jokes, he thought, but perhaps it should be. Most church people seemed to have a deficit in the humour department, but equally, he didn't approve of cringe-making jokiness. 'Geraldine', as he called her, meant well but had come down too far on the cringeworthy side. He tried to cover up his involuntary grimace with a forced smile. Only Bridget might have noticed.

The service progressed; Peter joined in lustily in the hymns. Was lust really the right word, Peter? One of the Seven Deadly Sins? Didn't you know? Of course he knew; that was why he had come to church. He was hedging his bets. What he had done with Beebee could be excused on a number of counts—principally that she had led him astray—but he relished the pleasure and wanted to do it again—over and over. No, it wasn't a sin at all. At worst a teeny weeny one—hardly worth mentioning. He was doing a kindness to a sad, lonely woman. It was an act of charity. But what of Vicky? Of course it was with her, too. But the Viagra, the ten-function Bullet Vibrator and the ten-function Rabbit Love Ring? Weren't those designed purely for pleasure? — Yes, but he was helping procreate. — But with a married woman? — No, she's divorced. — But you are married. — Yes, but Becky's not interested anymore. — So you think that lets you off the hook, do you, Peter? Haven't you heard this read in church by Geraldine? You would have if you'd come more often. *Know ye not that the unrighteous shall not inherit the kingdom of God?* — Come off it, I'm a good chap. — *Be not deceived: neither fornicators, nor idolaters, nor adulterers, nor effeminate, nor abusers of themselves with mankind, Nor thieves, nor covetous, nor drunkards, nor revilers, nor extortioners, shall inherit the kingdom of God.* — No! I don't do most of those anyway. Isn't God supposed to be love? — Yes, Peter. — Oh, sod it!

The people in the pew in front turned round and stared at him in view of the last utterance, made sotto voce but just loud enough to be audible. He stared back. *Screw you!* he thought. — No, Peter, that will not do. Why did you come to church if that's your attitude? Down on your knees. Confess to Geraldine.

The organist's concluding voluntary burst forth upon the unsuspecting congregation. Its solemn tones seemed to be admonishing the worshippers. Peter wanted to get out quickly to escape the censure of the music or was it the mockery of the organist? The second movement started softly, calmly,

146

soothingly. Peter began to feel at ease, relieved, forgiven—was he in paradise? Then crash—fortissimo—modulation—it was the judgment.

'Hello, Peter, fancy seeing you here,' Bridget said.

'I came to see the flowers—what a fantastic display! It must have taken you ages.'

'About an hour, but we had a lovely musical accompaniment. Robert played for us all the time—softly and sweetly—not like today, but isn't he brilliant?'

'I'm amazed. I thought the organist was an old biddy.'

'Far from it. He's got all the ladies after him.'

'The unmarried ones, I hope.'

'I don't think I stand a chance anyway. Let me introduce you.'

'Robert, this is Peter, Becky's husband.'

As they shook hands, Peter asked, 'What were you playing?'

'Mendelssohn's first Organ Sonata.'

Peter had his answer. He went out of the church and shook hands cursorily with Geraldine.

'I might need to come and see you about something soon,' he said.

'Anytime—we're always open.'

Later that morning, Jim phoned Isabelle.

'Jim here … What are you doing today?'

'Preparing for another subpanel meeting—English this time.'

'Well, don't forget this evening. I've got something interesting in mind.'

'Yes …' Isabelle said slowly and questioningly.

'Yeah.'

Isabelle was suspicious.

'It's in your best interests.'

'It always is with men.'

'There have been developments.'

'What? Since yesterday?'

'I'll buy you a vindaloo.'

147

'Oh, that's what you call it, is it?'

'Yeah. We're meeting at the Bombay at 6:30. I'll pick you up at 6:00. Be ready on time. It's in your interest.'

Peter wasn't sure what to make of his church outing. He had certainly got something out of it—a name, a name beginning with R, and an American connection to boot. — You got it, Peter. — No, you know I can't stand Americanisms. — It's not a glottal stop, Peter. — Yes, it is at the end, but even I use that kind. I confess. — Double standards, Peter. — I know, but I try to be strict. — But you aren't, are you, Peter? Not when it comes to morals. Double standards don't wash with me, Peter. — Oh, so it's all right for Becky, is it? But not for me? — Robert is kind to Becky. He looks after her and cares for her. — Well? It's still adultery. — I think that can be condoned, don't you? — Who's got double standards now? — I don't do double standards. — I don't want it to be him, though. — *He*, Peter. — Oh, eff off! — Was that all you got out of church, Peter? — No, I liked the music. — Robert is a good organist, Peter. What are you good at? — At what? … Oh, sod it!

Peter returned home, now more downcast than uplifted.

'How was church?' Becky asked.

'What do you expect me to say?'

'I don't know. What would a normal person say?'

'That's a bit below the belt … It was a change. Your boyfriend played well … Do you want a divorce?'

'Of course not.'

'Well, that's all right, then.'

'S'pose so.'

'You got it … Only joking.'

'Weird.'

Peter retreated to his study, now in an indefinable mood. The consolation of technology was all that remained. He turned on his computer with the intention of setting as many new exam questions as he could. — Open up the old files, Peter and change the wording a bit. No-one will know the difference. Jumble things up a bit. Use plosive for stop, spirant for fricative. Ask about allophones instead of phonemes. — That wouldn't be ethical. — Come on, Peter, the students won't ever cotton on. Maybe one has got hold of the old paper, but what's the likelihood that they all have? — All right, then.

A new email announcement flashed up on the screen:

Dr Beatrice Frensham

Cabriolet

Peter left the allophones and clicked on the email immediately.

Dear PL,

The cabriolet needs a spin.

What do you have in store for me today?

I'll be in Bluntingham at 2:30. Meet me outside the church.

Love,

Beebee xxx

Peter's mood was no longer indefinable. It was downright confused. Wasn't it bad enough that his conscience was plaguing him? That was only sin in thought, Peter. The real thing was at a respectable distance. You thought you had shelved the problem, but here it was, bursting upon you. — Seize the day, Peter. — Who are you? — Wouldn't you like to know? — A meeting in front of church, Peter? How could you? — What shall I do? — Do you have a conscience, Peter?

At lunch, Peter would come clean with Becky, he thought. Would the young goats be there? That might be tricky. — Tricky Vicky, Peter? — Oh, damn! I'd forgotten about her.

'What's for lunch, Becks?'
'Bread and cheese, Petes.'
'Where are the kids?'
'Out at football practice.'
'You know I went to church …'

149

'It hadn't escaped my notice.'

'Well, it wasn't just to look at the flowers.'

'No. You wanted to spy on Robert.'

'Well, yes, but I went for my spiritual needs.'

'Oh, yeah! Pull the other one.'

'I need inner peace.'

'Do you think Geraldine with her wobbly boobies can give that to you?'

'No, but a higher power can.'

'D'you think you should go and lie down?'

'After lunch, perhaps.'

'You might get indigestion.'

'I think I'll go for a walk instead. I may pop back into church. I found it hard to concentrate this morning. Too many distractions.'

'Geraldine in a surplice?'

'Among other things.'

After lunch, Peter went back to church and sat on a bench in the churchyard. 2:30 came, but there was no sign of Beebee. It was a warm autumn day. The temperature was nudging over 20 degrees. Peter heard the sound of a car approaching—a white cabriolet with the soft top down. A beaming Beebee with a fetching headscarf pulled up outside the lychgate.

'Anyone for a lift?' Beebee asked.

Peter looked all around for potential observers. There was no activity in Church Lane; he saw no-one. Nevertheless, he thought it advisable to appear as if this were a casual encounter with someone he didn't know. He went over to the car and chatted from outside for a brief while, occasionally pointing, as if to indicate something of significance, until he had decided that the coast was clear. He got in and gave Beebee a kiss on the cheek. They sat talking for a while about where they should go and what they might do.

'It's a pretty setting,' Beebee said. 'I've only ever once been to Bluntingham before. You're very lucky to live in such a lovely village.

'Yeah, I suppose we are. We moved here in the Nineties when the likes of us could afford to live in Bluntingham. It's amazing how it's changed, even since then. Backland development everywhere. Full of undesirables—nearly all nouveaux. I'm not a snob, you understand, but I draw the line at some things. Apparently, there are goings on behind the high hedges and electric gates that would make your hair stand on end. The police were called to a house in Manor Drive last month. Of course, I'm not interested in such sordid tales, but one can't help picking up these things.'

'Worse than what goes on in store cupboards in London Bridge?' Beebee said with a chuckle.

'Far worse.'

'I thought you enjoyed it.'

'Yes, I did. That's the problem.'

'Sorry, I don't see it.'

'I think it's got to stop.'

'For Goodness' sake, Peter, it hasn't even started. Today's your big chance. Let your inhibitions fly to the wind with the roof down.'

A sound of a clink was heard from the latch of the lychgate turning. Geraldine emerged through the gate, paused by the cabriolet and turned to see its occupants. It was too late for Peter to hide. He would have to brazen it out. He returned Geraldine's smile. She walked over to the car.

'It was lovely to see you in church today, Peter. I hope you'll come more often.'

'Yes, I hope so. I enjoyed the music—and of course your thought-provoking sermon,' Peter said hypocritically.

Beebee looked uncomfortable.

'Sorry, I should have introduced my colleague, Dr Beatrice Frensham. Beebee has come to help with some examining problems.'

'That's a work of supererogation, surely, on a Sunday,' Geraldine said.

Beebee chuckled. Peter looked uncomfortable. Geraldine turned to see if anyone was coming along the church path.

'Well, I must be getting back to the Vicarage,' she said. 'It's good to meet you. Come again. Do look round the church while you're here.'

Beebee thanked her, and Geraldine hurried away.

A few moments later, Robert came down the path. He cast but the briefest of glances at the cabriolet and walked on with no signs of recognition.

'Hm,' Peter said to Beebee. 'They were in church alone together. What do you think that means?'

'It was probably quite innocent,' Beebee said.

'What, you mean like us?'

'Just like us.'

What was that supposed to mean? Peter asked himself.

'I don't know whether I should be pleased or worried,' he said.

'Why do you always have to analyse?' Beebee said.

'Isn't that what all academics do?'

'Carpe diem.'

'Dies irae. Only joking, but it makes me stop and think sometimes. I can't quite get over the religion of my youth.'

'Have you tried?'

'Should I?'

'Come on, let's go and look round the church.'

They walked through the lychgate along the gravel path.

'It's a pretty corpse gate,' Peter said.

'Don't be so morbid. I came for a bit of cheering up.'

'No, lychgate is Old English. *Lych* means corpse, like German *Leiche*. Didn't you know?'

'Yeah, of corpse.'

'In the midst of life ... Do you know it?'

'For Goodness' sake, Peter, do you want me to go home again?'

'Purcell.'

'You're being weird.'

'Of course not.'

'Weird?'

'No, of course I don't want you to go home. I want you to do it to me again.'

'In church?'

'No, of course not.'

'Have you read the novel *Love among the Hymn-Books*? I've got it in the car.'

'No. Is it any good?'

'I haven't read it yet.'

'Who would want to do it among the hymn-books?'

'You'd be surprised. I'll lend it to you, and you can tell me.'

'Do you want to see Becky's flower arrangement?'

'Of course. Is it good?'

'Yes, she only joined the Flower Guild about a month ago, but she's learned very quickly. We all know the reason why.'

'Are you going to enlighten me?'

'I fear I'm a cuckold. Becky's got the hots for the organist.'

'Is that a problem? You've got the hots for the External.'

'That's different. We're colleagues.'

'Does that make it any better? Isn't it rather against the rules?'

'Whose rules?'

'The University's.'

'I don't think so. You're not under my supervision or someone I'm responsible for, are you?'

'Stop beating about the bush. Let's get on with it.'

'Not in church.'

'Of course not. Outside. The gardener's hut. You like tight spaces.'

'Love among the flowerpots.'

'Who said anything about love?'

'Oh, sod it!'

'Not in God's house.'

'Oh, shit, then!'

'I don't like that word.'

'Neither do I.'

They went round the back of the church and looked into the gardener's hut.

'I don't like spiders,' Peter said.

'Are you frightened they might crawl up somewhere they shouldn't?'

'That's more of a woman's problem.'

'Come on, get in the car. Where's the nearest wood?'

'I know a spot on the way to Ramsey.'

'Just the place for a walk, then.'

'Very funny.'

'I shall need directions. Put your seatbelt on. You're in for the ride of your life!'

They parked away from the other three cars, which Peter took to be dogging couples.

'Have you ever thought of joining in?' Beebee asked.

'You must be joking.'

'Don't you think it would be fun?'

'No, I can't think of anything more disgusting.'

'I can.'

'Don't tell me, please.'

'We're wasting time. Get out of the car. Do you want to take a picnic rug or is standing up OK again?'

'Whatever suits you.'

'We'll take one just in case.'

They walked for a good quarter of an hour into the interior of the wood.

'Got any white pebbles?' Peter asked.

'You've lost me there.'

'Hänsel und Gretel. So they found their way back.'

'I thought they got eaten.'

'No. That was the bread. They escaped and lived happily ever after. How's your gingerbread house?'

'Very tasty.'

They spread out the picnic rug and enjoyed what Peter believed was a taste of paradise.

Are you sure you've done the right thing, Peter? — Hast thou eaten of the gingerbread whereof I commanded thee that thou shouldest not eat? — The woman whom thou gavest to be with me, she gave me of the gingerbread, and I did eat … Oh no!

Jim picked up Isabelle from Rustat Road at 6:00, after first dousing himself in Eau Sauvage.

'Do you mind if I open a window, Jim?' Isabelle said.

'Bloody 'ell,' Jim said. 'You told me you liked the smell.'

'Yes, I do, but I think I might be getting a cold,' she said—a ploy that would serve for all eventualities. They met up with Philip at the Bombay. The waiter came to take their order of poppadoms, samosas, bhajis, and spicy rolls for starters.

'And what would you like for mains?' the courteous Indian waiter asked.

'Tikka masala, please,' Isabelle said.

'Chicken or lamb, madam?'

'Do you do vegetarian?' Isabelle asked.

Jim looked disgruntled.

'Yes, it's under "Vegetarian Mains",' the waiter said. 'And for you, sir?' he said, turning to Philip.

'I think I'll have the chicken korma, please. That's fairly mild, isn't it?'

'Yes, sir,' the waiter replied.

Jim's expression looked even more disapproving.

'What would you like, sir?' the waiter said to Jim.

'I'll have the vindaloo,' he said without a please.

'Are you sure you want to eat that, Jim?' Isabelle said. 'It's got three chillies for "very hot" on the menu.'

'Yeah, well, Jim's hot stuff,' he said.

'What about a chicken korma instead?' Philip asked.

'Definitely for wimps only,' Jim said.

'Oh, that's what I'm having,' Philip said.

'Don't take any notice of him, get him a vindaloo, too,' Jim said to the waiter.

'You'd better bring both,' Isabelle said. 'We can take the one we don't eat back home.'

'Well, it's very kind of you to invite me along,' Isabelle said, 'but I expect there's some ulterior motive.'

'Come on, Jim,' Philip said. 'Don't keep the young lady in suspense any longer.'

'Yeah, well, we've got a job for you.'

'Hey, steady on, Jim,' Philip said. 'It's got to go through College Council still, and we don't even know if we'll get the funding yet.'

'Look, Isabelle, you know Jim's got your best interests at heart. Philip's the facilitator. All you've got to do is help us out a bit with some clerical matters, like you do for the RRE. I'm going to see Paddy in London on Thursday, and I want you to come with me.'

'Sorry, Jim, I've got a meeting with Niamh then.'

'So, you don't want to be the Lubbins Fellow in Old European Languages, then. Give it some thought. Of course, if you'd rather be Niamh's assistant in Bristol, that's fine by me.'

'You drive a hard bargain, Jim.'

'Yeah, let's keep it hard.'

'That's a strange expression, Jim,' Philip said.

'Yeah, I'm a strange man.'

'You can say that again,' Isabelle said.

'Jim's Pad, 10:00, Thursday. We need to catch the 11:24. Don't be late.'

'I'll think about it,' Isabelle said. 'I'll need to sound out Niamh first.'

The three colleagues enjoyed their starters, dipping into the mango chutney and mint-flavoured yoghurt.

'Have we ordered any sides?' Jim asked.

'For goodness' sake don't let Peter hear you say that,' Isabelle said. 'It's another of his pet hates. He took me to one side over coffee in Ayr and gave me a lengthy exposition. It's just as well we weren't in Nando's. He'd be apoplectic.'

'What did he expose?' Jim asked.

156

'Not what you're thinking,' Isabelle said.

'Yeah, well, Jim's not an exhibitionist. Very discreet with the young ladies, that's me.'

'Exhibitionism's a funny thing,' Philip said. 'Whatever drives someone to do it?'

'Search me,' Jim said. 'Didn't you say Peter has a vacation place in Fuerteventura? It's full of exhibitionists there.'

'I think you mean naturists, Jim,' Philip said. 'I'm partial to a bit of that, too.'

'Maybe. What's your take on that, Dr Chesham?' Jim said.

'You're not catching me out on that,' Isabelle said. 'My lips are sealed.'

'Oh, yeah?' Jim said.

The mains arrived together with bowls of rice.

'You've got your sides, Jim. I hope they'll be to your liking,' Isabelle said. 'Shall we share the mains? Have a bit of each?'

'I'd rather have the korma,' Philip said.

'And I don't want any vindaloo,' Isabelle said.

'Yeah, well, that's extra spice for Jim, then. I hope you won't mind waiting for me.'

'Enjoy your meal,' the waiter said. 'Can I bring you any water?'

'Water's for wimps,' Jim said. 'I'll have one of your Indian beers.'

'A Cobra, sir?'

'Yeah.'

'We'll stick with the water,' Isabelle said.

The three colleagues enjoyed their mains.

'Here's to Peter, stuck up prick,' Jim said, 'with his hoity-toity ways and his bloody silly research on glottal stops. Perhaps we could get him to apply with us for funding on the old swear words.'

'I doubt it,' Isabelle said. 'He's far too refined.'

'Yeah, but he's still a randy bastard, I think you'll find, Professor Brown.'

'D'you think he's given Beebee one yet?'

157

'Eat up your curry, Jim,' Isabelle said. 'I need to get home for an early start tomorrow.'

'Stay the night at Jim's Pad—it's much nearer.'

'Sorry, Jim, you can give me a lift back to Rustat Road, but you're not coming in,' Isabelle said.

'Yeah, well, we'll see if the Passion Wagon is tidy. We couldn't have the Lubbins Fellow elect travelling in a messy carriage.'

'Must be getting back to Storey's Way,' Philip said. 'I haven't got a late pass.'

'Wimp,' Jim muttered.

They paid the bill and set off.

The Passion Wagon turned into Hills Road. Jim began to drive somewhat erratically and to clutch his stomach.

'Left here, into Cherry Hinton Road,' Isabelle said.

'I shan't make it,' Jim said. 'It must be the vindaloo. I need the loo.'

'I like the rhyme,' Isabelle said.

'I'm not joking,' Jim said. 'I need the toilet.'

'Don't let Peter hear you say that,' Isabelle said. 'It's strictly "lavatory" only for him.'

'Sod Peter,' Jim said.

'Hold on, Jim,' Isabelle said. 'There are some public loos up ahead, about a mile on the left in Cherry Hinton Hall Park.'

'Can't we go to yours? It's nearer, isn't it?'

'You'll be all right, they're open 24 hours—I've just checked on my phone. Left here. Park there and run. Straight ahead and on your left.'

Jim ran the 100 metres to the public conveniences, clutching his stomach and holding back the contents of his excessive chilli consumption as best he could. There was only one light on outside. A number of youths were gathered nearby, probably doing drugs, Jim thought.

'Are the toilets open?' Jim said.

'Sorry, mate,' one of the youths said. 'They close at 7. You'll have to use the bushes over there.'

Bloody 'ell! Jim thought as he saw a couple of men in the bushes. He was desperate.

'Sorry to trouble you,' he said.

'Do you want to join in?' one of them said. Are you up for a threesome?'

'No, not my scene, just carry on as before with the amorous activity.'

'Weird bloke,' the other man said. 'Who calls it amorous activity?'

'That's Jim Lubbins,' the first one said. 'I hope he didn't recognize me.'

'Sure not to have done in this light,' the other man whispered and carried on with the amorous activity. Relieved, Jim squatted behind the most suitable bush. A paper handkerchief came to the rescue.

'Good night,' Jim said to the men as he stumbled back to the car. The diarrhoea had temporarily subsided, but Jim's walking became unsteadier. Back at the car, Isabelle got out to help him.

'Everything OK, Jim?' she asked.

'Yeah, no, it bloody-well isn't. I've lost the feeling in my hands and can't stop my legs from shaking.'

'Just sit down in the passenger seat,' Isabelle said.

She eased him into the car and got into the driving seat.

'I'm taking you to hospital, Jim,' Isabelle said. 'I think you might have had a heart attack.'

'Yeah, well,' Jim said and passed out.

He came round an hour later in a diagnostic ward in Addenbrooke's hospital. A middle-aged nurse attended him.

'Hello, Jim,' she said. 'How are you feeling now?'

'Not too bright,' he said. 'I felt like I was dying. What's your name?'

'Sarah,' the nurse said. 'I've been assigned to you to look after you until we think you're well enough to go home. We need to run some more tests. The ECG has shown up some slight anomalies. The doctor will come and talk to you later in the morning. Get some rest now. Try to sleep.'

'Bloody 'ell,' Jim said.

'You're in good hands,' Sarah said.

'Yeah, well,' Jim said and drifted off to sleep.

In the morning, Jim was attended by Dr Pradesh, who explained the dangers of excessive chilli consumption.

'It seems you've been eating the Carolina Reaper, Mr Lubbins,' the doctor said. 'That's 2.2 million on the Scoville Scale. It can bring on symptoms of a heart attack, especially if you've been drinking.'

'Bloody 'ell,' Jim said.

'Yes, well,' the doctor said, 'we need to run some further tests on your heart. We need to repeat your ECG when you've got over the chilli poisoning, so we'll be keeping you in for a couple of days. Sarah will keep an eye on you.'

Jim's face lit up.

6. WEEK 4

Monday, 13 October

On Monday morning, Isabelle phoned the hospital and was put through to Z Ward. She was amused that Jim had ended up in Z Ward —Was that a ragbag ward for other patients and problem cases like on the RRE? she wondered. She scolded herself for her frivolous thoughts.

'Z Ward, Sarah Pascoe speaking,' the voice at the other end answered.

'Good morning, it's Isabelle Chesham here,' she said. I'm a friend of Jim Lubbins. I wonder if there's any news of him.'

'Yes, he's had breakfast and seen the doctor. He seems a lot better, but we're keeping him in for observation.'

'Have you any idea when he'll be discharged?'

'Not yet,' Sarah said. 'It'll probably be before the weekend.'

That won't please Jim, Isabelle thought. She would need to find out about the meeting in London.

'When are visiting hours, please?'

'Afternoons from 2 till 8.'

Next, Isabelle phoned Niamh and explained the predicament.

'I'm so sorry,' Niamh said. 'Let me know if there's any way I can help.'

'Well, I'm not sure if I can meet up with you on Thursday under the circumstances. I feel I ought to be on hand to

161

support Jim, and I know he has an important meeting on Thursday that he probably won't be able to attend now. I think he's hoping I might go in his place.'

'Well, we can reschedule our meeting for the following week if you like,' Niamh said. 'You go and support Jim.'

'Thanks, Niamh,' Isabelle said. 'Drop me a line next week when you're free, and I can give you an update on Jim as well.'

Next, Isabelle phoned Philip to tell him the news. After explaining the circumstances, she broached the question of the research fellowship.

'I hope Jim's illness won't derail our plans. I'm hoping to go and negotiate with Jim's former colleague Paddy on Thursday, as long as you think it's a good idea,' Isabelle said. 'The other problem is Jim's lecture on FIOB.'

'I'm sure we'll find a way round that,' Philip said. 'Tell Jim not to worry, and I'll sort it. It would be good if you could speak to Jim's colleague, too. Can you let me have a copy of Jim's article? He told me his lectures were based on that. I'm not sure how I get a whole hour's worth out of a quarter of an article, though.'

'You could read it very slowly and fill in a bit from personal experience,' Isabelle said. 'I'll email you over a copy of the article later.'

'Just one thing—Jim said it had a jokey title, something about a dog's arse,' Philip said. Can you fill me in on that? My period's quite a bit later.'

'"A dog's arse in your nose" is what he said it means … Funny lot, the Old Bavarians.'

'Maybe something to do with Lederhosen—I hear they get a bit sweaty in summer,' Philip said.

'I couldn't possibly comment,' Isabelle said.

'Try and get that tip at all costs—within reason, I mean, of course,' Philip said.

'Yes, well, I'll do my best,' Isabelle said.

Peter slept unsoundly on Sunday night. He kept thinking that he could feel undergrowth and insects beneath the sheets

162

and all around him. He daren't turn over for fear of making sticks break and twigs crackle. He was afraid that creepy crawlies were penetrating his orifices. He broke out in a sweat and whimpered, 'No, we shouldn't be doing this.' He reached out and briefly woke Becky, who muttered, 'Be careful, Peter.'

'I am being careful. Be gentle, don't chomp down on me,' he said.

'Whatever are you talking about?' Becky said. 'Turn over and get some sleep. You've got to be fresh for work in the morning.'

'Yeah, that's it, Beebee. I'm in deep, in deep trouble. Oh sod it, we must stop. Glottal stops. STOP. Give it to me. Oh, no!'

Peter shuddered, and his REM sleep came to a halt. He got up and went to the bathroom. When he returned to the marital bed, he couldn't sleep anymore. His thoughts were skitting about in many different directions. They started with his indiscretions with Beebee, soon switched to Becky, to Robert, the organ, the flowers, to Geraldine, to Vicky—*Damn it! that, too.* He had shelved that temporarily, back to Beebee, back to Robert, Becky, the Department, Frau Schmidt, Johanna, the RRE, the glottal stops. *Oh, damn it!*

He got up at 5 a.m. and went to his study.

As usual, he checked his emails first. There was only one of any note:

Dear PL,

You were fantastic today (well, most of the time), but I can't do it under these conditions anymore, and anyway, it'll be too chilly outside soon. We wouldn't want any bits malfunctioning because of the cold or worse still getting frost bite. Think of a better solution for the winter, please.

By the way, Alan says that Fiona is lodging an appeal and that I shall be required at the scrutiny meeting. Can't wait.

Beebee xx

Peter managed to complete Phonetics I and make a good start on Phonetics II, jumbling the questions up a bit, rewording here and there until he had passably different, apparently new, papers. It remained only for him to find suitable translation passages. Would he turn to his old pal, CD? He so liked that passage from *Great Expectations*, but he'd need something different this time, something more modern.

He glanced over at his half-finished campus novel, *Changing Places Again*, and leafed through the work, looking for a self-contained passage of about 250 words with some testing words and phrases. He put it down again and picked up *Love Among the Hymn-Books*, which Beebee had put in his pocket after their encounter in the woods. He liked the author's depiction of Darian and noted a certain similarity with himself: 'Darian was in his late fifties and had arrived at the stage where he was looking for a change of direction, not only in his job but more generally in life.'

This would be the passage. The full paragraph was about the right length, though it might need a bit of shortening. Roll over, Dickens. Poor Darian, he could empathize with him. Peter typed the passage into his computer and password-protected it. Johanna must not be given it until the last minute. She must be forced to swallow it like in a spy movie. Shouldn't that be *as*? he wondered. — It's a toss-up. — No, don't start on that, Peter. You need to have a shower and catch the train.

After showering, Peter went down to breakfast to join Becky.

'Everything OK, Becks?' he said.

'I'm not a bloody footballer, Peter,' came the curt reply.

'No, I suppose not,' Peter said and fetched himself some coffee and a stale croissant.

'D'you think you'll be going shopping today? If you go, can you get some fresh butter croissants from M & S?'

'I'll try to remember.'

'No flower arranging, I suppose, today.'

'Probably not. I'll ask Bridget. We may need to spray them.'

'What, with weedkiller?'

'Screw you.'

'Screw you, too. Like the rhyme?'

'Is it a rhyme?'

'Hm.'

'It's to stop them from going limp. A bit like you.'

'How's Beebee?'

'As far as I know, she's fine. I'll be seeing her on All Saints' Day. Actually, it's transferred to the 3rd this year.'

'All Saints' Day?'

'No, the scrutiny meeting.'

'Will she be wearing white?'

'What are you on about? Look, I've got to get to work. Say hello to Robert for me.'

Becky went into the kitchen. Peter left the house without saying goodbye. The kids came downstairs.

Peter trudged his way into the university, better known as ULB, which he often pronounced as a glottal gulp, in which usage he regarded it as a true acronym rather than an initialism. If anyone said the university was known by the acronym U-L-B, he would half wince, knowing that this usage was permitted by the OED, but just like that abbreviation, ULB was not properly an acronym, he firmly maintained. These linguistic reflections occupied him for but part of his journey. In the train, he was fortunate enough to find a group of four seats that was unoccupied, in which he could spread himself out until Stevenage, when there was usually an influx of a very different kind of commuter. Peter didn't often refer to these as the hoi polloi, since he knew that was a pleonasm, which grated against his linguist's conscience. Nevertheless, he allowed himself the muttered imprecation *damned hoi polloi*, though he would never allow this syntagm in English. But wasn't he speaking English? By the time he had settled the question to his satisfaction, every seat in the group of four was occupied, and Peter had to put his laptop with the password-protected exam papers away. Was *stockyards* too obvious a password? he wondered. Would

Johanna get the irony? Might a bright student like Belfield even guess it, if Johanna left her computer unattended but with the file locked, while she had a two-hour-long lunch break, thus necessitating another catastrophic resetting of the papers? No, *stockyards* would not do, nor even *Schlachthöfe*; the umlaut would cause Johanna too much difficulty, even though it might, together with the initial capital letter, provide extra security. He needed a better one. *Think, Peter. What have you been doing recently? Oh, no!* Memories of Warstow Wood came flooding back, but how did he get there? Ah! *cabriolet*—that was the perfect password, which only he and Beebee could ever guess. He smiled. A couple of the hoi polloi commuters—he shuddered at the construction—looked at him, wondering if he was crazy. Next, they would expect him to be muttering to himself.

At King's Cross—with an apostrophe today, Dr Compton—he allowed the hoi polloi to disembark first. Come off it, Peter, you don't disembark from a train. — Well, dismount, then. — No, it's not a bloody horse! — Damn it. I'll just let them get off, then. — Yes, often the simple Anglo-Saxon word's the best. — But this isn't simple. A phrasal verb by its very nature is complex. — You're splitting hairs, Peter. — I shall allow myself that luxury today if you don't mind. — It's your decision. — Don't I know it? — Bloody decisions. — I'm not making any today.

Peter felt he couldn't face the tube this morning. The many were already forming a slow-moving huddle around the entrance, like—*A.S.!*—at a football match, when the spectators queued to exit the ground. He made a decision, albeit a non-complex one, electing to walk and brave the discomforts of noxious exhaust fumes, the vibration and heat from the engines of London buses, the tooting of the black cabs, not imperious and bad-tempered like those of New York, but enough to say, 'look out, mate', or was it 'guv'? like the cheeky cockney cabbie inside.

166

At any rate, Peter would arrive in a better humour, albeit considerably later, than if he had fought his way through the crowds of subterranean Londoners.

When he arrived in the Department, he went straight to the staff pigeonholes and picked up his mail. A stiff, attractive envelope with a handwritten address had arrived from Germany. Peter wondered if it could be the invitation to receive his honour from the German Embassy. No, that was unlikely, he thought, it would come from London and anyway most likely not be handwritten. Johanna entered and greeted him ill-temperedly.

'Are the revised papers nearly ready?' Peter asked.

'No,' Johanna said without explanation.

'When is the deadline?'

'I don't know.'

'Well, make sure you find out from Alan today. We shall need them in good time for the scrutiny meeting.'

Johanna left without saying anything. Peter took his mail and went into his room. He sat down at his desk and turned his computer on. There were nine new emails, including ones from Vicky, Beebee, Harrison, and Niamh. He made another decision, to open the 'snail mail' first, contrary to his normal practice. Snail mail was one of the trendinesses that he allowed himself; indeed, he had warmed to this neologism, a part of the enrichment of the English language by the advent of the information technology revolution. Unlike phonetic alterations, he approved of additions to the lexicon—within reason, of course.

He opened the stiff envelope first and took out the attractively printed card. At the top was written 'Peter plus one'.

Printed underneath was:

Gisela and Michael
invite you to

SAVE *the* DATE

for their wedding on
Saturday, 1 August 2009
in Germany or England

formal invitation to follow

Oh no! Peter thought, after first feeling pleased for Gisela that
Harrison was going to make an honest woman of her, then
scolding himself for this horribly reactionary thought and also
considering that the child would be born illegitimate. But who
cared nowadays? Good luck to them both. *Oh sod it!* He returned to his first reaction. Becky won't want to go. That could
be embarrassing. No-one in these circles knew anything of his
marital difficulties. That was another one to shelve until later.

Next, Peter set to reading the emails. He read Niamh's first
since it was the earliest to arrive. Hers was a reaction to the
news of Jim's illness—a message to the RRE subpanel members, explaining the situation and hoping that he would be well
enough in time for the next meeting in May. She noted that
Jim's illness might mean extra work to be shared amongst the
other members. Peter's response predictably was 'Oh, no!' But
at least that didn't require a decision. Next, he opened Vicky's
and had a cursory glance at it. His eyes alighted on RRE; he
decided to read it properly later, judging that it was another
business email. He opened Harrison's next—I must stop calling him Harrison, he thought, but it suits him so much better
than Michael. Maybe he should tell him to adopt that as his
Christian name—he corrected himself—first name. It read:

Dear Peter,

I hope by now that you will have received the 'Save the date' invitation to Gisela's and my wedding. We so hope you will be there. You have been such a tower of strength during all our difficulties. I should like to ask you one big favour. Will you be my best man? There's no need to reply immediately.

Kindest regards,

Michael

Oh, no! Peter thought. That's the last thing he wanted to do. He would shelve a decision.

Next, he opened Beebee's email:

Dear PL,

Do you want to eat some gingerbread on 3 November? If so, I'll book a hotel. I can get a cheap one-night booking (stand?) via the University and claim it on my expenses as External, anyway. All you need is an excuse.

Love,

Beebee xxx

PS. It's getting cold, and I need warming up.

Oh, no! Peter thought. Of course I want to, but what should I do? He would shelve a decision.

Peter looked at his IKEA clock on the wall of his room. It was by now nearly 11:00, time for his Prose class. He wondered how many university language departments still called translation into the foreign language 'prose'. You had to know the code, he told his class, but you'll soon pick it up. 'Prose composition—translation into German to you and I,' he said and looked for a reaction. Belfield smiled knowingly. 'Is James the only one?' he asked. One or two more students began to smile without really knowing why.

169

'Since when has *I* been an object pronoun?' Peter asked, looking with as much menace as he could muster, at the timid young ladies in the front row who had not responded at all to his irony.

He invited Belfield to explain the hypercorrection and then went on to expatiate on the subject more generally, citing *whomever* for *whoever*. When they eventually got on to translation, a good twenty minutes of the hour had passed. Dickens's magnificent prose occupied them for the rest of the hour, after which Peter felt a great sense of satisfaction at having translated this arch-stylist's writing into equally stylish German prose. He retired to his room to relax after the nervous exertion of his class and sat for a while doing nothing. After ten minutes, he fired up his email program. A message flashed up:

Victoria Atherton

Urgent

Peter began to read:

Dear Peter,

I'm very concerned that you have been ignoring me and putting me off. You promised me that loan. I need it now.

Thursday, 7:00 at mine. Be sure to turn up prepared.

Vicky

PS. You can ignore the earlier email.

Peter no longer had the energy to utter an imprecation. He sat motionless in his chair and stared into space. Unfortunately, space for him reached only some four metres to his door, in which there was a portal that gave visual access to his solar system. Here heavenly bodies moved in mostly irregular motion as students and staff came and went to their lectures and Johanna could be seen flitting about the Department as a planet on a curious trajectory, mostly from her office to the post room, then to disappear for long periods at regular, predictable intervals three times a day, at 11:00, 1:00, and 4:00. Into this cosmos Peter stared while he pondered on the American pronunciation of that word and wondered why they felt the need to pronounce the second syllable with a long diphthong; after all, it was a short vowel in the Greek, from which the word was borrowed. He had his own theory, which he must test out sometime and possibly make the subject of his next major phonetic investigation: P. Lampton, *The cosmos re-examined*. Would it extend to 400 pages or to infinity and beyond? He decided not to venture outside his habitable sphere but to remain seated, cogitating on his options. Should he have decided not to make any decisions today? He couldn't decide. Prioritize, Peter. — You know I hate doing that. — Well, at least put them into categories for later prioritization. — OK, I'll just about manage that.

1. He would accept Harrison's invitation and give a witty speech at the wedding.
2. He would broach the matter with Becky.
3. When she declined to come, he would invite Beebee to accompany him.
4. He would write to Beebee and tentatively accept her invitation to gingerbread on All Saints' Day (transferred, but not really).
5. *Oh, damn!* He still didn't know if he could go through with the insemination attempt. He would write to Vicky later.

Having made his list, though not necessarily yet having prioritized, he looked up the patron saint of bakers. He had no idea why. It was totally irrelevant to his life, but did he somehow think that Saint Honoratus of Amiens would come to his aid with his baking problems? Wouldn't a Catholic pray to him for aid?

You're being crazy, Peter. Write those emails.

He wrote a simple, but friendly, email to Harrison. He'd love to come but feared his wife might not be able to make it, as she had to visit her parents in ____ (fill in the gap later) in August. He would do his best with a witty speech—they had glottal stops in common, after all!

He wrote to Beebee:

Dear Beebee,

I think you should book that hotel anyway. The gingerbread sounds very tempting. I like the chocolate-covered variety best.

Looking forward to seeing you on All Saints' Day. Pray to Saint Honoratus for me!

Peter x

Another email flashed up on the screen:

Professor D. Brown

Urgent

Dear Lampton,

Since I am writing on official business, I think it is appropriate to revert to surnames.

You will be aware that Dr Lubbins will be unable to act as External Examiner at Oxford, at least during the initial period. I hope you will be kind enough to oblige us by stepping into the gap. Your presence will be required at the scrutiny meeting on Thursday, 6 November.

Yours sincerely,

D. Brown

Oh, no! Peter thought. Another one for the list. The simplest way is to accept. That way he would also be able to insinuate himself into Brown's good books to his advantage in the RRE. He replied immediately:

Dear Derek Brown,

—That was sure to annoy him, he thought, if not for the forwardness, then for the ambiguity, and most of all for the maladroit formula Dear First Name plus Surname—

Thank you for your invitation to act as External Examiner. It will be a considerable extra burden, but under the circumstances, and in kindness to Jim, I am willing to act.

Yours sincerely,

P. Lampton

Peter spent the rest of the day dealing with departmental admin and completing his exam papers, which he gave to Johanna, with a stern warning that she should memorize the password and then destroy it. He didn't in the event have the courage to suggest that she eat it.

In the evening, he broached the subject of the wedding with Becky.

'You know I told you about Gisela being in the club. Well, Harrison's asked her to marry him, and we're invited to the wedding on 1 August. Harrison wants me to be best man.'

'Please don't use that expression, Peter. I find it most distasteful.'

'I must look up the etymology.'

'You're trying my patience.'

'Well, are you coming?'

'No.'

'Who's going to be my plus one, then?'

'Your girlfriend, of course.'

'I don't have a girlfriend.'

'Oh, no? I might come, then, after all. Where is the wedding?'

'They don't know yet.'

'Well, when you know, I'll tell you if I can come. I shall need a new outfit.'

Peter was disappointed at Becky's truculence, but it was what he had come to expect from her, especially since she had taken up flower arranging.

'I shan't be able to pick up the kids this afternoon,' Becky said. 'You'll have to do it.'

'You know I can't. I'll be in London. Isn't there someone else you can ask?'

'I'll work out something.'

'Try Robert.'

'I just might.'

'I'm going to check my emails.'

'Haven't you heard from her today?'

'Piss off!'

Little did Becky know that Vicky was the problem; in fact she didn't suspect any involvement with Vicky at all. Peter had barely mentioned her name in her presence.

'It's an RRE matter,' Peter said. 'Jim's been taken to hospital, and I may have to stand in for him. Incidentally, I've agreed to external in Oxford while Jim's ill.'

'More fool you.'

'You're so sweet.'

'Screw you.'

Peter went to his computer and typed in his password, which he had changed to cabriolet. Becky would never guess that. He typed:

Dear Vicky,

I was a little surprised to receive your email earlier today. I was in the middle of departmental business, so have not been able to answer until now. I'm not sure what you were thinking when you demanded my presence on Thursday at 7:00. I don't know if you realize that I'm a very busy man. As it happens, I can spare you a few minutes on Thursday at 6:00 to discuss the situation so that we can come to an amicable decision about your matter.

With kind regards,

Peter

A few minutes later, an email arrived from Vicky:

Dear Peter,

If you are not ready and willing to do the deed on Thursday, I shall need to take the matter out of your hands, which is a pity because I believe your academic genes would be particularly advantageous and complement my business genes perfectly.

Since I would not wish to put extra strain on Jim at this time, I am considering asking Derek to stand in. His robustness would be a procreational advantage.

Yours disappointedly,

Vicky

Peter was shocked at the thought of Brown fulfilling Vicky's needs and immediately wrote back:

Dear Vicky,

Don't ask Brown at any cost. You would always regret this. I will act. Although my equipment has become a little rusty since it has fallen into desuetude, I have had a little practice in the matter recently and trust that, with the help of additional aids, I shall deliver the goods to your satisfaction.

Fondest wishes,

Peter

A reply came:

Dear Peter,

You do talk nonsense! I have a supply of Viagra and a stock of adult films to get you in the mood.

We'll have dinner here: watermelon for starters, followed by chilli con carne, apples, bananas, and pistachio nuts for dessert, washed down with a bottle of fine claret. There'll be no stopping you after that.

Love,

Vicky x

PS. You'd better get in training with some finger exercises before Thursday.

Peter felt a warm glow at the thought of all the trouble Vicky was going to—to which she was going, Peter—but a feeling of terror overtook him. He Googled 'length of time Viagra takes to work'. About half an hour seemed to be the consensus of opinion. He would need to pay heed to this during the dinner. To make sure, he thought it would be wise to ask his friend, Perry Parker, who had personal experience of Viagra, albeit with men rather than women, but Peter couldn't see that that made a difference.

Hi Perry, Old Chap,

I have a rather indiscreet question, but I hope you'll be sympathetic with me for asking. I'm planning to trial Viagra on Thursday as a favour to a friend. Can you give me a few hints? What's it like? Do you get any side effects?

I hope you and Jaycee are both well and having a great time.

All the best,

Peter

Later that evening, Peter received a reply from Perry:

My Dear Boy,

Viagra can have nasty side effects: nausea, headaches, hot flushes, a red face, blurred vision, and you sometimes don't even get a stiffy. I often just get a semi, but with proper stimulation, I normally get hard. Oh, and by the way, you can sometimes get priapism. I wouldn't recommend it.

Happy screwing,

Perry x

Jim was becoming acclimatized to his hospital ward. Isabelle had been his only visitor to date. Where were all the other young ladies? he wondered. Had they not heard that Jim Lubbins had had a bit of a mishap with the old vindaloo? He supposed that word had not yet spread. He hoped someone would visit in the evening session. Sarah came over to chat.

'I'm going off my shift soon, Jim. I hope you're feeling a lot better. How's the hospital food suiting you?'

'It's shite,' Jim said.

'Now, now, naughty boy,' Sarah said. 'We can't have language like that in my hospital. You see that you behave.'

'Undes ars in tine naso,' Jim said.

'Are you sure you're all right? Do you need to see a doctor?'

'Bloody 'ell. Just practising for my lectures.'

'Eat up your delicious hospital food,' Sarah said. 'I shall be checking up on you.'

'What are you going to do if I don't?' Jim joked.

'I shall have to discipline you,' Sarah said. 'No more chocolate crunch for breakfast and a cold bed bath when I come on duty in the morning.'

'Yeah, well,' Jim said. 'Hot water's for wimps.'

'We'll try it out tomorrow,' Sarah said with a wink.

'Well, warm your hands first.'

'Now don't you start getting excited,' Sarah said. 'You've got to watch your ticker. The doctor says you need bed rest for the rest of the week and to take things easy after that.'

'Yeah, well, I'll cut down on the vindaloo.'

'You may need to cut down on more than that.'

'Bloody 'ell.'

Sarah gave him a smile and went back to the nurses' station. A few minutes later, Isabelle came into the ward and made her way to Jim's bed. She gave him a book.

'I thought you might like something to read,' she said.

'Hello, love,' Jim said. 'It's kind of you to come again.'

'Well, Jim, I've been sorting things out for you so that you can concentrate on getting better. I've told Niamh and Philip. Niamh's passed on the news to the RRE subpanel members, and Philip thinks I should go and meet Paddy on Thursday anyway without you. I hope you agree.'

'Yeah, well. Watch him. He'll try to flirt with you. He's married, though.'

'I think I can cope,' Isabelle said. 'Have you got his phone number? I ought to phone him first.'

'Sorry, love, I haven't got it on me. It's in Jim's Pad, next to the phone on my desk. You could go in and get it. The key's in my stuff in there. Water the plants if you go, and check the post.'

'I'll see what I can do, Jim.'

Isabelle took the key out of Jim's locker.

Peter came into the ward, looking flushed.

'Hello, Jim,' Peter said. 'I've come straight from the train. It's been a bit of a rush. How are you?'

'Nothing wrong with me. It's all the others,' Jim said. 'How's Mr Glottal Stops?'

'If you mean me,' Peter said, 'I'm just about coping with the new term and associated problems.'

'Becky being difficult, eh?'

'You could say that, but I'd rather not talk about it.'

'What about the glottal crap?'

'I haven't had any time for research except for checking a few references.'

'I hear you had intimate relations in the University Library.'

'Who told you that?'

'Jim has his sources.'

'Well, his sources are wrong. I had a meeting with a colleague about a very serious matter.'

'Oh, yeah! That's not what I heard.'

'Anyway, I can see that you are perfectly OK. I'm wondering why I've rushed home from London to see you. D'you want me to go again?'

'No, of course not. Jim likes pulling people's legs.'

'By the way, Derek has asked me to stand in for you at the Oxford scrutiny meeting. I hope that meets with your approval.'

'Yeah, well, if they can't have Lubbins, anyone's better than nothing.'

'Do you want me to hit you?' Peter said.

'I must be getting back,' Isabelle said. 'Lots to catch up on. I'll pop into Jim's Pad soon and report back.'

Philip arrived and swapped places with Isabelle.

'We haven't seen each other for a while,' Philip said to Peter.

'No, but I've come across your work a fair few times in the RRE.'

'Oh dear, that sounds ominous,' Philip said.

'Yeah, he's a hard bastard,' Jim said.

'Jim loves to joke,' Peter said. 'I can assure you we're scrupulously fair on the RRE.'

'What percentage of work gets selected for restructuring?' Philip asked.

'About 95%,' Jim said.

'Don't listen to him,' Peter said. 'That only applies to his work. I should think it's about fifty-fifty.'

'Yeah, well, we'll see you're all right, mate, if you play your cards right. Have you practised the Fucking in Old Bavarian lectures yet?'

Peter looked shocked.

'You haven't called it that, have you?' he said.

'Yeah, that was the old name, but we had to change it after a complaint.'

'Isabelle's offered to help with the conversion of the article into lectures,' Philip said. 'She can type much quicker than me.'

'I don't like to be pedantic,' Peter said, 'but I think you mean "than I". It's one of my hobby horses.'

'Stuck-up prick,' Jim said.

'Well, the stuck-up prick needs to be getting home to his devoted wife. I'm just not sure who she's devoted to,' Peter said.

'I don't like to be pedantic,' Philip said, 'but I think you mean "to whom she's devoted".'

'He's a prick, too,' Jim said.

'We'll see what Isabelle thinks when she helps me with the typing,' Philip said.

'Yeah, well, be careful,' Jim said.

'Oh, I will be—very careful,' Philip said.

'Did you mean shall?' Peter asked.

'Up yours,' Jim said.

'Bye, Jim, take care; bye, Philip, good luck with the lecture,' Peter said and set off home.

'You're very late, Becky said coldly.

'Yes, I called in to see Jim in hospital. He's his usual self; there doesn't seem to be anything wrong with him. He's probably just ducking out of his duties so he can chase after the young ladies more. Did the kids get home all right?'

'Yes, no thanks to you. We managed in the end.'

'I needn't ask who did it, I suppose.'

Well, don't, then,' Becky said.

'Do you enjoy being difficult?' Peter asked.

'Do you enjoy being such a prick?' Becky retorted.

'You're as bad as Jim,' Peter said.

'Stuff you.'

'Is there any dinner?'

'No. There was at 7:00. I've put it in the fridge. You can get it out if you like cold meals,' Becky said.

'I'll make a sandwich,' Peter said.

Oh, damn the lot of it! Peter cursed, as he left for his study with his sandwich and a glass of wine. *Bloody Becky! Bloody women! Why can life never be simple?* He went to his computer as if on autopilot. The first email was from Oxford with the details of the examining schedule. The second was from Vicky.

Dear Peter,

Just checking that all is still well. I have ordered some sexy underwear for Thursday—for me, that is. I assume you have your own. You'd better try out the V***** before Thursday and measure your blood pressure after half an hour. Eat plenty of fish before then. I've switched the starter to smoked mackerel. Remember the finger exercises, and NO screwing until Thursday!!!

Remember, all you've got to do is keep your nerve and shoot a few of those wriggly things. No pressure!

Love, Vicky x

'No pressure my arse!' Peter spluttered. For the time being, he would try out the 30mg pill. He washed one down with the remainder of his wine and fetched another glass from the kitchen. After half an hour, there was little reaction. He washed another down with his second glass. He had better take the 100mg pill after all on the night. He wrote back hastily to Vicky:

Dear Vicky,

There's no need to keep checking up on me. Now that I've made up my mind, I shan't duck out of it. I wasn't planning on wearing anything special on Thursday. I don't have any sexy underwear, I'm afraid. Becky makes me wear boxers from M & S. We like their all-butter croissants. I'm not very partial to smoked mackerel. It can be very repetitive. I think my finger exercises are in good order—you definitely don't have to worry on the other score. I have taken advice about the V***** and am titrating the dose. I'm sure everything will go swimmingly.

Love, Peter x

Peter went back into the sitting room where Becky was watching television.

'Can I get you a glass of wine?' he said as a kind of peace offering.

'Please,' Becky said unemotionally.

Peter returned with a glass of the red wine that he had been drinking.

'Here you are,' he said. 'It's rather good.'

'I can see that,' Becky said. 'Your face is as red as a beetroot.'

Oh, damn! Peter thought and felt discreetly down below through his pocket to check whether the Viagra had had much of an effect.

'Peter, what are you doing, feeling yourself?' Becky asked.

'I'm not,' he said, 'just adjusting my boxers.'

'Well, go and adjust them somewhere else, not while I'm watching TV, please, and not where the kids might see.'

Damn you! he thought and returned to his study, shutting the door behind him. He checked the effects of the Viagra. Yes, things were quite spectacular down below now. Should he put that to good use? Should he even try it on with Becky? *Damn!* Vicky had forbidden it. Bundle it up, Peter, and carry on as if nothing had happened. He went back to Becky.

'I'm watching something you wouldn't like,' she said.

'How do you know?' Peter asked.

'Well, if you'd prefer to do something a bit more adventurous,' Becky said, we could go upstairs, and I can record my programme.

Peter felt embarrassed. Had Becky supposed his erection had been caused by thoughts about her? She came over and acted seductively.

'Hello, big boy,' she said, feeling Peter's bulge. 'It's been a long time. I thought you'd lost interest.'

'Far from it, but this really isn't a good time,' Peter said.

'Why not?' Becky snapped back at him.

'I'm doing an experiment.'

'Oh yeah?' Becky said. 'And who might the object of the experiment be? Beebee by any chance.'

'No,' Peter stuttered. 'It's you.'

'Well, come and screw me, big boy' Becky said.

'I can't,' Peter whimpered. 'The experiment's not over yet.'

'Fuck you,' Becky said. 'There—look what you've made me say. Fuck you, Peter fucking Lampton.'

Peter retreated to his study in despair.

Thursday, 16 October

On Thursday, Isabelle set off for London on the train that had previously been agreed with Jim, after first having retrieved Paddy's details from Jim's Pad the day before. She gave Paddy a ring and established how and where exactly they should meet. Paddy explained what he would be wearing—a green tie with a shamrock. Isabelle explained she would be sporting her Girton scarf. They met at El Vino's and had lunch together, as planned.

'I'm so sorry Jim can't be here,' Paddy said. 'Is he still chasing after the young ladies?'

'Sadly, yes,' Isabelle said. 'I think he's hoping that I might be his latest conquest, but I'm not the right age group. I like Jim as a friend, but I don't want a romantic involvement. I'm not sure whether Jim does romantic anyway. He needs a nice caring lady of about his own age. You know he had some kind of heart attack. Well, hijinks in bed wouldn't exactly be the kind of exercise that the doctors would prescribe for his recovery, and anyway, he's not my type.'

'What is your type, then?' Paddy asked.

'Perhaps a tall, blond Scandinavian. I think it would suit my genes well. My dad did one of those DNA tests on a genealogy website, and it came up with quite a lot of Nordic ancestry. A Viking in his longship wielding his spear. Only joking. I'm not looking at the moment. My ex was a bit of a bastard—only interested in himself. He used sex to lure me, but I wasn't going to give in without some surety, if you'll pardon the financial allusion. Anyway, we shouldn't be talking about these things; we've only just met.'

'It never hurts to talk,' Paddy said.

'No, so tell me a bit about yourself. Are you married?'

'Yes. I was like Jim until a couple of years ago. Then I met the right person—at least, I thought so, but marriage does strange things to people. I think women give up trying when they've got a ring on their finger. Patsy has anyway.'

'I'm sorry,' Isabelle said. 'Are you going to tell me about this tip, then? I'm counting on that for my future.'

'Let me whisper in your ear. No-one must hear, you understand.'

'I hope I shall remember it,' Isabelle said.

'Well, you've got my number, and I've got yours. We can keep in touch if anything changes. Right, I've got two for you,' he whispered into her ear. 'Hadubrand Mining at 50p should double overnight, and Strandhill Assurance could be up to 5 Euro after an IPO price of 1.50€. Check the internet for the dates. No paper trail, you realize. If you phone me, erase the call history. No emails or texts!'

'Sounds worse than a James Bond movie,' Isabelle said.

'Good luck,' Paddy said. 'Wish Jim "Get well soon" from me. I hope we may meet up again one day.'

'Thanks, it's been a pleasure,' Isabelle said. 'I'm sure Jim appreciates it, too.'

Philip went along at 11:00 to a room of expectant students. His variations on a theme of Lubbins met with qualified success. Extemporizing on an intimate subject and remaining within the bounds of propriety was difficult for him. At the end of the lecture, he mopped his brow and staggered into his own lecture room for *Woyzeck*, hoping that few of Jim's students would be following him.

Peter spent the morning at home and left the house at lunchtime, with the excuse that he would be working in the library until late, checking references again. Becky needn't cook him any dinner. He had been invited by a colleague to dinner at Needham, at least, that's what he told her. If need be, he could ask Philip for an alibi. He wore a suit and took his gown with him in the car to prove the point. Before leaving, he put the Viagra, the ten-function Bullet Vibrator, and the ten-function Rabbit Love Ring into his briefcase and also added the last couple of bottles of red wine that he had had delivered from Bristol the week before. The condoms he put into his pocket. Maybe, Vicky would decide she didn't want to get pregnant after all. If he had worked up sufficient excitement in anticipation and were then denied his pleasure for fear of insemination, the condoms would be more than welcome. If he failed to give Vicky an orgasm, even with the help of the Rabbit Love Ring, of which he had no previous experience, there would always be the ten-function Bullet Vibrator. He thought he'd better check what the functions were and was disappointed to discover that it was only ten different speeds. At least, Vicky would be amused trying out the possibilities. Peter kept on reading the descriptions, in the hope of discovering more about the functions. He turned to the reviews on Amazon. One in particular from a disgruntled customer, whose vibrator was useless, owing to a broken button after only two orgasms, struck a chord: 'I nearly had to resort to sex with my husband.'—Patsy, London. Yes, he could sympathize with the frustrated woman. Sex with one's spouse was bottom of the league table, certainly at the moment for him. Sex with Beebee was great, but for how long would it last? Yes, that's right, Peter, not how long would it last for? But that's what you wanted to say, wasn't it? For Goodness' sake, Peter, why are you chasing after sex with women, when a ten-function Bullet Vibrator would do the job better? — No, it wouldn't. — Better than

Becky, though. — Better than Vicky, too? — We shall see. — *Oh, no!* Be sensible for a moment, Peter, and think. — Can a ten-function Bullet Vibrator make you happy, give you real happiness and contentment? Love, even? — What's in an orgasm? — You're right, of course. — We all think it will be better than it really is. — How many really satisfying orgasms have you had, Peter? — Don't answer that. — You'd better be going, Peter.

Peter parked at the Library and walked back into town first. He went into the Grand Arcade and looked round. He located the Ann Summers store. He looked all around him for someone he might know. Of course, there would be none of his students, and few colleagues from Cambridge would be around at the time, even fewer would know and recognize him. — Don't be a fool, Peter, he said to himself, as he walked past the door. Turn round and go back in. It's not a dirty-mac-brigade shop. You're not in Chesterton Road at the Private Shop. It's a bona fide adult store, catering for the Waitrose clientele of the adult industry. In you go, Peter. He stood in front of the window and tried to see past the displays of erotic, but not sleazy, lingerie—frilly rather than crotchless—he was sure that made all the difference. The coast was clear. He hurried in. The young assistant smiled at him but did not immediately ask if she could help him. Could anyone help him in his frustration and moral predicament? — Go out again, Peter. You don't belong in here. — I owe it to Vicky. — Well, hurry up, Peter. Ask the assistant. — I can't.

'Sexy underwear? Do you sell it?'

'For men or for women, sir?'

'For a woman.'

'We have these frilly red panties that are quite popular with the ladies and often bought by the gentlemen, too.'

'I want something for me.'

'I don't think we have them in your size, sir.'

'See-through briefs, leather thongs, posing pouches, sexy boxers? Do you have any?—Oh damn!' he added, sotto voce and wanted to run out of the shop.

'These boxers are quite popular, sir. It's a joke, you see— "Warning, may contain nuts." I assume you don't want me to explain it.'

Peter began to feel at ease. The assistant smiled and joked with him.

'Is this your first visit, sir?'

'Yes, probably my last, too.'

'There's nothing to be embarrassed about, sir. Which would you like to buy?'

'One of each,' Peter said.

'Card or cash, sir?'

'Card.'

'That will be £16, sir. Thank you, Professor Lampton.'

Peter went beetroot red and stumbled out of the shop, back to the Library. He put his purchases safely into the boot of his car, after first having extracted the boxers and put them into his jacket pocket. He next locked the boot. Now he had everything! What could possibly go wrong? Time to check references, Peter. He trudged up the steps, through the revolving doors, up the next flight of steps in the entrance hall and into the Catalogue Room. A few readers were struggling with the cumbersome guard books of the old catalogue. Peter felt a nostalgic glow. He distracted himself from the impending activity of the evening by locating the guard books for *L*. He looked up Lampton. There were one or two entries but none for Peter John Lampton. Did you really expect to find yourself in there, Peter? — No. — The old catalogue is pre-1978. You didn't publish anything before then, Peter. Why were you looking? — I thought it was worth checking. — That's illogical, Peter. — I know. It was really just for something to do and for old times' sake. You know how I loved this place. — That's understandable, then, Peter, but you'd be better concentrating on the business ahead. — Oh, fuck! — Not *in diesen heiligen Hallen*,

Peter! Moderate your language! — No, you're right. I'll go to the Tea Room and get a cheese scone. — They'll be stale by now. — Yes, you're right. — Sod it! I'll just get a tea.

Peter went to the Tea Room, which, that October afternoon, was already quite full of undergraduates chatting happily in their little groups—men trying to impress women, still early in the term, whom they had encountered in lectures or elsewhere, forging liaisons that might last for a whole undergraduate career or at least for the rest of the term. Then, there were the loners like himself, dotted about amongst the tables, trying not to appear lonely. Are you lonely, Peter? — Yes and no. — I prefer company when I come in here, but I've got lots of friends, just not in here. — Are you sure, Peter? Are they real friends, Peter? — Acquaintances, then. No, damn it, they *are* friends. — Where do acquaintances stop and friends start, Peter? Is Derek a friend? — What do you think? — It doesn't matter what I think, Peter. — No, Derek isn't a bloody friend. I hate him. — Steady on, Peter, it's not good to hate. — I don't really hate him. — Is Beebee a friend, Peter? — Yes, of course. — Is that why you fuck her, Peter, and not Becky? — How the hell do I know? — Are you going to fuck Vicky, Peter? — Yes, we have a deal. — Is it right to fuck friends but not your wife, Peter? — I'm going now.

Peter drank his tea and went up to North Wing 6. He checked the spot where he had had what Jim called intimate relations with Vicky. Damn it! They weren't intimate relations. — It was just a kiss. — But a passionate one, Peter. Do you think that will help when it comes to performing tonight, Peter? — I don't know what to think anymore.

He went to look for *Are German Nouns Oversexed?* But it wasn't there. Of course not, Vicky had borrowed it. — Are you losing your mind, Peter? — No, of course not, I just forgot. I'm nervous. — Yes, you are, Peter. Maybe you shouldn't go through with it, Peter. After all, it's a big responsibility, engendering a child and then walking away from the whole business.

— But I shan't walk away. — Shan't or won't Peter? — Aye, there's the rub.

Peter descended to North Wing 5 and stared out of the window with an open book in front of him. He rarely turned the pages. He watched the sun set. Of course, he couldn't see it on the north side. Before he left the library, he went into the men's lavatories—those glorious, high-ceilinged lavatories on the right-hand side as you left the building. He went into the middle cubicle—Good God, not stall! What an abomination that usage was! But why? Associations only. Why did the Americans use it? He didn't know. He glanced up at the glass globes of the lights, in which one could see indistinct reflections of other occupants of the room. Would one ever be able to recognize someone? He didn't think so. Better to wait until he was the only person in the room, though. He took out his neatly folded new boxer shorts with the suggestive legend. — Yes, Peter, they will appeal to Vicky, he chuckled to himself. He put them on and put his M & S ones into his jacket pocket and hoped the slight bulge would not look as if he had tried to steal a library book. He would never have done such a thing. The University's books were as sacred as the Library itself—objects of veneration within the great temple of learning. Before leaving the cubicle, he looked at the graffiti on the door. There were very few sexual graffiti. One or two classmarks, intended to lead the inquisitor to a book containing a contact on a slip of paper. Yes, he had looked one up once—purely out of curiosity. A casual sexual encounter, solicited in this way, was for desperate people. Peter had never been desperate, and even if he had been, he would never have had the courage to investigate further. Besides these, there were several 'academic' graffiti. Yes, 'Smash modern architecture!' was still there. It had been since he was an undergraduate. Its continued existence spoke to him. Was it intended to suggest that Scott's phallic masterpiece should in some way be destroyed? Surely not. Who wrote it? An undergraduate, no doubt. What prompted him to engrave this iconic exclamation, rune-like

189

into the door of the temple? Should Peter feel anger at the desecration? No, it enhanced the sanctity of the building. What are you going on about, Peter? Get a grip. Time to leave now. Have you done up your flies? He checked and walked down the stairway, past the security staff, his left hand held tight against his pocket with the boxers. The shame of having to reveal a pair of boxers upon being searched was unimaginable. But they never got people to empty their pockets, or did they? Maybe this security measure had been introduced of latter years, unbeknown to him. He exited the library as it was growing darker.

The elation at having done something so naughty as to change into a pair of sexy boxers in the holy halls was mixed with fear—fear of the unknown and impending doom. He had never felt under pressure to perform before, not even when he and Becky were trying for their first child; but this time, he had only one shot at it. If he failed, he might have to repeat the whole unsavoury process. Don't be silly, Peter. It will be fun. — That's what you think. — No pressure, Peter. — Just do what you normally do. — Oh, sod it! He got into his car and set off for Water Street. It's not too late to turn back, Peter. Drive home and make some excuse, Peter, if you've lost your bottle. No glottal stop, Peter, just for you. Turn back, O man. — No, I've got to go through with it. I've made a promise — Yes, Peter, but a promise to do what? — You know what. — Aye, there's the rub, Peter. — Oh, sod it!

Peter got out of his car and parked on the gravel beside the house. He retrieved his briefcase and purchases from the boot. He rang the bell, and Vicky appeared at the door. Peter went nervously into the house. Vicky grabbed him and extracted a timid kiss.

'Can't you do better than that?' she asked.

'I'm nervous,' he said.

He got out the two bottles of wine.

'Come and put them into the kitchen.'

Peter handed the Ann Summers bag to Vicky.

'I've brought you a little present. I'm sorry it's not wrapped.'

Vicky looked inside and took out the red panties. She gave Peter a passionate kiss.

'Wait there,' she said, 'while I go upstairs and put them on.'

Peter's nervous anxiety was subsiding gradually.

'Do you want to eat supper first? That was the plan. I was hoping we could have a glass of wine on the patio, overlooking the river, but it's too cold. Come and sit in the sitting room unless you'd prefer to get straight down to business.'

'As you please,' Peter said.

His anxiety had started to climb again.

'Of course, I shall have to be very careful when the baby's born, with the river being so close,' Vicky said.

Peter's anxiety levels reached new heights. Vicky went into the kitchen and brought out two glasses of wine, after first dissolving a 30mg pill in Peter's glass. She judged that that would have a beneficial effect on the evening's activities without causing undue haste or unnecessary embarrassment.

'How long do you think supper will take?' Peter asked.

'Why, are you in a hurry?'

'No, just thinking ahead. I need to have some idea of when I shall get home to Becky.'

'You're not hen-pecked, are you, Peter?'

'That's a leading question.'

'Well, are you?'

'Who bloody-well isn't?' Peter said. 'But I don't let her get away with it. We have armed neutrality.'

'We were constantly at war,' Vicky said, 'until I met Susan. I never thought I could have a lesbian relationship, but it was nice for a while.'

'I suppose it's different with women,' Peter said. 'Easier for two females to get on together.'

'Yes, until they disagree,' Vicky said. 'But I've always wanted a child, and that's where you come in.'

'Don't you think it will be a bit difficult as a single mum, especially at your age?'

'I think I'll cope all right. You'll visit from time to time, won't you?'

'It might be difficult.'

'Anyway, I'll go and get the starter. I've got you some king prawns, since you said you didn't like smoked mackerel.'

'I'm sorry, that was awfully rude of me.'

'Better to be honest than lie. I'll give you a rating later on— RRE-style.'

'Go easy on me, please.'

'You should be so lucky.'

'Have another glass of wine,' Vicky said. 'How are you feeling?'

'Fine,' Peter said. 'I think I'm gradually coming to terms with what's expected of me.'

Vicky went into the kitchen and returned with the wine bottle, suitably spiked. She poured a large glass for Peter, then went back to the kitchen to fetch the main course. Peter took this as his cue to swallow the 100mg pill. His face was starting to turn red; his speech became more slurred.

'Everything OK still?' Vicky asked after the main course.

'More wine?'

'Thanks, but I'm driving, as you know. Actually, I may be over the limit already.'

'No worries,' Vicky said. 'I can drive you home if you're overstretched in any way.'

'Please don't say "no worries". I can't take it.'

Vicky looked puzzled.

'Right, now's the time to start worrying! Is that better?'

Vicky went over to Peter and started to caress him from the chest downwards.

'You're embarrassing me,' Peter said.

He got up and tried to hide his priapic penis.

'No need to do that. That's what you're here for,' she said.

192

She beckoned him to follow her upstairs. Peter fetched his briefcase.

'You're very businessman-like,' she said. 'I hope you're not too business-like in the performance of your duties.'

She began to undress him slowly and caressingly, having stripped down to her bra and red panties. She started on his trousers.

'Now for the pants, she said seductively.'

'No! Don't call them pants,' Peter said.

'I was pulling your leg,' she said.

Peter insisted she leave the boxers in place and read the legend. His unrelenting erection made it difficult to read the text so that Vicky needed to move her head to one side.

'Open it,' Peter said, pointing at the briefcase. 'There's another little present inside.'

'Shall I fit it for you?' Vicky asked.

'If you think it will help,' Peter said.

They got into bed. Becky pressed the button on the ten-function Rabbit Love Ring. Peter turned off the light.

'I usually leave it on,' Vicky said.

'Becky insists otherwise—at least, she did when we used to do it.'

Half an hour later, Vicky got up, leaving a prostrate, priapic Peter on the bed.

'How was I?' he said.

'Lampton's performance showed a substantial proportion of emissions of international significance with a significant amount of rigour in need of only some restructuring.'

'Grades, please.'

'A- for Originality, A for Significance, A for Rigour.'

'Heavens!' Peter said. 'I've done it,' and fell asleep.

An hour later, Vicky woke her still priapic lover.

'Do you want to do it again?' she asked.

'Another time, perhaps.'

Vicky helped him get dressed and encouraged him into her car. She drove him back to Bluntingham and dropped him 100 metres from his house.

'I didn't hear the car,' Becky said.

'No, I had one over the odds and got a taxi.'

They retired to bed at 11:30. Peter got undressed in the bathroom, secreted his sexy boxers, and did his best to hide his persistent erection.

Did Becky suspect anything?

He supposed not.

Friday, 17 October

In the morning, Peter awoke, feeling decidedly groggy. He checked his penis for signs of continued priapism and was relieved that there were none. His joy at occasionally waking up with 'morning wood', a term of which he uncharacteristically approved, suspecting wrongly that it was of American provenance and thus to be eschewed, would have been out of place today and would have caused him added confusion, which he could well do without. He excused the construction and concentrated on the need to act normally, including with Becky and the kids. Normality could involve, and often did, arguments and sarcasms, especially when no young goats were present. But, leaving that aside, he needed to ensure there were no clues as to his activities of yesterday evening. That meant ensuring proper concealment of the boxers, Viagra, condoms, sex toys, and anything else that he might have forgotten about. Most of these artefacts were still at Vicky's so provided no immediate problem. The boxers would need washing, he supposed—easy enough to perform while Becky was out, though drying them might be more of a problem. Peter's main problem, however, was how to retrieve his car from Water Street. Becky could not be told, nor must she find out the precise location. As far as she was concerned, it was parked at Needham College. How would he get to the station, though? Fortunately, he could catch an off-peak train, since his first class wasn't until

194

11:00. He disliked having to use taxis, judging them to be much overpriced, but he would bite the bullet and phone for one later, preferably when Becky was preoccupied with the kids. He went downstairs and into his study. The boxers found their first refuge at the back of the bottom drawer of his desk. He resisted the temptation to check for emails. He really couldn't cope with any more complications this morning. He might just check on the train—he would shelve that decision for now. He drew a deep breath and went into the kitchen where Becky and the kids were already having breakfast. When the kids left to get ready for school, Becky turned her attention to Peter.

'How was it yesterday?' Becky asked.

A thought raced through Peter's mind. What did she mean by *it*? That was one of the shortest, if not *the* shortest, euphemisms for sex. Indeed, he had used it himself the previous night with Vicky. He would potentially need to lie—he hated that. Even if he no longer experienced religious scruples as in his youth, his sense of moral probity forbade him from lying. — Yes, Peter, it forbids you from lying but not from fucking someone who's not your wife. — You know the reasons. — I may know the reasons, but Becky doesn't and that occasions you to have to lie. — No, I won't lie. I'll just be economical with the truth.

Becky was concerned that his internal reasoning, of which she was unaware, had occasioned a significant pause before Peter could answer.

'Are you all right?' she asked. 'Did you hear what I said?'

'Yes,' Peter replied at length, 'I was thinking about the car parked at Needham and how I'm going to get it back.'

You're lying, Peter. — No I'm not; I've parked there in the past and no doubt shall do in the future. — That's a very poor excuse, Peter. Couldn't you do better than that? — Not at the moment, sorry. — That's not what you should be sorry about, Peter. — Oh, sod it!

'I'll run you over to Needham this evening,' Becky said.

'No, I'll manage somehow.'

195

'How was Beebee?'

'I don't get it.'

'That's where you were yesterday, wasn't it?'

'No.'

'Who were you with, then?'

Peter winced. Now's not the time for pedantry, Peter. —
But it might deflect her.

'I told you that I'd been invited to dinner by Philip.'

Very economical with the truth, Peter. — Well, I was last
year. — Oh dear, Peter. — Fuck off! — You don't speak to
me like that, Peter. — I'm sorry. — Really, Peter? — Are you
going to confess to Becky, Peter? — Sometime, perhaps. —
I'll be waiting, Peter. — Oh, shit! — Don't say that, Peter. You
know how I dislike it.

'Anyway, I've got to get to work. Will you be doing any
flower arranging today?'

Becky looked unmoved but understood the allusion.

'Have a good day,' Peter said.

'You, too.'

'I'll see you this evening after I've picked up the car.'

When Peter arrived at ULB, he managed to avoid speaking
to anyone, particularly Johanna. He sat down and turned on
his computer. Five unread emails greeted him. He turned first
to Vicky's:

Dear Big Boy,

I hope you got home safely last night and that you had a good
night's sleep, as I did. Did Peter's pecker go down in the end?
I hope so for your sake, but I could always use it again. We
shall know if the desired result has been achieved next month.
I'll buy a new packet of Clearblue to make sure. You've left
some of your stuff here as well as your car. I could pick you up
tomorrow, and we could try it again for good luck.

Let me know!

Love,

Vicky xxxx

Peter was naturally flattered that Vicky seemed to be satisfied with yesterday's proceedings. He hadn't often been called Big Boy. The time Becky did it was either flattery or sarcasm—it didn't really matter which. Was he really worthy of this designation, though? Psychologically, no. He, like most men, wished his penis were an inch longer. Of course, he had measured it and compared, both with scientific studies and with porn actors. Bad comparison, Peter. They're chosen for their larger-than-life proportions, are poorly paid, and have a generally miserable time. You know what a fluffer is, Peter. You're better off with Vicky and Beebee, even Becky. OK, so you used Viagra, but you could have coped without, and anyway, six inches is a respectable length. Has anyone ever complained?

There was a knock at the door. Peter hastily clicked on another email before he said, 'Come in.'

Johanna entered, and his heart sank.

'I have done all the exam papers now,' she said. 'They are all in the envelopes in the mail room.'

'Well done, Johanna,' Peter said. 'Have you sent them to the Externals, too?'

'Yes.'

'Thanks, keep up the good work.'

Peter returned to his emails. A new one flashed up from Beebee:

Dear Peter,

I have just opened the exam papers and discovered that my envelope contains 12 copies of the same paper. Would you be kind enough to investigate, please.

All best wishes,

Beebee

Copy to Alan Jameson

No, this was too much to deal with, Peter thought. He forwarded the email to Alan with an explanatory note. Next, he replied to Vicky.

Dear Ms Frilly Red Panties,

I'm pleased that my contribution to yesterday's proceedings met with your approval. I don't know how I'm going to get from my station to Water Street this evening. I suppose I could get a taxi, but I'd rather spend the fare on a token of my appreciation for anyone who might be willing to offer me a lift. Any ideas? My train gets in at 6:35.

By the way, if you're at a loss, look in my briefcase for another ten-function thingummy. I meant to give it to you yesterday. I hope you have lots of batteries.

Love from Big Boy (well, big enough)

A reply arrived ten minutes later:

Dear BB,

You drive a hard bargain, but I think I owe it to you. I'll be waiting outside the station at 6:35. Be prepared for more action.

V x

Hm, Peter thought. He was naturally pleased at Vicky's flirtatious banter but wondered whether he was wise for egging her on further. He didn't want to exhaust himself even with only a quickie. He couldn't run the risk of another priapic episode if he took more Viagra. There again, he feared the dreaded ED, about which he had read so much. He wouldn't be provided with the services of a fluffer. What's more, he didn't have his sexy boxers with him. He feared he might be a complete flop. Come off it, Peter, pull yourself together. When have you ever failed? — Never, but you know I haven't had much practice for years. — You were OK with Beebee twice and once with Vicky. Not just OK, but you were awarded a mark of distinction. — What if I've lost my nerve? Anyway, are you encouraging adultery for its own sake now? I thought you had moral standards. — I have shifting standards, Peter, but do you have?

After a hectic day's teaching and dealing with the additional problems caused by Johanna's incompetence, Peter arrived, exhausted, at King's Cross—he didn't give a damn about the apostrophe now, Dr Compton. He got into the train and fell promptly asleep. Fortunately, he was woken by the commuters alighting from the train at the station before his—yes, that was the word you were looking for a week or so ago, Peter. He joined the queue to cross the tracks via the footbridge and emerged, looking shagged, from the station building.

Having located Vicky's car, he flopped into the passenger seat.

'Are you ready for some more action?' Vicky asked.

'I don't think I can,' Peter said. 'Aren't you tired, too?' he asked.

'Of course, but we can take things gently tonight. The pressure's off. Let's see how we go.'

They set off for Cambridge. Peter was anxious, which was reinforced by a straying hand from Vicky, caressing his leg from time to time.

'Have you got those boxers on again?' she asked as her hand moved to the place where they might be located. Peter felt distinct stirrings. Vicky sensed these, too.

'Looks like you'll be OK then tonight,' she said.

'As if,' Peter said. 'I'm not sure, though.'

'Come on, Big Boy,' Vicky said. 'Keep Peter's pecker up.'

'Oh, whatever!' Peter said. Was that an imprecation or a bit of teenager speak? he wondered.

His phone rang.

'Excuse me, I must answer this; it's Becky. It could be important. She never normally rings.'

'Hello, Peter, it's Becky. When are you coming home? Geraldine has invited herself round this evening. She's got something to ask you.'

'What is it?'

'She's coming at 8:00. She'll tell you then. Hurry up and get back.'

'Damn nuisance,' Peter said. 'Bye, dear, see you soon.'

'Is there a problem?' Vicky said.

'I'm afraid so. A pastoral visit from the Vicar.'

'Has she got you in her sights for adultery? Deny everything. We'll catch up another time. Make sure that you're wearing something nutty.'

Peter packed his belongings in his briefcase.

'Enjoy the ten functions.'

'I shall.'

'Yes! You shall! I will it.'

He drove back to Bluntingham, relieved. *Damn!* he thought when he saw Geraldine's car parked in their drive. Didn't she realize that was his spot? He parked his to one side, so as not to block her in and went into the house as unobtrusively as possible, headed for his study. No, Peter, not *headed*; the word is *heading*. — I know, but everyone says *headed* nowadays. — Maybe. They also say *laying* when they mean *lying*, but you know better. You are heading for your study to lay your briefcase on the desk. — Steady on! I'm not going to lay anyone. — No, Peter? You've been doing a lot of laying recently—with anyone but your wife. Do you think this is what Geraldine has come about? — About which! — Go in and find out. — Oh, sod it!

Peter went into the sitting room, where Geraldine and Becky were conversing politely about flower arranging, the village, and other pointless topics.

'I'm sorry I'm a bit late,' he said. 'I had to pick the car up from Cambridge.'

Geraldine smiled.

'All well now?' she said.

'Yes, more or less,' Peter said. 'Have you been offered a drink, Vicar?' Peter asked with excessive formality.

'I always chuckle when people call me Vicar,' she said. 'Still, it's better than Reverend Mother, I suppose.'

'I think Peter's thinking of the Vicar of Dibley,' Becky said.

'Maybe,' Peter said. 'May I call you Geraldine?' he added in his state of confusion.

'If you must, but my name's Hermione.'

'I suppose you don't shorten it,' Peter said.

'No, I've always preferred the full form of names.'

Becky looked annoyed.

'To get back to my original question, Hermione, has Rebecca offered you a drink?' Peter said.

'Yes, but we haven't quite got that far yet.'

'What are you having?'

'I'd love a glass of red wine if you have any.'

'I'll go and look,' Becky said.

Peter made trivial chit chat with Hermione, as he would now have to call her, while Becky was in the kitchen, looking. She returned a couple of minutes later.

'Where are those last two bottles of red from Amory's, Peter?'

'I took them to Cambridge.'

'What? To a dinner at Needham? Was it PBAB?' Becky said facetiously.

'Something like that,' Peter said.

'Never mind,' Hermione said. 'I'll have anything you've got.'

'There's some Riesling in the fridge, left over from the departmental wine tasting.'

Becky fetched three glasses on a tray with the bottle of Blue Nun Riesling.

'Quite appropriate, really,' Peter said, 'what with you being a mother superior.'

Hermione smiled politely at his inane joke. Becky looked daggers at him.

'Where are the young goats?' Peter asked.

'Peter's sense of humour,' Becky said in answer to Hermione's inquisitive look. 'Young goats—kids.'

'Oh, I see.'

'Upstairs, doing their homework.'

'Well, this wasn't what you came for,' Peter said.

'Shouldn't that be "for which you came"?' Becky interjected.

Hermione sensed a tense relationship.

'Maybe I shouldn't ask you about that for which I came,' she said.

'Oh, please do,' Peter said, 'unless you want £1000 for the steeple.'

'No, the organ actually,' Hermione said, 'but it's not money we want, but kindness.'

Becky looked at the floor and took a sip from her glass.

'The organist needs somewhere to live. He's being thrown out of his lodgings and needs somewhere to stay for two or three weeks until he can find somewhere else. Becky said you have a spare room and might be able to put Robert up until he finds a new place.'

'It might be a little tricky,' Peter said.

'Yes, I quite understand,' Hermione said. 'It was only a thought.'

'By when do you need to know?' Becky asked, tongue in cheek.

'As soon as possible,' Hermione said. 'Perhaps you could tell me on Sunday after you've had a chance to discuss it.'

'Yes,' Becky said.

'No,' Peter said.

'We'll let you know,' Becky said.

Peter looked daggers at her.

'Well, I must be going,' Hermione said. 'Thanks for the Blue Nun.'

'I'll see you out,' Becky said.

Peter went into his study and avoided contact with Becky for the rest of the evening. His obsession with emails drew him like a magnet to his computer.

There was one from Beebee:

Dear PL,

Alan has contacted me about the exam papers. Apparently, Johanna had a problem with the collator on the photocopier. He's sorted it out now and has personally supervised the insertion of the right papers into my envelope.

Sounds a bit suggestive, eh? If you feel like a bit of insertion, my envelope is ready and willing. Or maybe you would like to practise orals in advance of the scrutiny meeting. The Premier Inn looks worth investigating—London or Cambridge. About £60 a night. Share the costs? Better than a cupboard, although that will always be dear to my heart.

Your willing External,

Beebee xxxx

Damn! Peter thought. Isn't life complicated enough with a truculent wife, who wants to install her boyfriend in the marital home, and a soon-to-be mother, of whose baby he was the father? He couldn't juggle two extramarital affairs of his own and cope with one of his wife's at the same time. Something would have to go. The simplest would be Beebee, but that in a way would be the saddest. She was the most fun, the most academic, the closest to his interests. She was exciting and great in a cupboard, even better in a wood. Vicky, on the other hand was good in bed; she had her own delightful waterfront house that, in the event of a split, would be the perfect base from which to continue life as nearly as possible as normal. He would miss Bluntingham and the young goats, but Ben was now 16 and Richard 14. They would be leaving the herd soon and anyway, they had Becky and whatever lover she took to herself. Yes, they would thrive without him. It wasn't so far from Water Street to Bluntingham, after all; the three of them would still see him regularly. The kids would soon be young bucks. The nanny goat would soon be a nan—though he thought that term rather common—when they had grown up and had kids of their own. Vicky was a sophisticated, urbane woman of the world and soon to be mother of his third child. She didn't expect any special responsibilities on his part, merely occasional visits, but he couldn't just abandon his paternal duties. He didn't yet know what paternal affection he might feel. He needed to be there for her and junior even if he wasn't involved on a day-to-day basis. Thus, Peter had worked out his priorities:

1. Go and live with Vicky and help bring up junior.
2. Stay with Becky and tolerate her having a permanent extramarital relationship.
3. In the case of 1, he would have to forgo Beebee (at least, he thought so).
4. In the case of 2, he would probably have to forgo Beebee, but he hoped he would be allowed 'conjugal' visits with Vicky and access to his latest kid.
5. Sell all the properties and found a happy, hippie commune where free love was not only possible but actively encouraged, not only man to woman, but woman to woman, man to two women, woman to two men, all together, even, and for anyone who wanted it, man to man, though he wasn't sure about that.

Upon completion of these musings—they were more than that, Peter; deliberations was a better word—he felt happy. He had it sorted. Number 5 was looking like a very good proposition. Unorthodox, but a solution to all his problems. Would the others think so, too? An alternative was open marriages. Hey, hang on, Peter, you and Becky are the only ones who are still married. — Robert is, too, but his wife's in the USA. — So you think you can discount her, do you? — Since I've never

204

met her, well, yes. — There's one other slight problem, Peter. Only two men to go round four women. — No, only three, practically speaking. We could invite another to join us, and if Robert's wife came over, add a fourth. — So, it's only about sex, is it, Peter? — Of course not. There's the kids, the cleaning, the shopping, the driving—we could all share. — I don't think it's that simple, Peter. — Look, I'm not going to discuss it further now. — All right, Peter. Best of luck.

As a consequence of his deliberations, Peter had omitted to click on any further emails. He had overlooked those from Vicky and Derek.

Saturday, 18 October

On Saturday, Peter awoke at 6:30, feeling a strong sense of shame. Becky lay beside him in the marital bed, albeit turned away and looking in the other direction. Her eyes were still closed. He wasn't sure if she was awake. The previous evening, they had gone to bed separately without speaking. They had not had a row but had given each other the silent treatment, something that Peter found unsettling. Normally, they made it a rule, even in their state of armed neutrality, to reconcile before going to bed. However, Becky had retired early, and Peter had remained shut away in his study until he was sure that the rest of the house was asleep. The stillness in the Lampton household set him thinking. Maybe he should accede to Becky's wishes, permit Robert to stay temporarily, and come to an amicable arrangement with his wife—a concordat between the two parties. They still had plenty to offer one another, even if sex was no longer part of the package. Sex was so important. People made such a big deal of it, but, managed properly, with understanding and sensitivity, it could be incorporated into a felicitous concordat to the advantage of all parties. Peter was a reasonable chap. He rarely acted impulsively but weighed up the pros and cons, just as he did with a student's work. He didn't like to disappoint any student by dismissing their work out of hand, so he usually added a comment along the lines that he could see some merit or that the student had made a valiant attempt. The only place he drew the line was in the matter of plagiarism, when the dishonesty of the plagiarist offended severely against his sense of probity. And so it was with Becky. She had made a valiant attempt to make their marriage work; it was not really her fault that they had drifted apart over the years. He had made less of an effort, but you know the reasons—he had to concentrate on his career and be the breadwinner. — What an awfully old-fashioned term, Peter. Do you think giving a few lectures and writing books about glottal stops can be compared to a man going out in the heat of the sun, tilling the ground, harvesting the crops and providing his family with something to eat? — Compared *with*? — No, *to*, Peter. — Yes, I see.

As it gradually got light and the sun's rays began to illuminate the sleepy village of Bluntingham, Peter resolved to make an approach to Becky and offer her a deal. — Hm, Peter, that sounds very American. Rather commercial, too. — Yes, it's no big deal, though. I'm easier about such things now. He felt a weight lifted from his linguist's shoulders as well as from his husband's. — Make Becky's breakfast, Peter. — No, that looks too contrived. — Yes, you're right. — Offer to get her a coffee. — Good idea.

He filled up the coffee maker with water, emptied the grounds container, and ensured there were sufficient coffee beans in the hopper. Next, he tidied the breakfast table and swept up the few crumbs that were left on the kitchen floor from the night before. He removed the dirty wine glasses and packed the dishwasher. The kids would sleep in on a Saturday. He would seize the moment as soon as Becky had her cup of coffee. She entered the kitchen glumly at 7:30. Peter supposed that her facial expression was as much due to her state of sleepiness upon rising as to the events of the night before. He smiled at her. She half-smiled back.

'Coffee? I've just made one. Shall I get you one?'

'Yeah, OK.'

206

Steady, Peter, don't expect politeness at this time of the morning, especially after last night. — Yes, you're right.

'Did you sleep well?'

'Yes, not bad.'

Shouldn't that be badly? — Don't tell her, Peter. Anyway, it would sound odd.

'I've been thinking about what Geraldine said. I'm prepared to give it a go if you are.'

'Yeah, might be an idea.'

'You don't sound too thrilled.'

'No, I am, I'm pleased. It will really help poor Robert. He's struggling over here on his own.'

'Look, Becky, I think we need to come clean with each other. Just because you're sleeping with Robert doesn't mean we have to abandon our marriage.'

'No, I suppose not. Are you suggesting a ménage à trois?'

'Something like that.'

'What do you get out of it?'

'Well, if I agree to Robert, you'll have to agree to something, too.'

'Beebee?'

'That's part of the deal. It would only be very occasional— she's very lonely, and it needn't affect our relationship.'

'So it's Robert in exchange for Beebee.'

'Yes, but there's another dimension.'

'Oh, yes?'

'Yes. I've entered into an arrangement with a colleague on the RRE. Her name's Vicky. She lives in Cambridge, so it's more of a hands-on arrangement.'

'Is that where you were on Thursday?'

'Yes.'

'Did you fuck her?'

'Yes.'

'And Beebee?'

'Yes.'

'And anyone else?'

'Of course not.'

'That's all right, then.'

'Are you sure?'

'No, but it's the easiest way out.'

'Yes. There is one other thing,' Peter said, drawing a deep breath.

'Hi Mum,' Richard, who had just entered, said, 'who's taking me to football today?'

'That will be your father.'

Peter decided to shelve the final confession. Becky thought it was also not worth asking him what it was that he had wanted to say when he was cut short. She had Robert now, Peter could have his 'bits'.

'Robert will be coming to stay for a couple of weeks,' she said when both of their sons were sitting at the breakfast table.

'Great,' Ben said. 'He'll be able to teach us baseball and take us to football.'

Cheer up, Peter. You're a decent-enough father, but you must admit you could have done better. — Yes, but I'll defer to Robert.

Peter went into his study, relieved. He had no need now to hide his boxers so carefully. He could mention Beebee and Vicky without dissembling and could even admit to meetings with them without interrogation. For the time being, he would remain circumspect, though.

Derek's email contained password-protected files of the Oxford papers, which he would work through over the next few days. Vicky's was multifaceted:

Dear Peter,

How are you? I think I can feel stirrings in my womb! I know it's silly and quite impossible so soon, but I'm sure your wriggles have already gone to work. If all has gone according to plan, the baby should be due around 17 July. I think I should start knitting and that you should prepare for fatherhood again.

I expect I'll be OK for the next RRE meeting in May, although the bump will have begun to show by then. Have you thought about how we're going to explain it? I had an email from Niamh a couple of days ago, which I haven't mentioned to you before on account of our personal 'business'. I hear the meeting has been switched to Ayr again. Apparently, Niamh and Derek were behind this. I assume they have personal reasons. It's just as well, as I didn't want to fly when pregnant. We're supposed to have finalized our grades before May, and I need to ensure that my summings up of the departments show a significant amount of rigour (!), without sounding too ridiculous. I realize they were a bit OTT last time. I understand that Derek is quite amenable to endorsing our ratings now. He is only querying one or two—possibly Jim's imprecations, but he may go easy on him in view of his illness. Jim's hoping to be well again by then, I understand. I expect you've heard that he has been discharged from hospital and seems to have fallen in love for the first time. Yeah, well! Her name's Sarah—she's the nurse who looked after him. No sex, though, for six weeks until Jim has been given the all-clear.

By the way, have you heard of Bisscoin? Apparently, it's the latest word on the financial street in Germany. Isabelle heard it from a friend of Jim's, who reckons it will go up exponentially. He recommended investing whatever you can afford in it. The starting price is 0.1 cent, so it's not going to break the bank. I'm buying $1000 worth.

That's all for now. I'm looking forward to seeing you again soon, but I think we must respect the baby and hold off from the intimate stuff until we know everything is OK.

With love from FRP to BB.

Peter wrote back:

Dear FRP,

I'm relieved to hear from you and to hear that all is well after the tempestuous events of last Thursday. It would be great if everything has worked out to your satisfaction. Thanks for the tip about Bisscoin. I'll probably invest, too, although I fear it may be a Ponzi scheme. Still, after the last tip I got from Jim that plummeted, I've got used to losing the odd thousand.

Becky and I had a heart-to-heart this morning. We 'fessed up' to our respective indiscretions, as the young people say, although I don't think they call them indiscretions. I think mine have given me a new outlook on life and possibly a new approach to linguistic matters. Why should the Devil have all the best words? Becky now knows about you but not about the baby. Please don't mention that to anyone. I'll drop it (not the baby!) gently when I get an opportune moment. I don't want the kids to find out that they will be getting a half-brother or -sister. Have you thought about names? I thought Victor for a boy and Petra for a girl, although the latter reminds me of the dog on Blue Peter. I'm not sure about the 'bump' and the RRE. That's really your matter. Of course, I'll stand by you, but I'd rather you didn't say how it came about at this stage.

Seeing Becky's boyfriend will be living with us for the next few weeks, I might be able to spend more time with you—that is if you will have me.

I must go and see Jim again next week. The poor chap must be very lonely and frustrated without s*x, but I don't think he got nearly as much of that as he intimated. I gather he's back at Jim's Pad now. I had already heard from Isabelle. His lady friend (Sarah) lives nearby and has taken him under her wing. She helps with his medication and rehab exercises. Isabelle is relieved that the pressure's off her.

I hope to go to church tomorrow with Becky. She does the flower arranging. In fact, that's how she met Robert (the organist). It will be odd having your wife's lover living in the house and pretending that it's totally normal. I'm less worried about that than the fact that he's American and that, despite my more liberal mentality now, his speech habits may cause some consternation. As I'm sure you know, glottal stops aren't much of a problem with Americans. I just hope he doesn't say *laying* for *lying*.

It's a pity that we shan't be 'getting together' in the near future, but, of course, I respect your wishes. I hope Becky and Robert don't rub it in by shrieking in the bedroom, especially not while the kids are at home, but I expect they'll be discreet and screw during the day.

Next week (Wednesday), I have to go to the German Embassy to pick up my medal. I'd like to invite you along, but I fear it might be misconstrued. If Becky ducks out of it, citing lack of suitable clothes or some such, I'll see if I can take another guest. Would you be willing to come under the circumstances?

Take care!

Peter xx

On Sunday, Peter persuaded Becky to go with him to church. 'It's the easiest way to sort out your boyfriend problem,' he said. 'I didn't want to go, but I thought it was best if we show a united front and speak to Robert together, preferably in Geraldine's presence.'

'I can't imagine anything more embarrassing,' Becky said, 'and anyway, I haven't got anything to wear.'

'I shouldn't bother—any skirt and top would do. You know Geraldine's not bothered about outward appearances.'

'Yes, but I am.'

'Does she know he screws you? She might think that's a bit anti-Christian, but on the other hand, she may be broadminded and modern. After all, why should morality be set in stone? It always amuses me that the Church doesn't advocate stoning adulterers anymore when they're so strict about who you can have sex with.'

Becky looked annoyed.

'I hope you noticed my sloppy construction. I'm trying to be less of a pedant in preparation for American speak in the home.'

'Well, I'm glad that's all that you're bothered about.'

'I'd prefer it if you two didn't screw in our bed and if you did it when no-one else is at home. By the way, I may stay a night or two in Cambridge while Robert's here. No worries. Vicky has forbidden sex.'

'Oh, why?'

'Something gynaecological, I think.'

'Poor Peter, there's always Beebee.'

'Don't rub it in,' Peter said. 'I'm being very liberal, letting you put your lover up in our house.'

'I wish you wouldn't refer to him as my lover or my boy-friend. It might slip out in company.'

'Fuck off!'

'Actually, I do appreciate it, but you didn't have much choice really under the circumstances.'

Becky gave Peter a smile and a kiss on the lips.

'Quite like old times,' he said.

They arrived at church ten minutes before the start of the service and went to find the same pew in which Peter had sat last time. Heads turned at the very uncommon sight of the two of them in church together. Geraldine smiled at them as she walked down the aisle from the vestry to the back of the church for the start of the service. She gave her usual greeting, with eyes fixed on Becky and Peter. Peter was sizing up the congregation and reckoned that they were amongst the young-est there.

'I don't suppose they get much adultery among this lot,' he whispered to Becky.

'You'd be surprised,' she said. 'There were rumours about Geraldine herself, Bridget told me.'

212

'Oh, so you're all right, then.'

Each time Geraldine mentioned sin, Peter looked at her to see on whom her eyes were fixed. There seemed to be no general pattern. He felt relieved. If anything, he thought, Becky and her organist lover might have come in for scrutiny. Did Geraldine even know? Did she suppose their relationship was innocuous, platonic? That ghastly word that he would never use! He began to count the times sin came up and scolded himself for the associations that *coming up* evoked in him. — Not appropriate in church, Peter. He lost count and drifted off into a daydream during the sermon, which nearly turned into a real dream. Becky nudged him with her elbow.

After the service, they waited in their pew, listening to Robert's concluding voluntary.

'Bach or Buxtehude?' Peter asked him when he came down the aisle.

'The Dorian,' Robert answered.

'Bach,' Peter said.

Robert nodded.

'Well played,' Peter said.

'He was good, wasn't he, Becky?' he said, tongue-in-cheek.

Did Robert perceive the irony?

'Yes, beautifully played. How lucky St Michael's is to have you.'

'It's great to see you guys here,' Robert said.

'We've come to talk to you,' Peter said. 'Do you know my wife?'

Becky looked daggers at him. *You don't need to rub it in, arsehole*, she would have liked to say to him. She smiled at Robert.

'I hear you're about to become homeless,' Peter said.

'Yeah, Hermione's trying to find me someplace to stay.'

'Somewhere,' Peter muttered imperceptibly.

'Do you guys know anywhere?'

'Becky's keen to offer you a bed.'

Becky's look was now one of thunder.

213

'That's fantastic,' Robert said. 'I could offer free music lessons and pay rent, of course.'

Peter thought he ought not to overplay his hand, so suggested they go and talk to Geraldine.

They agreed that Robert should move in on Saturday, 1 November.

'All Saints' Day,' Peter quipped. 'I hope your conduct will be saintly at all times.'

'Sure thing,' Robert said.

Peter reflected on how much more straightforward Americans were than the British, especially British intellectuals. Robert wasn't brash, but Peter supposed he evinced the superiority of that nation on account of its material successes that in turn manifested itself in an unquestioning ingenuousness of discourse, a superficiality even that suspected no hidden meaning. One might call it naïveté. Peter delighted in irony. He left the church, feeling happy that they had solved a problem and that he had scored a few points against Becky and Robert.

When they got outside, Becky gave him a glare and kicked him. They went home in silence.

7. WEEK 5

Monday, 20 October

Peter trudged into London as usual. Although he had that 'Monday morning feeling', he was still elated by the successes of the past week. Two of his personal problems were now solved. He pondered the remaining academic matters. The debacle with the exam papers had been righted, Johanna appeared to have knuckled down to the term's work now that they were approaching the halfway point. The ULB didn't have a 'division of term' as in Cambridge, an expression Peter regarded as pretentious and unnecessary. Although he regarded the prospect with foreboding, he checked in with Johanna and enquired if there had been any important messages since last week.

'No,' Johanna said curtly.

'Have you ordered coffee and biscuits for the examiners' meeting on 3 November, Johanna?'

'No.'

'Would you do that, please.'

'It's Alan's job.'

'No, Johanna, it's your job. I'm telling you to do it now. Coffee and biscuits for 15 at 10:00 on 3 November in OL 5. Do you think you'll manage that?'

Johanna stared angrily at him.

'You'll be taking the minutes, too, Johanna,' Peter said.

'That's the secretary's job.'

'You *are* the secretary.'

'The Exams Secretary.'

'Johanna,' Peter said in exasperation, 'you're walking on very thin ice.'

She turned and made as to leave the room.

'Three strikes and you're out, Johanna. That's number one.'

'Rude man,' she muttered. 'There was a message on Thursday from the German Embassy. You need to be there by 6:00, wear evening dress, and you can bring two guests. They wondered why you hadn't sent a formal reply.'

'I never received a formal invitation.'

'I put it in your pigeonhole two weeks ago.'

'But I never got it.'

'Maybe it got stuck in between all the junk mail.'

'Johanna, I despair.'

Peter phoned Becky straightaway.

'You'll never guess what's happened. That fuckwit Johanna has managed to lose my invitation to the German Embassy on Wednesday, so I didn't realize what the dress code is. Apparently, we have to wear evening dress. I assume that means DJs. Can you go and check mine please and see if I've got a clean white shirt.'

'I'm a bit busy at the moment,' Becky said. 'I'll check later.'

Peter wasn't sure whether the new marital arrangements had already come into effect—they hadn't officially, but he sensed a whiff of America in the Bluntingham air, accompanied by a stifled giggle. It didn't really bother him from a moral point of view that Becky was engaged in screwing the organist already, but he was put out that she hadn't waited until 1 November. It was sneaky of her not to wait for the agreed starting date of All Saints' Day, in which context, he reminded himself that Beebee was coming on the 3rd for the scrutiny meeting and that a hotel was booked. Of course, he would be perfectly within his rights—in accordance with the agreement—simply to announce his absence on account of amorous activity, but this seemed to him crass. He would tell Becky that he was staying the night in London (which he had never done before) and leave her to draw her own conclusions. At any rate, he wouldn't lie.

Peter's phonetics lecture at 11:00 went well. He had established a good working rapport with the students and even had them practising the various symbols of the IPA in class and diagnosing the sounds.

12 noon was the time when he caught up with emails. He dashed off a quick email to Vicky, inviting her to the Embassy. Since Becky hadn't said she wasn't coming, he assumed she was. He hadn't thought of inviting Beebee along anyway, so he assumed that Vicky would be his extra guest. After all, he had already suggested this to her.

The exams were uppermost in his mind, first and foremost the ULB papers, but also those from Oxford, for which he had already sent back his comments and suggestions in advance of their scrutiny meeting on 6 November. An email from Brown came up on the screen:

Dear Lampton,

I think you'll find that it will be best if you arrive at the Trainor Institution at 1:30 in time for the examiners' meeting at 2:00. These meetings have been known to go on for a long time— sometimes until early evening. I have therefore arranged for you to stay in St Mary's Hall. Ms Green, the Faculty Administrator, is dealing with the practicalities. You may wish to contact her in advance (details below). Marion and I would be pleased if you would join us for dinner after the examiners' meeting at 7 Portal Court. A pupil of mine, Miss Crashaw, will also be there.

I haven't yet had a chance to look at your reactions to the papers but should like to thank you in anticipation of your comments.

Yours sincerely,

D. Brown

Peter was taken aback. He hadn't been expecting to stay in Oxford. It would have been a simple matter for him to drive back home after the meeting. Why this apparent friendliness on the part of Brown? Why did he extend an invitation to meet his wife and his 'pupil' for dinner? Why did he refer to Miss Crashaw as his pupil and not his research student? Would they have anything in common at the dinner? He had never met Marion, he wasn't interested in the development of the European 'fairy tale' in relationship to romance, a topic with which Brown had burdened the unfortunate Miss Crashaw. What would he be expected to call any of them? He supposed he would revert to first names with Brown, but Mrs Brown and Miss Crashaw? The latter would no doubt be easy with first names. He would play it by ear.

When he got home, he found Becky in joyous mood. She had now had the chance to enjoy her lover's company in the family home with a clear conscience, although Peter begrudged her this on account of her lack of self-restraint in not waiting until 1 November. Although he himself was pleased with the progress made towards marital harmony, albeit not via the usual routes, his mood had been darkened by the events of the day.

'Did you have a good day, then?' Peter said.

Why did he say *then* and not address her by name? It would have sounded odd to use Becky at home—far too formal, he thought, even in this hypocoristic form of her name. One used real names in the company of others but not in the intimacy of the home. She had objected to Becks when he last used it; he wasn't going to tempt fate by repeating it. Gone were the days when he would have called her *rabbit*—the affectionate nickname that they used for each other—*bunny* seemed too crass then. *Dear* and *darling* were too intimate and hypocritical, *love* too common. He didn't explore further, so it was *then* for now.

218

'Yes, it was OK. I got quite a lot done,' Becky replied. 'Bridget and I checked the flowers and sprayed them. I went to Waitrose and bought some stuff for the week. They had an offer on wine—seven bottles for the price of six. Seeing you take ours all over the place, I thought it was worth restocking. There was a nice Rioja.'

'Good, I like that. Was that all you did? Did you look out my white dress shirt?'

'You'll have to wear an ordinary one; your dress shirt needs ironing.'

'Couldn't you possibly see your way clear to ironing it for me?'

'Can't you do it yourself?'

'I haven't got much time between now and Wednesday … OK, I'll wear a plain one. What are you going to wear?'

'What for?'

No, Peter, not now!

'For the reception on Wednesday. Will you be wearing your black cocktail dress?'

'I never said I was coming.'

'Aren't you?'

'Probably not. You can take Beebee or Vicky.'

'I'm allowed two guests.'

'Well, take them both.'

Bloody women! Peter thought. *Don't they just love to make things complicated?*

'Does Robert have any kids?'

'How should I know?'

'I thought you were intimately acquainted.'

'He hasn't told me.'

'I shall be away for the night on 3 and 6 November—just to let you know.'

'OK.'

Don't you want to know why and where? Peter thought she would want to know. Should he tell her? He was beginning to

wish the pre-concordat rules of suspicion and hostility oper-
ated again.

'Exams business,' he said.

'Great.'

Was that irony? Becky had been known to do irony. On balance, he thought it was indifference.

Damn her!

Wednesday, 22 October

When Wednesday came, Peter got dressed in his normal suit and packed his evening wear in a small suitcase. Upon entering his room, he hung his evening clothes up on a hanger on a coat peg beside the door.

When Johanna came in, she made a facetious comment about the evening's proceedings, which he ignored. She was known to make little digs in an attempt to get her own back for perceived slights. Peter's firmness on Monday was one such slight.

He decided to check with Vicky that all was OK:

Dear FRP,

Just checking that all is well for tonight. Shall we meet in the Department at 5:00? Does the cocktail dress still fit? Only joking, the bump can't have started to show, can it?

As expected, Becky isn't coming, so you can act as if you were my wife, but we mustn't say anything to anyone. Think of how you'd like me to introduce you. A colleague?

Looking forward to tonight.

Love,

BB x

PS. I'll get us a Danish in case you're hungry.

Vicky arrived on time, and they had a nibble of their Danishes together in Peter's room.

220

'I think I'll keep the rest for the train,' Peter said. 'Pity we can't go back together. Have you thought any more about "conjugal visits"? We'd need to get those in while Robert's living with us. I don't know how Becky will react after he's left—if he ever does. I don't know what the kids will make of him either. They really seem to like him. I think they prefer him to me. Not surprising really. He's quite hands on.'

'I'm going to ask my gynaecologist about sex while I'm pregnant,' Vicky said. 'If she says yes, we'll arrange some sleep overs. Are you sure Becky won't mind?'

'It's not up to her to mind. I'm allowing her bloody lover to live in our house. The only place I draw the line is screwing in the marital bed. There's a small double in Robert's room, so I suppose they'll use that.'

'Well, I've only got one bed, and you already know that.'

'Yes, I love the view, not that we got to see much when we did the deed.'

They set off for Belgrave Square in a taxi. Peter thought he could afford the luxury on the day on which he would receive his highest honour to date with the mother of his yet-to-be-born Petra or Victor, or maybe both. He held hands with Vicky in the taxi, something he had not done with a female for at least ten years. *Is she the one for you, Peter?* Suave, urbane, sexy, intelligent, but loving?

They got out at the Embassy, and Peter announced their arrival. They were shown into the room where the ceremony would take place. There were already a few well-dressed types, none of whom Peter recognized. Some of the men were already sporting distinctions. Peter wondered about the protocol of that, but they weren't at Buckingham Palace; in this respect, the Germans were much less formal, he supposed. The guests began to mingle, and the honorands were introduced to some of the VIPs by von Streibnitz.

'May I introduce the Minister for Education,' he said obsequiously.

'Professor Lampton is to receive the Cross of Merit, Third Class for his contribution to European linguistic integration and especially for his pioneering work on glottalization.'

Peter shook hands and began a conversation. He drew Vicky into the small group.

'May I introduce my colleague, Ms Victoria Atherton? We sit on a Research Restructuring Exercise panel together.'

Vicky smiled and shook hands.

'Vicky is an expert in corporate restructuring,' Peter said.

The minister tried not to look bored. Peter supposed that he had been given practical instruction in the matter. Von Streibnitz, with his air of supercilious German urbanity, was best suited in this regard. It was something the Germans excelled at, Peter thought. That *von* before the name said it all. A man with a *von* always lived up to his name, unlike a newly knighted political appointee in Britain or a Baron Gannex, elevated to the peerage by a Prime Minister who shared in the opprobrium of the recipient when he fell from grace. Peter disapproved of political honours but approved of academic ones. His highest academic aspiration was to parade in a procession of higher doctorate holders behind the Chancellor of the University of Cambridge on Honorary Degree Day, not that it was called anything so vulgar, but instead a Congregation of the Regent House for the conferment of Honorary Degrees. Peter could never aspire to a degree *honoris causa*, he supposed, but a Doctorate of Letters on the basis of his published work was something which he might yet attain. He could then strut in a scarlet gown, though, of course, he would never strut, merely follow demurely along with the others, knowing his place.

'Tell me a little about glottal stops, then,' the minister said.

'Where should I begin?' Peter said. 'My real interest is in their increasing use by politicians beginning in the later Twentieth Century. There have been not a few culprits, even at the very top.'

'Yes,' the minister said. 'My Sir Humphrey was complaining about this recently and was urging me to set an example in the

Department. I feel we could really use someone like you to lead the way. Would you be interested in chairing a quango? It might lead to public recognition and higher honours if you come to the appropriate conclusions.'

'Well, I'd never really seen myself as a public figure,' Peter said, 'but I have a strong sense of duty and honesty.'

'Duty's all-important,' the minister said.

'Yes,' Peter replied. 'I'll certainly think about it. How can I contact you?'

'We'll contact you next week,' the minister said. 'Thank you very much, Peter, I'm very glad we've met.'

'Thank you, minister,' Peter said.

'Do call me Michael.'

'Thank you, Michael.'

'Very good to meet you, Mrs Lampton,' the minister said.

Vicky smiled but did not correct him.

Von Streibnitz called the assembled company to order and introduced the Ambassador.

Peter listened to the tedious speeches and the brief citations for the honorands. He was glad he didn't have the responsibility of thinking them up. When his medal was pinned on his lapel, he felt a sense of pride. His career could only go upwards from now on. Did Becky want to accompany him on the ascent? She wasn't keen, he thought. Should he encourage her? Vicky, on the other hand, would make the perfect consort— intelligent and urbane, and good in bed. Could he combine the two officially?

Thursday, 23 October

On Thursday, Jim felt up to resuming his lecture series on FIOB. The title had been changed, but the rumour had circulated among the students that Jim had been unable to give his lecture last week owing to a stress-related illness following the complaint. Philip, after kindly stepping in the previous week, had informed last week's attendees that Dr Lubbins would resume his lectures on Old Bavarian Dialects (formerly Fucking in Old Bavarian). Word had spread amongst the students that these were very near the knuckle and not to be missed. Jim consequently encountered a large group of about fifty students, waiting outside the door of the Raised Faculty Building, holding a banner on two poles to form a triumphal arch for him, with the legend, 'Long live Lubbins!', which they chanted as Jim approached.

'Yeah,' Jim said. 'You thought old Jim wasn't coming back, did you? How many are coming to Fucking in Old Bavarian?' All the students put their hands up. Jim smiled. 'We shall need a bigger room, then.'

A student volunteered to go to the Faculty Administrator, who grudgingly moved Jim into a lecture room with a seating capacity of 80. The students formed a procession, with the banner leading. The persistent chant 'Long live Lubbins' could be heard in the neighbouring faculties, to the consternation of some of the crustier dons. Jim smiled and found his place at the lectern, as the students took their seats.

'In the immortal words of Dr James Lubbins,' he began, 'the Old Bavarians liked to fuck a lot.' A loud cheer ripped through the lecture hall.

Jim's lecture was a triumph that was reported in the student newspaper *Varsity*, with the result that the audience doubled for the next week and an even larger room had to be found. At the end of the lecture, Jim concluded, 'In the immortal words of J. W. von Goethe, trans. Lubbins, "There's nothing so good for a pretty young chick as a shiny gold bar and a glistening prick." Yeah, that will show the stuck-up pricks in the faculty.'

Jim assumed that he would receive rave notices in his student assessments at the end of the term. There was no way the stuck-up pricks could make a case for dismissal, he thought.

224

8.   WEEK 6

Wednesday, 29 October

One week to the day since Peter had the conversation with the minister, he received a letter on official notepaper:

Rt Hon Michael Worsfield CBE MP

Minister of State

Dear Peter,

Following our most successful conversation last week at the German Embassy, I have taken soundings with the Secretary of State and the PM and have received the green light to appoint you as Chairman of the Commission for the Regulation of Spoken English. You will report to the Secretary of State.

In the event that you are willing to take up this duty, you will have free rein to choose the members of your Commission and will be eligible for office space in Westminster and full secretarial support. We anticipate that your Commission should be able to submit a report by 1 December next year, before the New Year Honours List is published.

The Secretary of State and I would welcome the opportunity to work closely with you in regulating the excrescences that have of late crept into the pronunciation of Her Majesty's English.

Yours ever,

Michael

Peter's first thought was to contact Vicky. She was as it were his partner in crime; after all, the minister had mistakenly called her Mrs Lampton. Peter scanned the letter in and sent it as an attachment to Vicky:

Dear Vicky,

I feel I should address you properly now in the light of recent developments. Please read the attached and tell me if you would like to be a member of the Lampton Commission.

This may necessarily curtail my work with the RRE, although I will make every effort to attend the final meeting.

With best wishes,

Peter

Professor P J Lampton
Chair elect, Commission for the Regulation of Spoken English

Saturday, 1 November
On Saturday, the Lampton boys were full of expectation. They were unaware that it was All Saints' Day—they had not enjoyed the religious upbringing of Peter's youth, which, while leaving him with a sense of probity and honesty in his adult life, had also contributed to doubts, superstitions, and insecurities, but above all, a guilty conscience. For the meantime, however, his conscience was clear. Both he and Becky were adulterers, but to commit adultery with the full knowledge and consent of one's spouse was certainly not adultery in the spirit of the Act, merely a technicality. Peter was a pragmatic person. He would need to be when he chaired the Lampton Commission on Spoken English. Its initials had already led him to refer to it by the pet name Elsie.

He dashed off a quick email to Vicky at 7:00:

Dear FRP,

I think we can permit ourselves the liberty of using our special names for private correspondence. As you can see, I have set up a Gmail account, which I intend henceforth to use for all personal correspondence. I shall use my university account only for business now. I don't want to confuse the two now that I have a public persona as the Chairman of a Government-sponsored Commission. I hope you like the name I've given it—Elsie. It's an evocative name with a homely feel to it. Do you remember Elsie Tanner? No, I expect you're too young. She wasn't one of my favourites, but I think she had a heart of gold beneath the brash northern exterior. But I digress.

Robert is due to move in chez Lampton today, which fills me with some disquiet. Of course, he will have to show greater respect towards PJL and not call me 'Lemon Juice' to Becky now that I'm chair of an important Commission. Nevertheless, I don't want to be around when he moves in, and I'm certainly not going to help carry in his boxes from the car. He has bought himself a Vauxhall Astra. I can't think of anything more middle-class and boring. Of course, he's not a brash American who'd drive a Chevy Camaro or a Ford Mustang, but I think an Astra hardly suits the bow-ties and Harvard spectacles.

Anyway, I was hoping I might pop over and see you today. I think it would be a good opportunity to discuss future plans. Would you mind if I left a few things at Water Street? Even though Becky is fully aware of our relationship, I'd rather not run the risk of Robert discovering my nutty boxers or any of the things I bought at AS a couple of weeks ago, not that I expect we shall get much use for them until you have found out more about your 'condition'. If you agree, I'll be over at about 10:00. Robert is supposed to be moving in around 12:00. Ben and Richard can carry his boxes!

227

Have you decided whether you will be a member of Elsie yet? It will help to have your business input—amongst other things.

See you later, I hope,

PJL (BB) xx

A positive reply from Vicky at 8:30 put Peter in a good mood. At breakfast, he mentioned to Becky that he would be away and that he hoped she and the boys would cope with Robert's move.

'Where are you going?' Becky asked.

'To Cambridge,' Peter replied.

'To Vicky's?'

'Yes, we're going to be discussing the Commission. She's agreed to be a member,' Peter said.

'Oh, that's what they call it now, is it?'

'You can call it what you like. You might like to come up with some suitably American name for it now that Robert will be a permanent fixture.'

'He's only temporary.'

'Whatever.'

No, Peter. First, you don't adopt sloppy speech habits, unbecoming a quango chair, just because you think you can now cavort freely with your lady friend. Second, you need to show respect towards Becky in case the thing with Vicky doesn't work out. You don't want to be left high and dry. Think about it, Peter. — Yes, you're right. I was getting above myself.

Before setting off for Water Street, Peter checked his emails once again. There ought to be a name for this, Peter—Obsessive Email Syndrome? It's a recognized psychological fact. Should your Commission investigate it? — No, I don't think so, everyone does it. — Probably not, Peter, only a certain type of person. You're obviously one of those, Peter. — What type? — That's for you to decide, Peter.

228

Oh, no! One from Beebee. I'd been shutting that problem out. — Face up to it, Peter. — Can you really cope with two mistresses and a baby, not to mention a wife and a quango?

Hi Peter,

Where have you been? I haven't heard from you for ages. Have you forgotten about little Beebee? The cabriolet's ready and waiting anytime you are. How about tomorrow?

Anyway, we must make arrangements for our post-scrutiny get-together. I've booked the Premier Inn. I don't know if they serve gingerbread officially. I think we have to make our own arrangements.

I've sent in my comments to Johanna. I hope you all got them.

Let me know about tomorrow.

Love,

Beebee x

Peter replied immediately:

Dear Beebee,

It's lovely to hear from you. Life has been a little hectic recently—domestic arrangements, etc. Becky's organist friend will be staying for a few weeks until he finds a new place to live. I've seen quite a lot of Vicky recently. In fact, I really ought to explain. She and I have come to an agreement—to our mutual advantage. I'd rather not put it in writing but will explain when I see you. It needn't affect our relationship. As you know, I can't offer an exclusive relationship anyway. I don't quite know where I stand with Becky. Things are not really looking good, but I can't afford to burn bridges, and I've also got the 'kids' to think about. Added to that, I've been appointed to chair a quango. You might be interested in serving on it. We can discuss when we meet.

See you on Monday—sorry, but tomorrow's too busy.

Love,

Peter x

9. WEEK 7

Monday, 3 November

Peter's day in Cambridge with Vicky had been enjoyable. There had been plenty of opportunity for affection, kissing, caressing, in fact everything except intercourse. Yes, Peter, we mean fucking, although you pedantically maintain that *intercourse* is a perfectly innocuous word with no outright sexual connotations; we were just trying to be polite, as befits a man in your exalted position.

Vicky was able to give a demonstration of the ten-function Bullet Vibrator, but, for understandable reasons, the ten-function Rabbit Love Ring was not brought into play. Pregnancy was a difficult time, not only for the woman, Peter thought. No, he wasn't just being selfish, he recognized his duties and responsibilities, but now, at the beginning of a new week, he had to concentrate on the Department of Other Languages at ULB. Today, however, he was not in charge. That responsibility was devolved to Alan. Even though Alan had only published a handful of articles and was not working on a groundbreaking book on glottal stops that had led to international prominence among scholars and national importance in the highest Government circles, today Peter would have to defer to him and, if necessary, call him Mr Chairman, though these niceties were being dispensed with in the more intimate context of the departmental exams board.

Johanna had succeeded in ordering the coffee and biscuits for 10:00. She even managed to take minutes of decisions, keep careful track of corrections, amendments, and reformulations of questions, discreetly backed up by Dr Compton, who in addition to being the departmental expert on commas and apostrophes, made notes on the proceedings, as Secretary of the exams board, and verified the often-inadequate minutes of the Departmental Secretary. The day went without a hitch. There was an hour's break for a sandwich lunch, provided at departmental expense, and a further break for refreshments in the afternoon, so that the day's business concluded at 4:00, and colleagues were free to leave the Department or continue with their own work while Johanna assembled the corrections and began grudgingly, at the behest of the Chairman, to modify her files of the revised papers while the corrections were still fresh in her mind.

Peter felt it incumbent on him to check with Alan that everything was in order. He also looked in on a bothered Johanna, for whom this was one of the most stressful days in the academic year. Satisfied that all was in order, he left the Department with Beebee, doing his best to make their intercourse— no, not fucking—look as collegial as possible. He politely opened doors for her and stood to one side to let her pass. He made a pretence of saying goodbye to her when they left the building and turned into the busy City street, allowing her to walk some fifty metres from him before he set off in the same direction. He was embarrassed at this subterfuge, but he felt the ends justified the means. So what if people suspected something? There was no reason why their suspicions should be confirmed. As soon as Beebee had turned the corner and was out of sight of the ULB building, Peter sped up and caught up with her.

Once they had reached the Premier Inn, they felt able to relax and calmly proceed to their room. Peter explained about the LCSE, and Beebee showed interest.

'I suppose it will be like the RRE all over again,' she said.

'I expect there will be similarities,' Peter said, 'but I intend to chair it very differently from Niamh, and we shan't have Derek looking over our shoulders.'

'Don't you think it would be rather fun to invite him to sit on it?' Beebee asked.

'Not really,' Peter said, 'but it would be a way of righting past wrongs, should these occur. I think on balance, though, I'd rather not have him.'

'Who have you invited so far?'

'Whom.'

'All right, whom?'

'Just Vicky and you. Do you two get on well together?'

'Yes, we can sing from the same hymn-sheet,' Beebee said, tongue in cheek.

'Is that *Ancient and Modern*, by any chance?'

'You've lost me there.'

'You've heard of the hymn-book, no doubt, but I want the Commission to take a similar approach to the English language—preserve the old while accepting the new, provided that the Commission sees value in each.'

'Talking of hymn-books, did you read that novel I gave you?'

'No, I haven't had time yet. I'm keeping it for holiday reading. Getting back to Vicky, you remember I told you we had an arrangement. You can keep a secret, can't you?'

'I've always managed to so far.'

'Well, Vicky asked me to impregnate her, but she doesn't want anyone to know.'

'Is that a big deal?'

'It is for her. Isn't it for you? I didn't want to upset you.'

'No, of course not, the more the merrier. Only joking, but I'm prepared to share.'

'Phew! That's a relief! Becky is also proving amenable—so far, at least. You know she's moved her lover in, pro tem.'

'No, I didn't. That's very magnanimous of you.'

'Yes, or foolish. I don't know whether I still love Becky. She's grown cold over the years, and I've sought refuge in my work. I've got a lot to thank her for—for which, sorry—but the spark went long ago.'

'I think it happens to everyone. At least you're not divorced and lonely like me. What do you think it's like going home to an empty flat every day, with nothing for comfort but a fuck in the woods or a grope in a cupboard?'

'We must make the best of what we have, I suppose. Sometimes, I wonder whether marriage is suited to modern life. My view is that morality needs periodically re-evaluating—without the input of religious people. They seem intent on spoiling everyone's fun, though that's not the case with our local vicar. She's a bit of a goer, I believe, but we hardly ever see beneath the surface—or into the inner depths of the woods.'

'Shall we look for our gingerbread house?' Beebee asked.

'Why not?' Peter said.

After they had explored the possibilities that a bed in a Premier Inn afforded them, Peter began to have pangs of conscience, not at all on Becky's account, but because of his special affinity with Vicky and their unborn child. He tried to justify his infidelity to her, using the same arguments as before, namely that Beebee was sad and lonely. The concept of concupiscence never entered his consciousness. The pangs subsided with rapidity when Beebee said how much she had enjoyed it, how much good he had done her, and how charitable his actions were, but above all when she suggested they go out for dinner and make an evening of it together. They had a bistro meal and enjoyed a concert at the Barbican.

In the morning, Peter said goodbye to Beebee after breakfast. They kissed and agreed to maintain their relationship on an occasional basis. Either could call the other when the need arose to enact a scene from Hänsel und Gretel. Peter insisted on the umlaut.

Buoyed by the recent successes, Peter went in early to the Department the following morning and supervised the finalizing of the exam papers by Johanna.

'Please make sure that you put the right papers into the envelopes this time, Johanna,' he said.

'Of course,' she said.

Peter trusted that this request would have succeeded in ensuring compliance.

Thursday, 6 November

On Thursday, Peter drove to Oxford and parked at St Mary's Hall, where a space had been reserved for him. He found his room and unpacked his things before walking to the Trainor Institution. He had underestimated the amount of time it would take to get there and arrived at 1:38. He found Brown's office and knocked on the door.

'Good afternoon, Lampton,' Brown said. 'I had wanted to go through some of your suggestions for revisions, but now you've arrived rather late, we shan't have a chance. I think you'll find that some of your reformulations are inappropriate and that you don't understand the way our system in Oxford works.'

'I'm very sorry, Derek,' Peter said, 'but I was drafted in at the last moment without adequate explanation of your system, which apparently differs from every other university in the country, or am I mistaken?'

'I expect you will learn as we go along, but I would recommend that you withdraw all the suggestions of substance unless I mention them and that you concentrate on punctuation.'

Peter felt it was not worth arguing the point with Brown.

'It will be a much shorter meeting in that case, if the External's comments aren't taken into account,' he said. 'I hope to explain the circumstances in my report, that is, if I am still acting in the summer. I believe Jim is now back in harness—news of his successful lecture series in Cambridge has recently reached me, and in any case, I'm unlikely to be able to spend much time on examining. I don't know if you've heard, but I've been appointed to chair a Government Commission on the Regulation of Spoken English.'

'Congratulations, Peter. That's splendid news,' Brown said, clasping him behind the back with one hand in an awkward gesture of friendship. 'Let me know if there's any way in which I can be of service. We can talk further over dinner.'

'Thank you, Derek. It's early days yet. I've only just started recruiting people. I need to balance seniority with scholarly acuity. The criteria are very tough. I was very surprised that my work was singled out. Maybe the preliminary findings of our RRE panel have been leaked. What do you think?'

'I couldn't possibly comment, but we are very fortunate to have you on board here in Oxford.'

'Yes, I suppose you are, but the Commission will be strictly impartial, rather like your approach on the RRE. Anyway, I'm glad I shan't have to get involved in the complexities of formulation of your exam questions.'

'Feel free to say whatever occurs to you.'

Peter smiled. They went into the meeting.

Upon conclusion of the business, in which Peter had been restrained with his comments, restricting them largely to Oxford commas, quotation marks, italics, missing apostrophes, and prepositions at the end of sentences, Derek looked pleased and thanked him publicly for his valuable contribution. It was agreed that Peter should go back to St Mary's Hall and freshen up before dinner in Portal Court at 7:30. Peter assured Derek that he would not be late this time, which met with a surprisingly accommodating response.

'I think you'll find that Marion has been well trained to cope with such domestic situations, Peter. A few minutes either way won't be a problem. I've got in a few bottles of Château de la Tour Verte, which I think you'll find to your taste. You won't be driving back tonight.'

'Looking forward to it Derek, especially to meeting your wife and Miss Crashaw.'

Peter went back to his room, freshened up, and changed into what he felt were more appropriate clothes. He availed himself of the computing facilities in his room to check his emails. Amongst these was the University of Cambridge Job Opportunities Weekly Email, to which he subscribed. He frequently cast his eye over the jobs, one of which caught his eye: Master of Needham College. He clicked on the link and read:

Needham College has begun the search for its next Master in succession to Professor Dame Annemarie Kuhnstoff. A committee of fellows, under the chairmanship of Dr Philip Hitchinson, has instructed Rational Restructuring of Cambridge to spearhead the process of finding suitably qualified candidates who have achieved distinction in their professional field. For further information and person specification, please follow the link below.

Despite his initial reaction of distaste at the vulgarity of the commercialized process and the awful term *person specification*, Peter made a mental note. He had indeed, he thought, achieved distinction in his professional field. Moreover, he had recently met Hitchinson. It might be worth making further enquiries. Was it just coincidence that it was Vicky's firm that they had employed as part of the process? He supposed so. It was strange that Vicky hadn't mentioned it, but it was a sizeable firm, and she was probably not involved. Nevertheless, she would be able to keep him informed of the field and report on progress.

Peter's mind drifted away to his installation as Master of Needham—'Black Rod' (he assumed there was such a College functionary) knocking on the sturdy oak door of the College, while he waited outside in his scarlet gown and squared hood, his doctor's bonnet positioned demurely on his head, the gold tassel hanging to the left, only for the door to be shut in his face, to be opened again when his credentials were presented to the assembled begowned fellowship inside. The applause, the adulation, the—dare he say—adoration of the new Master was almost overwhelming. Peter's work on the glottal stop, his chairmanship of the Lampton Commission on the Regulation of Spoken English, all these had at long last been appropriately recognized. Peter was now a Head of House. Henceforth he would be at the forefront of University processions. Could he possibly go any higher? The chant of the students lining the way of the procession to the College chapel rang out in his ears 'Long live Lampton, Long live Lampton.'

It was only when Peter had taken up his stall in the chapel—no, not that kind of stall, Peter—that the chanting died down, the organ began, and the process of his installation stopped abruptly, for Peter came out of his daydream and set off for Portal Court. He timed it exactly, having checked the distance on Google Maps. At precisely 7:35, Peter rang the doorbell. A beaming Derek greeted him.

'Come in, my dear fellow,' he said. 'Come and meet Marion and Miss Crashaw.'

Peter stepped cautiously into the booklined hallway and went into the sitting room, which resembled a library. A few of the books even had classmarks on their spines, which reminded Peter of the jape in Ayr. Was that *Comparative Phonology of Sonorants*? Peter wondered.

'Come here, Marion,' Derek called out to the kitchen. An unassuming woman emerged, flustered, and smiled as she entered the room. 'Meet Professor Lampton, Marion.'

'Peter, please,' Peter said to her.

They shook hands.

'Professor Lampton chairs the Commission on the Regulation of Spoken English,' Derek continued. 'Would you bring him a sherry and fetch the peanuts, Marion.'

Marion smiled hesitantly, Peter looked embarrassed, Miss Crashaw, who hadn't yet been introduced, looked on timidly from further away. Marion returned with the drink and the peanuts.

'All right, put them down there, Marion,' Brown said. 'I think you need to get back to your kitchen now while I introduce Miss Crashaw.'

Peter shook hands with Brown's pupil.

'Please call me Peter,' he said.

'I'm Jenny,' Miss Crashaw said.

Peter wondered how long he would have to endure the awkwardness of dinner at the 'Brown house'. He smiled as he remembered Jim's 'How now, Brown cow?' and the unamused response that that evoked. The conversation became a little more animated after the first bottle of Château de la Tour Verte. The question of academic jobs in relation to Miss Crashaw came up. Peter asked her where she looked for jobs. She replied that she consulted the online bulletin boards but also looked in the newspapers in the common room. Brown laughed.

'Have you seen that Needham are advertising for a new Master? They're using one of those dreadful recruitment agencies, in fact, the firm that Ms Atherton works for—she's someone who sits on the RRE panel with us, he explained to the ladies. I can't imagine that they'll get a suitable candidate this way. All that seems to interest colleges nowadays is commercial and media experience, oh, and a bit of government influence for good measure—anything but academic excellence. I don't suppose I'll be applying.' Peter smiled as if to agree with Brown's pessimism and resolved that *he* would apply.

'Thank you for a lovely evening, Marion,' Peter said after the dinner, mustering as much sincerity as possible. 'Thank you, Derek, most enjoyable. It was good meeting you, Jenny. Good luck with the job search. If I can help in any way, please feel free to get in touch. Just Google me.'

Peter hurried back to St Mary's Hall through the Oxford streets. The cold of the evening was alleviated somewhat by the inner warmth provided by the wine, which, however, caused Peter's path back to his accommodation to be a little erratic. He went up to his room and wrote an email to Vicky:

239

Dear FRP,

You will notice that I'm using my Gmail account. Please ensure you reply to this and not my ULB one.

I've just experienced the most boring dinner of my life chez Brown. For some reason, he decided to entertain me to dinner at his house rather than in college. Poor Marion, his wife, she seems to be treated more like a housemaid—something from Upstairs Downstairs, but I suppose that fits in perfectly with his general approach to life. I also met his research student, Jenny, whom he calls Miss Crashaw. I pity both of them.

Ironically, he's been very friendly towards me since I have been appointed chair of the LCSE. I think he's trying to get appointed to the Commission himself, but I shan't give him that satisfaction. I'm keeping him in suspense.

He mentioned the Mastership of Needham. Apparently, RARE are involved with the search process. I'm surprised you didn't tell me. I hope you can find out more, as I'm thinking of applying.

Are you getting any comfort from the old ten-function thingummy? It's very lonely in my room here. They don't have a porn channel in St Mary's Hall, not that I ever watch one of those!

Looking forward to seeing you at the weekend.

Hope all is well with the little one.

Peter x

Vicky sent him a reply later that evening:

Dear BB,

I'm sorry to hear you're lonely. I'd love to cheer you up.

Yes, I only heard yesterday about the Needham retainer. I'm not directly involved, but I know the man who's leading this. I'll have a word with him.

I'm off to bed soon. I think I can feel stirrings already. Anyway, I may pay a visit to No. 10 before going to sleep, thinking and dreaming of you, of course.

Love,

FRP

PS. I haven't worn them for a long time!

Peter went to bed, happy that his visit to Oxford had been a success. He lay in bed, thinking of how he was going to apply for the job at Needham. Dare he call it a job? That rather depended on who was appointed, or as colleges quaintly say, elected, though he had to acknowledge that there was an election process, which could no doubt be fixed. It worried him that the fixing process might equally include blackballing, not just the promotion of a favoured candidate. With this in mind, he set about planning his strategy. Would Derek prove to be an ally rather than an adversary if he were to be appointed to the LCSE? He might, under the right circumstances, be one of Peter's referees.

Friday, 7 November

Early on the following day, Peter drove into London. He very rarely took this step. Seeing that there was very limited parking at ULB, he had arranged for a reserved space, available only to senior staff on special occasions. He parked his car and walked leisurely to the Department, savouring the freedom and sense of importance that a journey to work by car afforded him. The awful battle with taxis, buses, bus lanes, traffic lights, congestion charges, and possibly other things, which presently did not occur to him, seemed to pale into insignificance with the freedom of having his own car in which later to leave at any time he wished and not be dependent on connections and timetables. Thus, Peter was a happy man, and the happiness was one that a Derek or a Jim could not possibly experience, situated as they were so close to work that they could be there in under twenty minutes.

Peter went along to Johanna's office and enquired whether she had sent the corrected exam papers off to the Exams Registry.

'Do you take me for an idiot?' Johanna said.

Peter decided that, rather than answering this in the affirmative, he would trust Johanna not to have cocked things up this time. He kept his disparaging assessment of her competence to himself.

Saturday, 8 November

On Saturday, Peter got up early and set about writing his application to Needham. He first revised his CV; at the top were his degrees and letters: *Peter John Lampton, MA, PhD (Cantab.), FIRSE.*

He was glad that he had progressed to Fellowship of the Institution for the Regulation of Spoken English and was no longer AIRSE, which often got mistaken when people read his qualifications hastily.

Next, he listed Verdienstkreuz dritter Klasse der Bundesrepublik Deutschland, together with a translation. Below that, he added his Chairmanship of the LCSE, above his next greatest achievement to date, namely membership of Subpanel Z of the RRE.

Satisfied that he had listed everything of importance, he revised his List of Publications, giving special prominence to his magnum opus that had formed a major part of the ULB submission to the RRE: Peter John Lampton, *Glottal Stops in Twentieth-Century English Political Discourse: A Phonetic Perspective* (350 pp. + 400 pp. transcriptions). This he marked AT PRESS, which, while not strictly true, certainly made a better impression than 'in progress' or 'forthcoming'. Underneath the book, were listed six articles, including 'The Glottalization of Sonor-ants in Thirteenth-century Romance and Germanic' (revised edition of the original, unpublished article, 1978, 33 pp.), being prepared for submission to the *Zeitschrift für vergleichende Phonol-ogie*.

He listed minor distinctions, a long-service award from ULB, a handful of reviews, and trusted that his application might, God willing, find favour with the appointments com-mittee.

10. WEEK 8

Monday, 10 November

Jim continued to make a good recovery, buoyed by the tremendous reception of his lectures, the second of which had attracted well over 100 students, so that there was standing room only. At the end of the lecture, the familiar chant of 'Long Live Lubbins!' continued for a good five minutes. The local TV stations had sent a film crew, and Jim had become a regional sensation after he had appeared on BBC Look East and ITV's News Anglia.

Jim had been persuaded by Sarah to take things easy, especially in view of the excitement caused by his lectures. Sarah and he had grown closer together in under a month, and Jim was already envisioning a settled family life with a wife and kids. Sarah stayed overnight in Jim's Pad and helped to make it more homely, adding the caring female touch to the furnishings and ornaments. She removed some of Jim's 'artworks' reflecting his former 'conquests'—mainly photos of himself in the company of one or more young ladies—and replaced them with more appropriate pictures of calming scenes of the countryside and family life from his and her past. In short, Jim's Pad was being transformed into a home fit for Mr and Mrs Lubbins, although Sarah had set her sights on a bungalow in one of the Cambridgeshire villages, preferably Caldecote, should their romance ever blossom into a full-blown love affair, however restrained it would have to be in view of Jim's heart.

While Jim had been in hospital, he had, of course, kept in touch with Isabelle, who had given him much support and let him down very gradually by pointing out how desirable a union with a more mature woman was, while not making comparisons. They could still be friends and colleagues and work happily on projects together, but Isabelle could give no guarantees that she would stay in Cambridge, even if she were successful in gaining the research fellowship that she coveted. Isabelle maintained links with Paddy, too, and received regular tips from him. The IPO tips that she had passed on to Philip had doubled the investment made by the shrewd bursar at Needham, so that at least one research fellowship was a distinct possibility. The College Council had, however, baulked at the idea of a restricted fellowship. There was talk of a second research fellowship, which this time could be restricted to Arts or Science, to a specific discipline even, but not so narrowly as to ensure that Isabelle got it without any competition. The only way this might happen would be if someone were to endow a named fellowship, and that was unlikely to happen. This formed part of Isabelle's discussions with Jim and why he would be better settling down than entering into an uncertain relationship with her.

'Yeah, well,' Jim said. 'I'm going to ask Sarah to marry me, anyway, but I'll also see you're all right. Jim's set to become a millionaire, all thanks to Bisscoin. Jim got Paddy to buy $10,000 worth, and it's doubling each week. I reckon there'll soon be enough to endow the James Lubbins Research Fellowship in Old Bavarian Dialectology. If no suitable candidates present themselves, it can be broadened to include young ladies of any Arts subject who would otherwise not be able to gain an academic post or finish their research project. That'll be one in the eye for the stuck-up pricks.'

'You'll never get away with it, Jim,' she said, 'but thanks.'

'Yeah, well, if you don't fit into the first category, you'll fit into the second.'

Peter was putting the finishing touches to his application to Needham in between teaching and supervising departmental business. He decided to wait until the weekend before finalizing it at home. He would discuss it with Vicky before sending it off. Before leaving the Department, he got Johanna to show him the envelopes with the exam papers, intending to ensure that the right ones went off to the Registry.

'Would you mind showing me the papers before you take them to the Registry, Johanna. At the very least, I want to cast an eye over them and count them,' he said.

'You can't,' Johanna said. 'The envelopes are sealed.'

Saturday, 8 November

Owing to the new domestic arrangements, Peter and Becky had not managed to get much time together to discuss events and plans for the future. Each of them assumed that things were carrying on as normal, with the exception of Becky's now firmly established liaison with Robert and Peter's freedom to spend as much time at Water Street as he liked, without explanation or a guilty conscience. They both acquiesced in the status quo and were happy to see this continue. The kids thought the arrangement was wonderful. Even if they came in for some ragging at school about their mum's boyfriend, they enjoyed having 'Uncle Robert' to take them to football, a Guy Fawkes Party, or an excursion to London, to play baseball with them in the park, and generally to fulfil the role of older brother, uncle, and young, enthusiastic father all rolled into one. Robert had not made much effort to find alternative accommodation but was applying for permanent jobs, having got wind of his wife's infidelity in the USA.

Peter hadn't yet mentioned to Becky that he was thinking of applying to Needham, so on Saturday, when the kids were out at football practice with 'Uncle Robert'—not that they ever used that old-fashioned, bourgeois appellation—Peter decided to broach the subject of his application to Needham.

'I've seen a job advertised in Cambridge,' he said after the kids had departed with Robert.

'Oh, yes?' Becky replied with her typical lack of enthusiasm for anything to do with Peter's career. She decided against speculating about what the job might be since she wasn't sure whether to tease and possibly insult him by suggesting too lowly a position or to mock him by suggesting one that was too exalted.

'Yes,' Peter said. 'Now that I'm Chair of the LCSE, I'm likely to be taken much more seriously—even by you, I should have hoped.'

'Let me guess,' Becky said, 'Vice Chancellor?'

'No, Master of Needham,' Peter said.

'Well, good luck with that,' Becky said dismissively.

'I think I stand a reasonable chance of getting it,' Peter said.

'Oh, yeah?'

'Screw you! You're not going to hold me back with this one. Anyway, Vicky's firm's handling the recruitment process, and Philip, whom you don't know, is chair of the search committee.'

'Oh, so it will be a put-up job, then, will it?'

'No, of course not, but it's always best to know people under these circumstances. That's where I've gone wrong before.'

'Not the only place,' Becky said unkindly.

'Well, I'm going to apply, anyway, and if I get it, it will mean some changes. We shall have to move into the Lodge.'

'Beaver's or Gatekeeper's?'

'Piss off!'

'Sorry. I don't mean to disappoint you, but what's the likelihood of you getting it?'

'Your.'

'Huh?'

'Quite high, I think.'

'That might create difficulties, I'm pregnant.'

'Oh, no! It can't be mine … Robert?'

'Yeah.'

'Do the kids know?'

'Of course not.'

'Anyone else?'

'Only Bridget.'

'Geraldine?'

'I hope not.'

'When's it due?'

'In about eight months' time, sometime in July.'

'I'm going to be a father again.'

'Sorry, but we'll have to come clean and acknowledge Robert as the father.'

'No, really. Vicky's pregnant. She's not expecting me to leave you, though.'

'Oh, great! Shall we tell the kids when they get back?'

'Piss off!'

Peter was glad that they had both kept their cool despite the barbed comments and insults. A few minutes later, he apologized to Becky, and they went back to their state of armed neutrality. When Robert returned with the kids, Peter took his cue and drove to Water Street. Along the way, he phoned Vicky to check if all was OK for a visit.

'Hi, it's Peter. Are you free for lunch today? I thought we might grab a bite at the Plough and look at my application to Needham beforehand.'

'I'm doing the hoovering,' Vicky said. 'But you can come and help if you like. I'm afraid I don't have a sexy housemaid's costume.'

'Pity, there are other ways.'

'What time will you be here?'

'In about twenty minutes.'

When Peter arrived, Vicky had progressed to dusting and general tidying.

'I've tidied the desk so you can open up your files.'

'Was that the spellchecker?'

'Huh?'

'I thought you meant flies.'

'I expect you to behave. Just imagine if you were the Master of Needham. You would have to be on your best behaviour all the time and very boring, too.'

'I'm boring enough at ULB.'

'Yes, but not with me.'

'If I were the Master, you could be my mistress.'

'Hm. You have a wife.'

'Yes, it's so old-fashioned, so stick-in-the mud, don't you think? Do you remember that famous Sinologist at Caius? What was his name?'

'Surely you remember.'

'It'll come to me. Give me a feather duster, Fifi.'

'I'll switch the computer on. Have you got your file?'

'Yes, will you insert it in the right slot for me, please.'

Peter went through his application with Vicky.

'Do you think it can be improved in any way?'

'I'm sure there are lots of ways, like make up five books that you've written about important subjects.'

'Apart from that.'

'Stress your forward-looking approach to education.'

'Do I have one?'

'Lie!'

'I never lie.'

'Well, think of something.'

They agreed on a personal statement that stressed the importance of innovation beside preserving tradition and the maintenance of the highest linguistic standards.

'Should I enclose a photo?' Peter asked.

'Do you think looks matter?' Vicky said. 'Give me your phone, and I'll take one anyway.'

'I think you deserve a nice lunch now,' Peter said. 'Who's driving?'

'You.'

After lunch, Peter and Vicky sat and chatted about their future. The RRE, relationships, work all came up for discussion. Peter told Vicky about his discussions with Becky this morning and how he was relieved there were no more secrets to be kept hidden.

'How did Becky take the news?'

'She told me first?'

'Huh?'

'That she's pregnant by Robert. That makes three babies for the Department of Other Languages at ULB. Gisela will be first, Becky second, and you last. Maybe we could have a departmental creche.'

'How will Becky cope?'

'With difficulty. It's a geriatric pregnancy—quite unexpected. She thought that she was past child-bearing age and didn't take precautions.'

'It is with me, too.'

'Will you have a hospital birth?'

'Of course, at the Rosie, I expect.'

'I hope I'll be allowed to be present.'

'Yeah, that would be nice.'

'Anyway, I'd better be getting back and get this application in the post.'

'Good luck, Master Lampton.'

'You wait.'

11. NOW IS THE MONTH OF MAYING—ALMOST

Monday, 20 April

The exams term at the University of London Bridge began with two weeks' teaching, during which time the students attended revision classes and tried to catch up on missed, neglected, or botched work. The staff were expected to compensate for the students' failings by holding these supplementary classes, which most duly laid on. Peter disapproved of this system, maintaining that he had taught them all they needed to know the first time round, he had nothing to add, and that it was up to them to decide whether they had understood it. Consequently, he offered himself only for question-and-answer sessions or, if they really wanted it, a brief new topic. If they didn't know what a phoneme was by now, they shouldn't be in his Department.

In Cambridge, the Easter Term would start on the next day. Cambridge had done little to change or modernize since Jim and Peter were undergraduates, so that the traditional pattern of four weeks' teaching, followed by exams in the latter part of the term, leaving the students time to enjoy themselves while in hot years the dons sweated in overheated offices, marking the scripts of those whom they had taught a few weeks ago, having now morphed from benevolent teachers into nit-picking, pedantic, exacting examiners. The timetable at London

Bridge differed from that at Cambridge and at Oxford, where everything took place later, but the principle of examining was the same.

Peter was a sympathetic examiner. He was a pedant, admittedly, but his pedantry was to be regarded in a positive sense. He favoured students who did not end sentences with prepositions. He looked favourably on those who used apostrophes correctly. Good spelling and punctuation were rewarded almost as highly as good content. Peter's acute sense of fairness, however, led to his awarding marks in the tens and twenties for very lacking answers, whereas many of his colleagues would have given 43 or 45. In such cases, Peter gave 28 or less. At the other end of the scale, he would occasionally go higher than 80, having been known even to award 95 for an answer of brilliance. If a candidate emerged on a borderline, he usually bumped him or her up into the higher class, but he gave a II.2 mark where it was due and deprecated the practice of giving everyone a II.1 for fear of the consequences and the way in which the marks might be taken to reflect the quality of the teaching.

Prior to the start of term, namely on 15 April, the restructurers assembled again in Ayr to finalize their decisions. They had less time for personal activities and socializing but had to concentrate on the league tables and paragraphs of justification. Peter was astounded that his book on the glottal stop emerged as the highest-rated research in the linguistic category. Jim's imprecations were further down the list, but neither was deemed in need of restructuring. All the decisions were reviewed and approved by Derek. The results would be published at the end of June, in time for researchers and departments to take necessary action before the long vacation took people into libraries or onto beaches.

Peter would by then, of course, be anticipating fatherhood for the third time. Nevertheless, the excitement with which he anticipated his new child would be tempered by the anxiety surrounding Vicky's geriatric pregnancy, which applied even more to Becky's. He was in a quandary. Hitherto, he had seen his place as being in the home at Bluntingham, acting as if he still had a functioning marriage, playing the part of the expectant father of his wife's new child, being there for Becky and the kids and acting as if all were well. They had a lodger, who remarkably fitted so well into the family circumstances after they had, out of the kindness of their hearts, offered him a roof over his head in his time of need. To an outsider observing the scene in Bluntingham, the picture was one of normality, but as Becky's pregnancy began to show, the rumour mill began churning out stories, which in this case were not far from the truth—Becky had had a longstanding affair with Robert, which was why he, an accomplished musician, had accepted the post of a humble village organist when he might have been in contention for a top job at a cathedral. He was almost immediately identified as the father of Becky's expected baby. The situation became embarrassing for all, not least for the kids. Peter reasoned that, since Robert was the father of Becky's child, Robert ought to take full responsibility rather than acting in a merely subsidiary role. This was reinforced by the fact that Vicky was alone and needed Peter's support. She had welcomed his offer of being there at the birth, but there was a lot of time to go before that, and she needed more than occasional support. Ergo, he ought to move in with her at Water Street and allow the Bluntinghamites to have confirmation of the rumours. The opprobrium of the situation would soon be lived down, he thought. Anyway, he didn't really care about what the locals thought. He was Chairman of a Government Commission and a Very Important Person, something of which he was becoming increasingly convinced in his own mind. He resolved therefore to explore the possibilities with two of the three women in his life. First, he offered his support to Vicky and was somewhat taken aback when told that she was quite capable of coping on her own and had never expected him to leave Becky for her. She wanted the child and was prepared to go through the whole process on her own, including the raising of the child. As a compromise, she suggested that Peter stay over at weekends. This seemed to him like a good idea, which he would broach with Becky at an opportune moment. Upon obtaining her approval, Peter became what is sometimes referred to as a weekly commuter, although his commuting was between two different women, with the added complication of having also to commute to London from a different station on a Monday morning and return to it on a Friday evening. But for the time being, the examinations process would occupy most of his time.

Monday, 11 May

On the third Monday of term, the ULB students were standing nervously in a sort of queue outside the examinations hall, waiting to be admitted, in order to demonstrate how much of the teaching of the past year they had absorbed and whether they had been able to contribute any added value. Peter's subject was not one for speculation and discursive analysis. Even if he didn't proclaim with Jim that he dealt in hard facts, not intellectual pap, his subject did not afford even the bright student the chance to propound his or her own theories about linguistics, except in exceptional cases; instead, it relied on sound knowledge, well ordered, and well presented, with lots of relevant examples. The theory was simple, the practice not always commensurate with the theory. Peter believed in setting exam questions that the students could answer well if they had done the required amount of work. He used to quip that, even if the candidates had known the questions in advance, the results would still be the same, the very good ones would get firsts, most of the others II.1s, and the really weak ones fails. With this in mind, he went to the exams hall at the end of his examination to pick up the scripts, so that he could get to work marking them as soon as possible before the next batch came along on Wednesday. He took the envelope back to his room and had a brief look inside. All appeared to be in order. Next, Peter ventured out onto the streets of the capital to fetch a sandwich from Pret à Manger, which he took back to his room and settled down to read his latest emails. One had arrived from Michael.Harrison65@gmail.com. Baby Michaela Petra Harrison-Schmidt, weighing 3.6 kg, had arrived, born in the Geisenhofer Frauenklinik on Sunday, 10 May. Harrison, as Peter still called him except to his face, explained how they had chosen Petra in his honour and how both names would work in either German or English. Peter felt a warm sense of being appreciated. He thought he would send a card to Munich rather than just an email; however, he sent a quick congratulatory email pro tem.

When he had finished the email, while eating his sandwich, he went back to the envelope of exam scripts, armed with his red pen. He began to read the first script at the top of the pile. He thought he recognized the handwriting of the anonymous script but not the style of writing. He read the answer through to the end before checking the question paper. It was a near-perfect answer to the question, but the question was not the one that he had set in the revised paper. He got out his copy of the new paper and compared it with the question paper before him. A sinking feeling came over him. The paper they had sat was the original that Johanna had supposedly lost. The handwriting was that of Fiona Stanhope, one of the weakest students. The answer to the question set was first-class. Peter assumed this was a one-off. After all, Fiona had been accused and found guilty of plagiarism. He would assess the problem when he had marked the whole batch. He put them away in his briefcase for marking at home, where, he hoped, circumstances would be less hectic, and got on with departmental admin.

Through the portal in his door, he looked out into the departmental solar system and saw a wandering star—Johanna passed by the window and looked in to gauge the mood inside. A few minutes later, she repeated her trajectory and observed a more agitated-looking Peter. When Peter did not confront her, she supposed that the Head of Department had not discovered her mistake, which she had realized upon checking the spare question papers that had been returned to the Department. If challenged, she resolved to be confrontational and to deny everything.

This time you'll be firm, Peter. She will have to go. — I'll attend to it in the morning.

When Peter arrived home at Bluntingham that evening, he found a familiar official-looking envelope, which Becky had placed on his desk. He opened it and read:

Rt Hon Ernest Globes MP

Secretary of State for Educating Britain

Dear Professor Lampton,

Following a review of English-language teaching in our schools, it has been decided to establish a new post of Chief Linguistic Adviser to Her Majesty's Government. You may be aware of the existing post of Chief Scientific Adviser. The intention is to put linguistic advice on a par with scientific. In view of the successful preliminary reports of the Commission on Spoken English, which you chair, and the keenly awaited findings of the Research Restructuring Exercise, I should greatly value your input in the search for a suitable person to fulfil this role; indeed I would welcome an application from you.

I look forward to hearing from you.

Yours sincerely,

Ernie Globes

Peter went excitedly to Becky, who was conversing in the kitchen with Robert. He was annoyed at Robert's presence, whom he was beginning to view as a usurper. Now would not be the time to tell her.

He glared at both of them.

'I've got something to tell you,' he said curtly to Becky. Robert took the hint and left the room.

'What do you think? I've practically been offered the post of Chief Linguistic Adviser to the Government. Isn't that fantastic?'

'I'm very pleased for you,' Becky said unemotionally.

'I thought you might have shown a bit of enthusiasm,' Peter said.

'Wonders will never cease,' she said.

Peter left the room, downcast. He would phone Vicky instead for the enthusiasm Becky had denied him.

'Wowee!' Vicky said when she heard the news. 'That's amazing. It should clinch the Needham post. I got a list of potential applicants from Robin a couple of days ago. I can't send you a copy, but we can look over it together at the weekend. There are quite a few great minds amongst them.'

'Great minds?' Peter said. 'Is that a criterion?'

'It seems to be at Needham. Don't you think it applies to you, then?'

'You know I'm too modest to say.'

'Don't forget, you have many other qualities.'

'Hah!' Peter said. 'Not what you're thinking of.' He was too elated to wince at his construction.

'You'll have to promise to be on your best behaviour now.'

'I'll do my best,' Peter said. The excitement had almost made him at a loss for words. He couldn't think of anything witty to say, so he returned to Becky and watched TV for the rest of the evening with her and Robert.

Peter fell asleep in front of the TV. He began to dream that he was reading the Needham College Annual Report for 2012. Below a photograph of the Master standing in front of the Master's Lodge in his scarlet gown, flanked by his wife and close friend, Ms Victoria Atherton, with two three-year-old children standing in front of them, he read:

The Master, Sir Peter Lampton, LittD, FBA, FIRSE and Lady Lampton hosted a garden party for honorary graduates and new fellows. Amongst those present were: Professor Derek Brown, MA, PhD, Hon. LittD (for services to Other Languages in the Research Restructuring Exercise); Dr Robert Harnwell, PhD (Harvard), Fellow in Music; Dr James Lubbins, MA, PhD, Honorary Fellow and munificent benefactor; Professor Beatrice Frensham, BA, PhD, Professor of Other Languages, University of Oxford, Honorary Fellow; Ms Victoria Atherton, MA, Fellow, Director of the Rebecca Lampton Institute for Relationship Restructuring; Dr Isabelle Chesham, MA, PhD, James and Sarah Lubbins Research Fellow in Old European Languages; Ms Gisela Harrison-Schmidt, Staatsexamen, Language Teaching Officer; Mr Michael Harrison, BA, Research Fellow in Phonetics, Dr ...

'I'm going to bed, Peter,' Becky said as she got up when the programme had finished.

'Oh fuck!' Peter said as she went upstairs. Tomorrow he would deal with Johanna.

Printed in Great Britain
by Amazon